SHE HAD TURNED TO FACE HIM . . .

"You must think me a shameless hussy," Madeline said, as she put her drink down and moved closer.

"Right now, ma'am," replied Longarm, "I'm not thinking much at all."

She smiled wickedly. "I know. You're just looking."

She was right, of course. And Longarm had no excuses to offer. Madeline had been wearing only a long, filmy nightgown by the time he reached her place for that nightcap she had promised him . . .

Also in the LONGARM series from Jove

LONGARM
LONGARM ON THE BORDER
LONGARM AND THE AVENGING ANGELS
LONGARM AND THE WENDIGO
LONGARM IN THE INDIAN NATION
LONGARM AND THE LOGGERS
LONGARM AND THE HIGHGRADERS
LONGARM AND THE NESTERS
LONGARM AND THE HATCHET MEN
LONGARM AND THE MOLLY MAGUIRES
LONGARM AND THE TEXAS RANGERS
LONGARM IN LINCOLN COUNTY
LONGARM IN THE SAND HILLS
LONGARM IN LEADVILLE
LONGARM ON THE DEVIL'S TRAIL
LONGARM AND THE MOUNTIES
LONGARM AND THE BANDIT QUEEN
LONGARM ON THE YELLOWSTONE
LONGARM IN THE FOUR CORNERS
LONGARM AT ROBBER'S ROOST

TABOR EVANS

LONGARM
AND THE SHEEPHERDERS

A JOVE BOOK

Copyright © 1980 by Jove Publications, Inc.

All rights reserved. No part of this publication may be reproduced or transmitted in any form or by any means, electronic or mechanical, including photocopy, recording, or any information storage and retrieval system, without permission in writing from the publisher.

Requests for permission to make copies of any part of the work should be mailed to: Permissions, Jove Publications, Inc., 200 Madison Avenue, New York, NY 10016

First Jove edition published June 1980

10 9 8 7 6 5 4 3 2 1

Printed in the United States of America

Jove books are published by Jove Publications, Inc., 200 Madison Avenue, New York, NY 10016

Chapter 1

Marshall Billy Vail was leaning over his clerk's newfangled writing machine, watching the pale young man go at it, when Longarm entered. Vail turned quickly at Longarm's entrance, his eyebrows lifting in surprise.

"On time for a change! I can't believe it," the chief marshal cried happily. He straightened up and almost rubbed his hands together in glee. It was obvious at once to Longarm that his boss had an assignment for him and was looking forward to sending him off. He never liked to see dust settling on Longarm's Stetson.

"What have you got for me?" Longarm inquired, stopping in front of the marshal. His chief wasn't all that much to look at, and that was the truth. The man was running to lard, trapped as he was behind a desk. In his own time, Marshal Billy Vail had shot it out with a passel of borderland desperadoes and a considerable number of Comanches, north *and* south of the border. But all that was in the past. Though Billy Vail wasn't more than fifteen years older than Longarm, it was a sobering experience for the tall lawman to see what could happen to a man in that short span. It was one very good reason why Longarm did not mind that Billy Vail kept him on the trail.

"Get in here, and I'll tell you," Vail answered, marching ahead of Longarm into his office and moving around behind his desk.

Longarm followed in after him and closed the door.

5

Slumping into the red leather chair in front of Vail's desk, he glanced at the banjo clock on the oak-paneled wall. Longarm was startled. He was indeed early. Ten minutes early. He hadn't realized he was that anxious to get into action.

Longarm took out a cheroot and lit up as he watched Vail poke doggedly through the pile of paperwork that just kept settling on the poor man's desk—a blizzard from Washington, D.C., was what it was, and there was no end to it that Longarm or Billy Vail would ever get to see.

"Here it is," Vail said exultantly, pulling out a folder and opening it. He read a few paragraphs silently, then glanced up at Longarm. "Ever hear of Ruby Wells, Nevada?"

Longarm shook his head. "Can't say as I have. Should I have heard of it?"

"No reason in the world," Vail said. "It's in the middle of the Ruby Mountains. You know that territory. That's why I'm sending you back there."

Longarm nodded. He remembered, all right. He had passed the Rubies on his way to the headwaters of the Humboldt and into the Great Basin, where a ruthless logging combine had been bent on stripping the mountainsides of every tree and shrub.

"I remember the country, Billy, but not Ruby Wells. What's the trouble? More loggers?"

"Train robbers."

"I'm listening," Longarm said, leaning his head back and puffing contentedly on his cheroot. The skinny cigars were a weakness he occasionally chided himself for, usually when he wasn't on a case, and his confinement in the overly civilized—to his point of view— city of Denver began to get on his nerves.

"Outlaws boarded a train in California, waited until they were in the middle of nowhere, then forced their way into the mail car."

"By 'nowhere,' I take it you mean Nevada Territory."

"That's right. Once they were inside the mail car, they gunned down the postal clerk in cold blood. They had no provocation; the man wasn't even armed. Then they looted the safe of gold coins being shipped from the U.S. Mint in San Francisco. After that, they pulled the brake cord. There were riders waiting at trackside with spare mounts, and the outlaws disappeared into the Rubies."

"And you think they're holed up in Ruby Wells?"

"I've looked at the map," Vail said, leaning back in his chair and watching Longarm carefully. "The Rubies would make a fine place to hide out until the heat dies down some. But when it does, they'll have to board a train at Ruby Wells to get out of there. They sure as hell couldn't ride out. Water holes are miles apart, and they don't have mules, they have horses. You got any idea how heavy that gold is?"

"Okay. So you want me to go to Ruby Wells and nose around, see if I can get a line on where those jaspers might be hiding out."

"That's the ticket. Keep an eye on the occasional trains that pass through. We'll have other deputy marshals at other widely spaced stops. This is one case where almost every federal office west of the Mississippi is sending men. That murder of a federal employee has the Post Office and Washington screaming for action. Since you know the area, we're sending you to the town where they're likeliest to show up, so keep a lookout for any suspicious strangers you see riding into town."

Longarm took the cheroot out of his mouth. "Since when do you have to tell me my business, Billy?"

"Hell, I'm just repeating what I was told. The heat's on for this one, Longarm. Washington wants action."

Longarm stood up. "Just don't tell me my business, chief. I don't care what those lard-assed bureaucrats write on those reports. I know what to look for, and I know how to stake out a town. I'll watch the trains and I'll keep my eyes peeled for strangers, and I'll keep my ass down and my mouth shut. If those buzzards are in the Rubies, I'll sniff them out."

As he stood there with his cheroot clamped in his mouth, Deputy U.S. Marshal Custis Long was an imposing sight. His lean frame stretched to well over six feet tall, and looked as tough as saddle leather. His John L. Sullivan mustache, his hair, and his Stetson were brown, along with his tweed vest and suit. His shirt was blue-gray, and he wore it with a black shoestring tie knotted at the neck—the tie he wore only as a grudging concession to Justice Department regulations, which required such neckwear to be worn by all field personnel. He tended to discard it as soon as he was out of sight of Denver. His boots, of cordovan leather, were low-heeled army issue. His Stetson he wore with the crown telescoped flat on top, tilted slightly forward, cavalry-style, above his dark-browed, gunmetal blue eyes.

Vail sighed. "I know you'll do your job, Longarm. No need to get your bowels in an uproar. Take the train from Fort Douglas, Utah, and bring a horse with you. I figure that's the best and quickest way to get there. Now get your vouchers and rail pass from that clerk of mine, and get out of here. And I'll be remembering what you just said—if those buzzards are in the Rubies, you'll sniff them out."

Longarm snugged the snuff-brown Stetson down securely onto his head and left Vail's small office, wondering if just maybe he hadn't bitten off a little bit more than he could chew. But then again, he didn't chew tobacco, he smoked it. And all he had told the chief was that *if* those murdering sons of bitches were in the Rubies, he would flush them good and proper. And he would. *If* they were there.

• • •

Longarm arrived in Ruby Wells four days later, supervised the unloading of his horse, and then went to find a livery. His impressions of Ruby Wells were not at all encouraging. He had come to the place in search of unsavory characters—riders who looked and acted suspiciously. The difficulty was, that description fit nearly every citizen of Ruby Wells. It looked to Longarm as if the town of Ruby Wells was where old and unwashed gunslicks and desperadoes came to die—more than likely in a flash of gunfire and amid the tinkle of exploding glass.

As soon as Longarm had found a hotel and a barber shop with a bathtub, in that order, he searched out the town marshal and found him on the porch in front of his small frame jailhouse, sitting on a wooden chair with his legs crossed in front of him on a hitch rail. A toothpick was sticking out of one corner of his mouth. Like Longarm, the marshal sported a John L. Sullivan mustache, but there the resemblance ended. The marshal looked like bread dough on the rise, with his clothing exerting a frantic but futile effort to keep him in some rough semblance of human shape.

As Longarm paused beside him, the fellow made a truly herculean effort, managing to uncross his legs and get to his feet. By the time he was standing in front of Longarm, he was perspiring freely and his grimy face was beet-red.

"Name's Custis Long," Longarm introduced himself. "You should have had a wire that I was coming."

"Sure, I got the wire," the fellow replied, almost as if Longarm had just suggested he couldn't read. "You're here about that train robbery."

"That's right, Marshal. What can you tell me?"

"You want to go inside my office? Cooler in there, and I got a bottle."

Longarm shrugged and followed the man into the

small office-jail. The place stank of slop jars that were not kept clean, and stale vomit. The marshal, of course, noticed nothing. He reached into a drawer as soon as he was sitting behind his desk, and brought out a somewhat depleted bottle of rye whiskey. The two glasses he brought out after it were full-sized.

"Say when," the marshal said as he poured Longarm's drink.

"When."

The marshal pushed Longarm's drink across the desk to him, and Longarm sat down on a wooden chair beside the desk. As Longarm took the drink, the town marshal said, "My name's Wills Toady, but I 'spect you knew that." Wills had poured himself half a tumblerful of the whiskey. He threw it down as if it were fresh spring water, made a quick face, and then looked cheerfully at Longarm.

"And all I can tell you about that train robbery is that I don't know a damn thing. I been sittin' out there keepin' my eye peeled for any mean-lookin' strangers. Trouble is, they're all mean-lookin', what with this damn range war heatin' up."

"Range war?"

"Sheepmen comin' in—or trying to." Wills wrinkled his fleshy nose in distaste. "This here's cattle country. Ain't no room in it for them grass-killin' sheep."

"How many were in that train robbery for sure? I'd like to know that, Wills."

"Six. Four on the train, two more with the horses along the right-of-way. They're up there in the Rubies, I'm thinkin', just bidin' their time, waitin' for all this federal heat to let up some. With all that gold, they got good reason to hole up and wait a bit."

"Unless they get anxious to spend a little of the loot," Longarm reminded the man.

Wills Toady looked at Longarm carefully, through watery eyes. "I suppose they might get a trifle anxious, at that. But, like I said, this town's fillin' up with undesirables, so it's harder'n hell to figure out who's a train robber and who's in here to cut up them sheepherders."

Longarm thought he ought to try to get the range war straight in his head—find out who was who and what was up—but he didn't like talking to this fat lawman any longer than he had to, and he was in this country to find those train robbers. Killing an unarmed postal clerk was not only a federal offense, it was an outrage that Longarm was anxious to avenge. Longarm finished his drink and stood up.

"You figure those robbers are still up in the Rubies, eh?" he asked.

Wills Toady tilted his head so he could peer up at the tall lawman. "Maybe they is, and maybe they ain't. I figure the best way to find out would be to go up there and take a look-see." The man's broad face broke into a yellow grin. Then he reached for the bottle to pour himself a second libation.

Longarm thanked the man and left the little office. *Trouble is, what that tub of lard suggested is right on the money,* he thought. *The only way to find out where those varmints are holding up is to hightail up there to those Rubies and start sniffing around.*

Longarm was already more than anxious to get the smell of this mean-looking town behind him. On the single main street, running at right angles from the train station, he counted eleven saloons. His hotel was at the end of that street, with a sheer bluff scrubbing its back. If the saloons stayed open through the early hours of the morning, Longarm was going to have some difficulty in getting to sleep. For a moment he considered the possibility of riding out that evening, then thought better of it. He would get what sleep he could. That train ride had been no pleasure.

● ● ●

Longarm sat bolt upright, his double-action Colt .44 swinging out from under his pillow, the muzzle searching the darkness of his room. And then the woman screamed again. It came from the next room and had that shrill, cutting quality to it that always made the hair on the back of his neck rise straight up. Swiftly, Longarm swung back his covers and padded on bare feet across the floor, kicking aside the pieces of crumpled paper he had scattered there earlier as a safeguard. Pulling open the door, he stepped out into the dim hallway. A single wall lamp cast a yellow glow over the dank passageway; there was enough light to show Longarm the open door next to his room.

Even as he started down the hallway to the door, a third scream issued from the open doorway and Longarm heard a low, guttural laugh, punctuated by a sharp, stinging slap. He heard the woman's gasp of pain.

"Go ahead," the man's voice said to the woman. "Let out another scream if you've a mind to. They ain't no one goin' to hear you in this town!"

"That so?" Longarm asked, stepping into the room. He had not bothered to climb into his britches, and now stood in the doorway in his longjohns, his sixgun gleaming blue in the light from the single kerosene lamp on the dresser.

The man and woman were on the bed, neither of them wearing very much. The girl had a profusion of long dark hair, setting off a pale, almost alabaster complexion. Both of her full breasts were exposed, the nipples erect from the excitement of her battle with the lean, blade-faced individual who was atop her.

"What the hell do you want, mister?" the fellow snarled.

"Sleep," Longarm replied. "I want to get some sleep. Get off that lady and out of this room."

The man was furious. His long blade of a nose

seemed to get even sharper as he pushed himself back off the woman to stare fully at the tall intruder. His lidded eyes were cruel, and the line of his lean mouth contemptuous. He fairly bristled with an unashamed, perverse energy. Had Longarm found him in the act of murdering a neighbor with a dripping ax, the fellow would have been no more outraged at Longarm's interruption. He was a man who did what he wanted, *when* he wanted, and brooked no interference from anyone.

"Well, damn your eyes!" the fellow snarled. "If you want sleep, get back into your room and get to sleep, then. And leave us be! Now git!"

Longarm was almost amused at the man's truculence. He seemed to pay no heed at all to the pistol in Longarm's right fist. Longarm looked at the girl. "You want this jasper out of here?"

She seemed confused. The man had already slapped her around, and there was no way she could tell how effective Longarm was going to be in dealing with her assailant. She did not know on which side to place her chips. Longarm realized her dilemma instantly and made her choice for her.

He strode into the room grabbed the back of the fellow's nightshirt and flung him off the bed. The man landed on his back, the rear of his skull banging harshly against the wall. For a moment the man lay stunned. Longarm heard the girl's gasp of dismay.

When the fellow's confusion cleared up and he was able to gaze up at Longarm, the lawman said quietly, menacingly, "I'll tell you this once more. Get your things and get out of this room. Leave this girl be. I suggest next time you pick a girl who's partial to a man of your talents."

For just a moment, the fellow regarded Longarm with his cold, lidded eyes; then he struck. Like an uncoiling rattler, he flung himself from the floor and, fastening both arms around Longarm's waist, he burrowed his head into the lawman's midsection and bore him relentlessly back. Longarm felt the breath explode from his lungs as the wall slammed him with stunning force, cracking his head smartly. The Colt dropped from his fingers as he sagged, his senses on the brink of unconsciousness.

His opponent stepped back swiftly and brought his right fist around with sledging force, catching the meaty part of Longarm's jaw. Lights exploded deep within Longarm's skull, and he glimpsed the face of the girl, her dark eyes wide in her pale face, as he slipped sideways to the floor. The man proceeded to kick at Longarm's body then, with vicious, meticulous care. Longarm covered up his head while the blows rained on him, his head clearing slowly, his rage at this treatment building to an exultant fury as he contemplated what he would do to this vicious bastard. Abruptly, his hand snaked out and caught the man's foot, almost upending him.

The fellow pulled free of Longarm's grip, snatched up the lawman's dropped Colt, and regarded the still-prone Longarm with his lidded eyes. "You gettin' much sleep now, mister?" he inquired. His narrow face creased into a humorless grin. He raised the revolver and leveled it at Longarm. "Think maybe you'll be takin' that sleep right now!"

It was then that the girl decided on which side to pitch her penny. She flung herself off the bed and onto her attacker's back, one pale arm circling his neck and pulling him abruptly around. The fellow's gunhand went up as he fired. The bullet smashed a hole in the wall just over Longarm's head. Longarm hurled himself up off the floor and caught the man with a murderous, chopping blow to his midsection, just below the breastbone, sending him reeling, the girl still clinging to him frantically, his knees buckling under their combined weight. The girl flung herself away, and before the fellow sagged to the floor, Longarm brought up a stiff left to the man's face, swinging his head around sharply, then finished him off with a roundhouse right to the point of his chin. When Longarm completed his follow-through, his back was to the man.

The fellow went back with such force that his head slammed through the room's thin wall, and when he came to rest finally, his scraggly hair was gray with plaster. Longarm looked down at the slim, unconscious man with something bordering on admiration. His figure was slight, there was little heft to him. Yet he had proved to be a fierce opponent, whose malice gave him a kind of supercharged energy.

In his arrogance, however, he had tried to shoot Longarm down in cold blood. He had the heart and the soul of a killer, and no matter how admirable his fury might seem, it was a force that Longarm realized he could not allow to range freely—for his own and for other's safety. He reached down, grabbed the man's nightshirt, and hauled him upright, grunting only slightly with the exertion; then he turned, faced the window, and hurled the man out through it. The explosion of shattering glass was followed by the sound of cries from the street below.

Longarm went to the window and looked down. The girl's assailant had landed on the porch roof just under the window, then rolled off. The still-unconscious man appeared to have landed on two men passing by. Longarm could not be certain of this. All he could see in the dimly lit street were three sprawled bodies, two of whom were shouting angrily and twisting about on the ground. A crowd quickly gathered about them. The two men were hauled to their feet, then all eyes were directed upward at Longarm, standing with his upper torso leaning out through the broken window.

Longarm paid no attention to their shouts, and when

he saw the man he had just hurled from a second-story window stir and get groggily to his feet, then slink off through the gathering crowd, he ducked back inside the room, closed the door, and turned to the girl.

"Who was that?"

"That bad man, oh yes!" the girl cried.

"I know that, ma'am. But I would like to know his name."

"Cal Wyatt," she told him.

Heavy footsteps sounded in the hallway outside the door, followed by an impatient pounding. "Open up in there!" demanded the town marshal.

Longarm pulled open the door as the girl hastily covered her nakedness with a blanket. "What kept you, Toady?" the weary lawman demanded.

Startled to see Longarm facing him, the red-faced marshal pulled up abruptly. There was a sixgun in his right hand. He hastily dropped it back into his holster. "Marshal Long!" he cried. "What are you doing in here?" And then his eyes caught the figure of the girl, reclining now on the bed, the bedsheets held up about her neck. He looked with alarm at Longarm, then. "That's Carmen! Carmen Montalban!"

"Is that who she is? Thank you, Wills. A little while ago, she was rassling with that piece of human garbage I tossed out the window. Her screams were not being noticed worth mention by you or anyone else in this town. And I was trying to sleep next door. Now why don't you just go back to your office and let me get back to sleep?"

The man swallowed, then nodded quickly. He backed up a step, turned, and hastened down the corridor. Longarm closed the door and turned to the girl.

"Why was the marshal so upset to see you, Carmen?"

"My father is Pablo Montalban, and it is known what he would do to any man who molested me."

"I see. And what would he do?"

"He would kill him."

"Do you think he will kill Cal Wyatt?"

"He will try, if he learns what that man tried to do tonight."

"Pardon this question, ma'am—but what were you doing in here with Wyatt? Did you come up here to discuss the weather?"

The girl's face darkened. "You are right," she admitted. "I was a fool. I should never have trusted Cal Wyatt. But he promised to tell me what had happened to Manuel."

"And who is he?"

"He is my intended. But for too long now, he has been missing in the mountains. I am certain that Cal's boss, Slade Barnstable, is responsible. I just know he is. He will do anything to stop those of us who herd sheep. Cal said he knew what had happened to Manuel. He said he would tell me." She looked up at Longarm then, and he saw the tears streaming down her cheeks. "I had to know. We were soon to be married, at the next shearing." She looked away from Longarm then, her thick, luxuriant hair cascading down over her face as she lowered her head. Longarm thought he heard a sob.

"What did he tell you, Carmen?" Longarm asked softly.

Her voice was muffled as she thrust the knuckles of her right hand up to her mouth. "He said Manuel is dead. He said all the sheep are gone too. The entire flock, all of it, was rimrocked!" She looked up at Longarm then, and flung her hair back, her eyes wide. "And then, the pig, he laughed at me and tried to take me!"

"That's when you started screaming?"

"Yes."

Longarm went to the window and looked down at the street. A small crowd was still milling about in front of the hotel, and every once in a while, one of the crowd would turn and look up at the shattered window, Cal Wyatt's recent exit from the hotel was still the hottest topic in town. Longarm turned from the window and looked at Carmen.

"Is this your room?"

She nodded.

"You came into town alone and checked into this room?"

Again she nodded.

"You must love Manuel very much."

She bowed her head. "But Carmen is such a fool!" she said heatedly. "My father . . . he will say I am spoiled now. Even if Manuel is alive, I will not be allowed to marry him!" This last came out as a despairing wail.

Longarm went over to her and placed his hand gently on her shoulder. "I'll go with you to your father's camp tomorrow and try to explain. Maybe I'll be able to lie some, as well."

Carmen looked up at him. *"Señor!"* she cried. "How can I thank you?"

"By going into my room and sleeping there. I'll sleep here, just in case Mr. Wyatt returns. Tomorrow you'll ride with me into the Rubies. Maybe we'll find that Manuel is alive and well—and I'll get a line on six men I'm looking for."

"Six men?"

"I'll explain that to you later, ma'am. Now why don't you go on into my room? I think we can both use the sleep. It's going to be a long day tomorrow."

She nodded and got up from the bed, her ripped dress held in place by one hand. Before she darted past him and out the door, she reached up quickly and kissed him on the side of his face.

Longarm saw her safely into his room, took his own clothing and gear into her room, and then closed the door. He was still thinking of the warmth of that peck on his cheek when he fell asleep for the second time, the sound of the crowd in the street below his window reminding him of the roar of a distant beast.

Chapter 2

Already dressed by dawn the next morning, Longarm was standing close to the shattered window, inspecting his weapons. One of the surprises he kept in store for those who took an interest in burying him prematurely was a double-barreled .44 derringer, which rode in the right-hand pocket of his vest. A gold-washed chain, leading from the brass butt of the derringer, draped across the front of the vest and was attached to Longarm's Ingersoll watch, which he carried in the left-hand vest pocket. As a watch fob, the derringer was most effective. As a lifesaver, it had proved its worth countless times in the past.

At the moment, Longarm was inspecting the derringer carefully, having already gone over his Colt Model T .44-40, which now rested in the open-toed holster of his cross-draw rig. Satisfied that his ace-in-the-pocket would respond promptly when called upon, he dropped the small pistol into his vest pocket, tucked a clean linen handkerchief into the breast pocket of his frock coat, and took his snuff-brown Stetson up off the edge of the bed. He was putting it on when he heard a hurried, soft rapping on his door, followed by the whispered, urgent voice of Carmen Montalban.

"Marshal Long! The hotel manager, he is here—and with him is Mr. Barnstable!"

Longarm finished putting on his hat, and pulled open the door. He saw a small, plump man, his round face stamped with disapproval, standing behind Carmen. And to one side of the manager stood a tall, sardonic-looking individual dressed in black frock coat and trousers, a bright white shirt, a velvet vest, and a black, flat-crowned Stetson. He was smoking a cheroot, and the aroma from it reminded Longarm of his own desire for a smoke. This tall fellow was obviously Cal Wyatt's employer, and the smoldering look in his dark eyes did much to confirm that impression.

Longarm smiled at the manager. "Yes, sir. Can I be of any help?"

The man was taken aback by Longarm's genial manner. He swallowed in confusion. "Sir, this is not the room I gave out to you yesterday. And the window . . ." He paused in confusion and looked back for help to the man Longarm knew was Slade Barnstable.

Slade took the cheroot out of his mouth and returned Longarm's smile. His teeth were dazzlingly white in his healthily tanned face. "Good morning, Marshal. What this insect beside me is laboring to bring forth is his outrage at your destructive proclivities. It seems you amuse yourself by storming into other people's rooms, interrupting their play, and visiting cruel punishment upon their persons, after which you hurl them through the window—without bothering, of course, to open it. The man is outraged by your use of his property, as am I by your treatment of a trusted and loyal friend. We have both come up here to set matters straight."

"A mite early in the morning for that, ain't it, old son?"

Slade's smile was wintry now. "Indeed, but it is, as you know, the early bird that catches all the worms."

Longarm looked down at the manager. The disapproval on his face had congealed into a kind of nervous despair. Slade had taken matters completely out of his hands. "I'll pay for the window. The man I threw out of it was disturbing my sleep. Miss Montalban here was being molested by the turd that Mr. Slade Barnstable here describes as his 'trusted and loyal friend.' I'll see the town marshal before I leave this morning, and swear out a complaint against Mr. Wyatt. Molesting a woman and attempted murder should still be indictable offenses, even in a place as backward and uncivilized as this one."

The man took a hasty step back, glancing again for aid in the direction of Slade Barnstable. It was obvious to Longarm, now, that it was Slade who had forced the poor little fellow into making this deputation. Longarm took Carmen's arm and drew her gently behind him into the room. She too was alarmed at the low-keyed but bristling antagonism that flew between Longarm and Slade.

Slade frowned at Longarm's words, and appeared to reconsider his previous attitude. "A complaint, did you say?" he demanded. "Against Cal?"

Longarm smiled. "You heard me, Slade."

"And you say Cal . . . molested this girl?" An ironic smile played for a moment on the man's face. It was obvious he was about to say something concerning the girl's status, but when he caught the iron gleam that sprang into Longarm's eyes, he held himself in check and contented himself with a shrug. "And tried to murder you? Really, Marshal, I find all that quite hard to believe. You know you will need witnesses, and this girl quaking behind you is not really in a position to convince anyone of the truth of what you have just charged." He smiled suddenly, expansively. "But I will take your word for it and see to Cal myself. In his cups, the man has been known to whoop things up a bit. I am sure it was nothing more serious than that."

"Then you'll take care of him?"

"Most assuredly, Marshal. You can count on that."

"Yes, I know I can. Meanwhile, old son, you tell that son of a bitch that he'd best steer a wide course around me the next time we clap eyes on each other. I'm ordinarily slow to anger, and I don't usually bear grudges. But that 'trusted and loyal friend' of yours has worked a kind of mean spell on me, you might say. Now if you two gentlemen will excuse us, Miss Montalban and I are about to ride out of Ruby Wells. Good day, sirs." Longarm smiled again, to take a little of the sting out of his words.

He waited, still smiling, as the two men began to back up. It was the manager who turned first and scuttled ahead of Slade down the corridor. Slade did not scuttle, and as he followed after the manager, he turned and smiled coldly at Longarm, touching the brim of his black hat as he did so. Longarm understood the smile and the gesture. The man was assuring Longarm that although this particular round belonged to the lawman, Slade would not concede anything more than that.

Longarm turned to look down at Carmen. She had worked some kind of magic on the torn dress, so that she was now decently covered. She carried her belongings in a beautifully embroidered carpetbag. A red ribbon had been threaded through the crown of her luxuriant hair, and contrary to current fashion, she allowed thick curls to cascade freely down upon her shoulders.

"Can you ride, Carmen?"

She almost bristled, then announced with pride, "I can ride better than most men, *Señor*."

Longarm laughed.

Carmen, it turned out, had not been exaggerating. Riding beside Longarm on the powerful bay she had ridden into Ruby Wells the day before, she kept pace easily with Longarm, who was mounted on a big buckskin. She rode astride, her long, flowing skirt billowing out behind her, a floppy-brimmed hat on her head. She had fished it out of the carpetbag, which now hung down from the cantle.

As they rode across the semi-desert toward the Rubies, Carmen told Longarm almost more than he wanted to know about the range war that was now beginning to rage across the juniper-pinyon hillsides and sagebrush flats of this territory. The problem, as Longarm realized after listening to Carmen, was economics. This open range, owned by the government, was coveted by both sheepherders and cattlemen. Until now, the cattlemen had had things all their own way. They were here first, as they saw it. The sheepmen were the interlopers. No one seemed to be keeping track of the amount of cattle and sheep grazing on these foothills and flats, with the result that both sides were overgrazing. And it was the sheepherders, naturally, who took the blame for most of it.

By a stream shaded with cottonwoods, the two made their noon camp. After they had tended to their mounts and made a modest meal from the biscuits and jerky Longarm took from his saddlebags, Carmen took off her boots, lifted her skirts, and went wading in the cold waters of the stream. She teased Longarm into following her example. Longarm found the icy water bracing, and at last the two sat side by side on the bank, their backs to a tree, and continued their conversation.

"My father," Carmen explained, "worked long years for Mr. Mooreland, who has been here as long as many of these men who run the cattle. Each year my father took his pay in ewes, and Mr. Mooreland, he let my father run his own sheep with Mr. Mooreland's sheep. Soon my father have a big flock, and now he is a sheep rancher too, like Mr. Mooreland."

"Does Manuel work for your father or for Mooreland?"

"He works for Kyle Erikson. He is a new man on the range, and he bring many Basque people over to help him run sheep for a big company in Kansas City, I think." She wrinkled her forehead in concentration. "I do not know him much. He is a funny man, very tall, very handsome—only he is not a good rider, I think. He is cruel to his horses, not like you—and other good riders."

"So it's Erikson, your father, and this oldtimer, Mooreland, against the cattlemen. Where does this Slade Barnstable come in?"

"I do not know. He is the owner of the Drover's Palace, where the cattlemen all go to get drunk and gamble. Some say he is the big man behind the cattlemen, but I do not know this. But I know he hates sheepmen and sheep—like Cal Wyatt." She turned suddenly to Longarm, unhappiness crossing her face like a cloud obscuring the sun. "Do you think he lies when he says Manuel is dead?"

Longarm knew what the girl wanted him to say, so he said it. "It's sure likely, Carmen. He knows how you feel about Manuel, and used that knowledge to get you up into that room. Maybe he just told you Manuel was dead so you wouldn't see any reason for holding out on him."

"Yes," she said eagerly. "That is what I think. He is a cruel, terrible man. I think the devil lives in him often." She shuddered at the thought, then crossed herself quickly.

"I haven't thanked you yet, have I?"

"You thank *me, Señor* Long?"

"Of course. If you hadn't jumped Wyatt when you did, I'd be a dead man right now."

"Oh," she said, blushing, "that was nothing. I should have struck him sooner. He hurt you bad, did he not?"

"He was a tough one, all right. Maybe you're right. There might be some devil in that fellow, after all."

She nodded thoughtfully. "Yes," she said, "I think so."

She pulled up her skirts suddenly, and eased her feet into the icy water. Longarm watched the swift water coiling about her calves. She strode out deeper, and soon the water was lapping at her thighs. He pulled his boots on hurriedly, then got to his feet. It was time they got back on the trail.

Longarm was finding it somewhat difficult to keep reminding himself that this girl and her troubles were not his—that his assignment was to collar six no-account train robbers. With a shrug, he clapped his hat back on and walked through the shade to where their mounts were hobbled. At least he was heading in the right direction—toward the Ruby Mountains.

In the shadow of the Rubies, they halted and Carmen pointed to the cluster of ranch buildings at the head of a valley far below. "That is Mr. Mooreland's ranch," she said. "I remember it well. His wife, before she died, taught me English, and much else besides. She even tried to teach me to ride sidesaddle." Carmen smiled at the thought.

"I'd like to meet the man," Longarm told her.

"Yes," Carmen said. "I would also like again to see the old man. He was always kind to me and my father. It is not far."

Longarm let Carmen lead the way as they left the ridge and picked their way carefully into the valley. Here, the grass was lush and mostly free of sorrel, dock, and other weeds Longarm would have expected. This did not surprise him. He knew there were many who maintained that sheep not only did not destroy pasture, but actually improved it. Indeed, John Chisum and other big ranchers had their own herds of sheep. Cows prefer grass, whereas sheep prefer to browse on brush and weeds. The pastureland through which Carmen and Longarm were now riding bore ample testimony to that fact—directly contrary to the growing nonsense about the supposed inability of cows and sheep to prosper on the same range.

Still, as Longarm and Carmen neared the ranch buildings, Longarm looked far and wide in search of sheep, but found not a one. He glanced at Carmen.

"Is this man Mooreland still raising sheep?"

"Oh yes."

"Where are they?"

"Some flocks must be in higher pasture. It is strange, though. Many sheep are usually found in these foothills. I wonder where they have gone."

Longarm asked no more questions. Already he could see how he had alarmed the girl. Remembering what Cal Wyatt had told her about Manuel and the flock he was herding, Longarm felt a slow, cold finger of dread stealing up his back as he rode closer to the seemingly deserted ranch. He saw sheep wagons near one of the barns. And then he caught sight of something bloody and very white lying half in and half out of a barn doorway. He reined in quickly.

"Stay here, Carmen," he said, his voice sharp.

She pulled up also and glanced at him, sudden fear blazing into her pale face. "What is it, *Señor* Long?"

"I don't know. Just stay here."

And then both of them heard what the sound of their movement earlier had obscured: the distant, mournful blatting of terrified sheep. It was coming from a flat well beyond and below the barn, out of sight of the riders. Carmen uttered a suppressed cry and spurred her horse toward the barn, with Longarm pounding after her.

Both came in view of the stream-fed pastureland below the ranch at the same time. At once, Longarm understood the reason for Camen's dismayed cry. The sheep they had been looking for were crowded around a sheep wagon. It was a large flock. But the frantic bleating was coming from only a small percentage of the flock—the rest made up an ugly, mutilated mass of bodies. Longarm realized, then, what he had glimpsed in the barn doorway behind him.

"Dynamite," Carmen whispered. "They use dynamite on the sheep. I see it before. It is terrible! Sticks of dynamite they throw into the flock!"

"Don't go down there," Longarm said. "Stay here."

Carmen nodded as she quieted her restless mount. "I will not go down there," she agreed. "It is too terrible. But hurry, *Señor* Long! I worry about Mr. Mooreland."

The closer Longarm got to the mutilated sheep, the uglier the scene became. The gray fleece was streaked with livid banners of blood. Flies buzzed about decapitated, tangled corpses. The sight of the young lambs was particularly disheartening. Even more terrible were the few young lambs still alive that persisted in nudging and butting at the remains of what had once been their mothers.

Longarm found the old sheep rancher on the far side of the wagon. He was sitting on the stained ground, his back to one of the wheels, and in his lap was the dead body of a black-and-white border collie. The old man was stroking the dog's shattered skull, unmindful of the persistent flies and the blood that stained both his hands. As Longarm dismounted, he feared for the man's mind. The oldtimer was not crying out or saying anything to the dead animal he cradled in his lap. He was simply staring down at it, stroking it over and over again.

"Mr. Mooreland?" Longarm inquired softly, as he went down on one knee beside the old man.

At first it appeared as though the old man had not heard him. But then his hand stopped stroking the dog's head and he looked with wide, uncomprehending eyes at Longarm. "Dynamite they used," he said, his voice soft, filled with pain. "I don't understand. Why?"

"Who was it, Mr. Mooreland? Who did this?"

"Gunnysackers."

Longarm reached over and took the body of the collie away from the old man. Mooreland did not resist; he just watched as Longarm stood up with the animal's broken body in his arms. "Why don't we go back to your ranch?" Longarm suggested gently.

Mooreland nodded obediently and rose slowly to his feet—a tall, gangling man in his early sixties, Longarm judged, with a face seamed and baked from countless suns, his hatless head covered with a light fuzz of snow-white hair. Even the man's brows were white, his still-wide, uncomprehending eyes a sky blue.

Longarm stepped back and let Mooreland pass him as he walked up the slope toward his ranch. Still carrying the dog, Longarm followed. Twice the sheep rancher turned to look at the dead dog Longarm was carrying. The second time, he looked from the dog to Longarm and said, "They clubbed him to death when he went for their horses. I tried to hold him."

Longarm just nodded. Mooreland turned about and continued up the slope, his long, lean frame bent forward, his eyes glancing not once at the bleating remains of the once-huge flock to his left. Longarm did not glance at the bloody carnage either. It was enough to hear the pathetic bleating.

Carmen ran to Mooreland's side and flung her arms around him, sobbing. Mooreland patted her on the head and did his best to comfort her. "They got Ranger," he told her. "Old Ranger. But it's all right. He went down fighting."

Then the old man pulled away from Carmen and walked on toward the ranch. Longarm joined Carmen, who shuddered when she saw the way the dog had been mutilated. He put the animal down. "Gunnysackers," he told Carmen. "Do you have any idea who might have been inside those gunnysacks?"

Carmen started to say something, then shook her head. "No. I cannot say that. If I am wrong, it would be terrible. After all, who could do such a cruel thing?"

Longarm decided not to press the girl, but he knew she was not telling all she knew. For the moment, however, they had to think of Mooreland. He seemed to be taking the loss of his sheep very hard, almost as if he had lost a loved one.

And then he realized. It was not the loss of the sheep; it was the death of the border collie.

"I'll get a shovel," he told Carmen. "I don't reckon Mooreland is in any condition to bury this animal. Why don't you go in and see if you can comfort him?"

Carmen nodded and hurried after the old man, who was already entering his ranch house. Longarm started for the barn. As he neared it, the bloody body of the sheep he had seen earlier became visible. It looked as if the animal had been shot once through the neck. It had bled profusely. A cloud of green flies filled the air surrounding it like an obscene, buzzing cocoon.

The sound of a rifle shot punctured the unnatural stillness of the yard. Longarm spun to see Carmen, about to mount the low porch, freeze in sudden dismay. Before he could cry out to her, she broke into a run, mounted the porch, and burst into the ranch house. Her scream filled the air, blotting out even the cries of the wounded and dying sheep below in the meadow.

Old Mooreland had turned a rifle on himself, Longarm had no doubt. He broke into a run for the ranchhouse.

It was late that same day when Longarm and Carmen left the two graves on the rise overlooking Mooreland's ranch buildings. Carmen had fashioned the crosses that stood at the head of each grave—a large one for Mooreland, a suitably smaller one for the smaller grave of Mooreland's dog. Longarm had not known what to say, but Carmen, a devout Catholic like all Basques, had prayed beautifully, her words coming from the heart, her voice throbbing with genuine feeling.

Below the ridge now, they stopped and looked back at the two crosses outlined against the still-bright sky.

"He must have really loved that dog," Longarm mused aloud, still finding it difficult to believe a man would end his life over the loss of a dog.

Carmen looked at Longarm and saw his confusion. "You do not understand," she said, "about a sheepherder and his dog. It is many years since Mr. Mooreland tended his flocks alone with that dog, but Ranger was his best dog. There is a saying among us, *Señor* Long: a shepherd will sigh to lose his friend, groan if his wife or child dies, but if his dog is lost by death, his grief is overwhelming and his anguish cannot be borne. It was so with Mr. Mooreland."

Longarm nodded. He guessed he understood. What had happened here at this sheep ranch had not been at all pleasant, and he felt himself being drawn into this conflict between the sheep ranchers and the cattlemen. He felt it—and fought against it. He was after six train robbers, and the solitary men who herded their sheep in the foothills and high ranges of the Rubies would be the ones most likely to notice any gang of six men holed up hereabouts. This was the reason, he told himself, that he was taking Carmen to her people; he was hoping he could enlist their aid in his search.

And then he glanced down upon that bloody meadow and wondered if he could keep himself to that resolve.

It was late the next day when they reached Pablo Montalban's sheep ranch. It was a sprawling affair, a mixture of low corrals and pens and sheds, with the main house a tall, clapboard affair, the barns and pens constructed of lodgepole pines. The pens were empty of all but a few sheep, their distinctive smell hanging over the place. On the flank of a hill to the south of the ranch, Longarm saw a small herd of cattle; and in a pasture close by the stream that wound through the valley, there were more than a dozen fine-blooded horses grazing.

As Longarm and Carmen rode into the compound, Carmen's father and her brother Pedro walked stiffly, reluctantly across the yard to greet them. Carmen's father did not ask either of them to dismount, and his grim visage left no doubt that Carmen's fears had been justified. She was close to being an outcast from her own family.

Longarm reined in and gazed down at the Basque patriarch. He was a short, powerfully built individual. He reminded Longarm of an Indian. His eyes were black slits in his face, his expression impassive. On his head he wore a wide-brimmed sombrero, and over his shoulders a multi-colored, wool serape.

As Carmen pulled up beside Longarm, she said, her voice clear with just the hint of defiance in her tone, "This is Marshal Long. He will tell you where I have been."

Montalban turned his cold gaze on Longarm, who said, "This daughter of yours is a very brave woman, if maybe a little foolish. She demanded that Cal Wyatt tell her about Manuel. What he told her was very bad, and now Cal Wyatt is a shamed man in Ruby Wells as a result of your daughter's fury. I thought it best to escort her at once from the town and back to her family, where she will be safe. And where she will be loved for her bravery and consoled in her sorrow."

The Basque looked from Longarm to Carmen. Longarm could not be certain, but he thought the man's face had softened. There was no doubt that her brother Pedro had relented a bit, and it was he who moved forward to greet Carmen. Proudly, almost regally, the girl dismounted to greet her brother.

Pablo Montalban looked back at Longarm. "Dismount and rest, *Señor*. Pedro will see to your horse."

A meal was rustled up swiftly for both of them despite the lateness of the hour, and around the table the entire Montalban clan sat listening to Carmen's tale of what Cal Wyatt had told her and then of the terrible slaughter at Mooreland's sheep ranch. There was general agreement that Cal could have been lying, but not much hope that he was—after considering the events at Mooreland's ranch.

"If Cal Wyatt was telling the truth, Carmen," her brother said, "then he must have been a party to what happened to the sheep Manuel was herding, and perhaps also to what happened at Mooreland's."

"Yes," she said softly, her voice barely audible. "I know."

Theresa Montalban, Carmen's mother, reached out gently, then, and rested her hand on Carmen's shoulder. Carmen turned to her mother suddenly and buried her face in her bosom, her sudden, deep sobs filling the kitchen.

Pablo got to his feet and looked down at Longarm. "I will show you to your room, Marshal Long," he told him.

Longarm finished his coffee and left the table. Nodding curtly to Pedro, he followed the sheep rancher down a long corridor to a tiny but neat room. A lamp was lit on a small table by the bed. The bedclothes were turned down for him. The room had no luxuries, but it was immaculate.

Longarm thanked the man, who left him without a word as he closed the door firmly. Wearily, gratefully, Longarm began to undress. He was looking forward to sleeping in a bed once again.

He was almost asleep when he heard the door open. He was facing the door and opened his eyes to see Carmen, dressed in a long white nightgown that reached all the way to the floor, coming toward him. This Longarm had not expected, and it was something he did not want. Basque hospitality was legendary in the West; what was also legendary was the fierce pride they took in their women.

"Carmen, what—"

She swiftly placed her fingers on his lips to silence him. Then she was on her knees beside the bed, her luminous face close to his. "I come to thank you, *Señor* Long," she said.

"That's all right, Carmen," Longarm whispered hastily. "You don't need—"

She stopped his words with a warm kiss, a kiss that lasted longer than Longarm's resistance to it. When the kiss was done, Carmen's hands held Longarm's face gently. His senses reeling, Longarm tried to protest, but found he could not utter any words that might send Carmen from him.

"I cannot stay longer, *Señor* Long," Carmen whispered. "Manuel is still my intended, and I do not want to believe he is dead. So I will not. And you are in my father's house as his guest." Her eyes were wide, appealing for Longarm's sympathy and understanding. "So I must go. But you see, I do like you very much and thank you for all you have done for me these past few days. Good night."

She rose swiftly and was gone like a ghost, the door shutting silently behind her.

With a sigh, Longarm settled himself back into sleep. It was not easy, however. At last, smiling slightly at Carmen's words, he dropped off, the pressure of her warm lips still fresh on his own.

Chapter 3

Longarm did not sleep through the night. He was awakened by the silent figure of Pablo Montalban standing beside his bed. That he had gained entry to Longarm's room without alerting the light-sleeping lawman disturbed Longarm for a moment as he sat up and studied the impassive figure, who was regarding him closely, somberly.

Longarm glanced out the window. It was not yet light and there was no hint of dawn in the eastern sky. He looked back at Pablo. The man was holding a lantern, its sharp light in the dark room casting long shadows and plunging the Basque's eyes into deep, fathomless hollows and transforming his hooked nose into a sharp beak. The man was obviously troubled as he regarded Longarm.

"It is time for you to go, *Señor* Long," the older man said. "The virtue of my foolish daughter demands it."

Longarm did not want to argue with the man, or to make matters worse by protesting that Carmen had only come into his room to thank him, and that all that had passed between them was a harmless kiss, since Longarm knew enough about the Basques to realize that there was no such thing as a harmless kiss between an unmarried Basque woman and a man.

Without a word, Longarm nodded and threw back his covers. "Give me some time to dress," he said, "and I'll be gone shortly."

The old man nodded, pleased at Longarm's quiet acceptance of his situation. "You will not go alone, *Señor* Long," the man explained. "I will go with you. My daughter told me of your mission in this troubled country. It is the six train robbers you seek. Is this not so?"

Standing up in his longjohns, Longarm nodded quickly. "It is."

"Then I shall take you to them."

Longarm was flabbergasted. "You know where they are?"

The man's smile was a thin one, his beak of a nose growing even more birdlike. "Pedro saw them after the robbery of the train. In a valley they were dividing their spoils. There was much argument and shouting." The man shrugged. "Pedro did not stay to watch more. Perhaps they are still there."

"When did Pedro see this?"

"Two, three weeks ago."

Longarm sighed. That was a long time. More than likely, the trail was stone cold by this time, despite the old man's optimism. Nevertheless, it was something, and he was grateful for it. "Good," he told Pablo. "I'll be dressed and ready to go in a few minutes."

The man nodded curtly, placed the glowing lantern on the small table by Longarm's bed, and left the room.

For better than three hours, Pablo Montalban had ridden beside Longarm without a word as they climbed steadily into the verdant foothills of the Ruby Mountains. Longarm accepted the old man's silence without resentment, and contented himself with looking about him, enjoying the landscape and the ride into this cooler land. Occasionally he caught glimpses of cattle grazing on distant hillsides, and twice they rode close by flocks being tended by Basque sheepherders as dark and as taciturn as Pablo Montalban, who rode past them with only a single wave of his hand and without introducing either to Longarm.

It had not bothered Longarm, though he would like to have known if these herders were working for Kyle Erikson, the sheep rancher Carmen had mentioned. But Longarm had contented himself with studying the two herders as he rode on past, noting the poverty of their dress and the lonely, stoic cast to their faces.

Both herders were as tanned and weatherstained as any cowpokes Longarm had known, but it seemed almost unnatural to see such sturdy specimens afoot in such rough country, with only their sheepdogs for company.

The dogs were a delight to watch. Sensing any restlessness in the flocks, they seemed to anticipate the herder's commands as they moved quickly and decisively in among the sheep, or swiftly skirted the outer fringes of the flock to bring back any wandering woolies that appeared to be in danger of going astray. The herders communicated with their dogs, Longarm noted, as much through whistling and hand signals as by spoken commands.

It was fascinating to observe this partnership between man and dog, and as Longarm left the second of the two sheepherders behind, he found himself recalling old Mooreland, sitting disconsolately on the ground amid his slaughtered sheep, his dog's crushed head cradled in his lap. How long the man had been sitting there, Longarm could only guess. Hours, perhaps. He remembered Carmen's explanation of Mooreland's anguish and thought now that he understood why the old man had taken his life.

They were cresting a ridge, their horses laboring a bit. As they topped it finally, Pablo reined in and with a quick motion of his dark hand, pointed to a small cluster of shacks in the valley below.

Longarm pulled up also and studied the buildings. They did not appear to be lived in, but that didn't mean much. Longarm was always astonished at the poverty and filth that men on the prod accepted as a matter of course. The corrals were in poor repair; there was a gaping hole in the roof of one of the buildings, which might have served at one time as a bunkhouse. What was obviously the main house no longer had windowpanes, and the stovepipe chimney was hanging by a wire.

Longarm turned to Pablo for an explanation. The man spoke sparingly: "Three weeks ago they were here, like Pedro say. Pedro see one run from corral, another shoot him. Then they ride off." The rancher pointed north to a trail that led through a narrow pass.

"How many?"

"Five riders. They use horse of man they killed for to carry heavy load. They ride slowly. Much gold they carry, I think. Pedro think so too."

"Did he recognize any of the men?"

"They were too far away, I think."

Longarm nodded. "Thank you, *Señor* Montalban. I'll take it from here."

The man nodded and pulled his mount around. He held his hand up silently in parting and rode back down the slope. Longarm watched the Basque ride for a moment, musing on the man's laconic, taciturn nature. The solitary business of tending flocks most of his life had left its mark on him, as it undoubtedly did on all those who took up this lonely way of life.

Longarm looked back down at the ranch buildings below him in the valley and nudged his horse forward.

Three-quarters of the way across the valley, Longarm came upon the badly decomposed body of the outlaw Pedro had seen shot down. The vultures had not quite finished with the remains, and as Longarm skirted the unpleasant site, he saw the neat black hole in the rear of the man's bleached skull. Pedro had reported accurately what he had seen: the poor son of a bitch had been fleeing from his fellow outlaws at the moment he was cut down. They had needed his horse.

Continuing on to the ranch buildings, Longarm dismounted and stepped inside the ranch house. The place was a shambles, its wooden floor broken through in places, a single filthy table resting on only three legs, two chairs lying on their side, a pile of food-encrusted tin plates piled into a wooden bucket that sat on the sideboard next to the pump. Filthy mattresses were piled in one corner, the stuffing of one of them pulled loose by some nest-building pack rat. The entire building was one large single room, the far wall consisting of a huge uncompleted fireplace. A single wooden ladder led up into the straw-filled attic. Tufts of straw poked down through a few holes in the ceiling. As Longarm stood silently in the middle of the room, he thought he could hear the sound of mice scurrying about in the hay above his head.

As he bent to pick up a lantern lying on its side near the table, he spotted a single gold coin. Even in the musty, dim light of the place, it had the unmistakable gleam of a newly minted coin. Forgetting about the lantern, he plucked the coin off the floor and examined it closely, turning it around in his calloused fingers.

No doubt about it—the coin was part of the shipment from the mint in San Francisco. Longarm pocketed the coin, glanced once around him at the miserable room, then went quickly outside. Pedro had seen the men ride north through the pass. Their trail was as cold as a whore's heart by now, but it would do no harm to ride through the pass and see what he might discover. So far, he had been very lucky. Maybe his luck would hold.

● ● ●

It did.

That first gold coin had not been dropped simply through carelessness. The outlaws had poured their ill-gotten gains into a leaking saddlebag, or whatever. Halfway to the pass, another coin winked up at Longarm from the grass. He retrieved it and, forewarned, rode much more slowly toward the pass. Before he had reached it, he had recovered two more gold coins.

Inside the pass he found another coin, then no more for a full mile, when he saw two coins less than twenty feet from each other, winking at him from a tuft of grass beside the trail. The trail they were using was well-defined and led toward a distant canyon. Not until he reached the canyon did Longarm's searching gaze pick out another coin.

Sundown brought Longarm's treasure hunt to a halt. His saddlebag a good deal heavier than when he started out, he dismounted beside a swift stream, supped on jerky and coffee, then crawled into his bedroll and slept almost instantly, a bemused smile on his face.

He was still amused at noon the next day when, high in the Rubies, he came across fresh tracks. The trail of gleaming gold had suddenly become sparse; for the past mile or so it had dried up completely. The significant fact was that this sudden lack of blazing gold coincided with the appearance of the new tracks. It was obvious what had happened.

Belatedly, the fleeing outlaw band had discovered the leak in their saddlebag and had sent riders back to retrieve what gold they could. It was quite simple for Longarm to read the sign. Two riders were engaged in the retrieval operation. He could see clearly where they had reined in and jumped down, their bootheels digging into the soft ground, and plucked the coins off the trail. It must have been a time-consuming job, since the riders seemed to have been off their horses almost as much as they were on. The small leak in the saddlebag must have become a hemorrhage by this time.

The second set of tracks was easier to follow than the first, since there had been no rain to wash them out, and by sundown of the second day since he had left the abandoned ranch, Longarm found himself still in the Rubies, traveling through a land pockmarked with granite outcroppings, stunted juniper, and sage. So dry and rocky had the trail become by then that the sign he was following had vanished, and Longarm had found himself on his own. But he was not discouraged. He had already used up more luck than a riverboat gambler with a marked deck. It was about time for him to scramble some.

He was still scrambling that evening when he made camp in a rocky land punctuated with narrow gullies and boulders as big as hotels—a high badlands that offered as many places for human concealment as the hair on a sheepdog offered to fleas. He lit a fire to brew some coffee and was not a bit shy about the smoke he raised in the process. At this altitude the coffee did much to warm his insides. He lingered over it, then fixed a dummy of stones covered with a single blanket alongside the fire, after which he found himself a spot of high ground overlooking the campsite and lugged his bedroll to that spot and curled up in it. He was not expecting any visitors positively, but he was certain to be closer to that band of outlaws now than he had been the night before. His hope was that they were not so foolish as to neglect to cover their trail, or at least to keep an eye out for the smoke of campfires set by any unwary pursuers. That they were in this area seemed likely. Seldom had Longarm stumbled upon a land better suited to the task of concealing a contingent of train robbers.

With his right hand closed about the grips of his sixgun, Longarm shut his eyes and was soon asleep.

Longarm opened his eyes. The position of the moon told him it was well past midnight. He did not move. He just lay in his soogan, listening. The sound that had awakened him came again. Turning his head slightly and removing his revolver from under the blanket, he looked down at the still-glowing embers of his campfire, which he had purposely built up after constructing his dummy. A movement in the darkness just beyond the campfire's glow caught Longarm's attention. He looked more closely and saw someone dragging himself with almost infinite patience along the ground toward the dummy Longarm had fashioned. The sound he had heard was that of a gunbelt's buckle being dragged over stony ground. This fellow approaching the campfire was evidently in some distress, Longarm realized suddenly as he saw how slowly and painfully the man pulled himself along.

Longarm watched as the man circled the fire while still flat on his belly, and then reached out to grab the blanket-covered pile of rocks. As his hand closed about the unyielding stone, he uttered a soft cry of dismay—then looked quickly, warily about him.

At that moment a shot from the rocks above Longarm sent a slug into the campfire beside the man. As the sound of its report echoed and reechoed, the glowing cinders erupted. Frantically the fellow tried to ward off the blazing embers that showered down upon him.

A second shot found not the fire, but the man crouched beside it. The fellow cried out once, cursing his assailant, then lay still. A third shot was fired. Longarm could hear the bullet as it thudded into the man's body.

Then the assassin turned his fire on the dummy Longarm had fashioned. Two rounds ricocheted off the rocks under the blanket, and at once the rifleman realized his mistake. Longarm heard the scuffing of bootheels on rock and the chink of spurs. The sounds faded. A moment later, the quiet night was disturbed by the distant, rapidly fading mutter of swift hoofbeats.

Longarm left his soogan and with his Colt held out before him climbed warily down the rocky slope to his campfire and the dead man. But the man was not dead. The moment Longarm placed a hand on the fellow's shoulder, he groaned audibly. Longarm pushed him gently over. The man's eyes opened. The moonlight gleamed on his staring eyeballs.

"He's kilt me!" the man gasped up at Longarm.

"Who was it?" Longarm asked.

"Trampas! He's killing us all off! Everyone of us! The dirty son of a bitch!"

"Why? Why is Trampas killing you?"

The man looked up at Longarm for a moment without responding. Despite his condition, he was wary of the question. And of Longarm. "Who . . . who the hell are you?" he gasped.

"Never mind that now. Tell me who you are and why this man Trampas is trying to kill you."

The man grinned weakly, then began to cough. "Name's Patty—Patty Wormser. An' Trampas ain't *tried* to kill me. He's done it. An' he'll find the rest in Ruby Wells and kill them too! He done hid the gold and now he wants it all to hisself!"

"Where did he hide it?"

"You a lawman, ain't you." It was not a question, but a statement.

"Yes, Patty, I'm a lawman. Now where's the gold hid? I'll keep it from Trampas. You can beat him yet."

"Aw, shit! You a lawman and you're tryin' to help

me? All you want is that gold. You don't care none about Patty or Stan Bucker. Don't you tell me no different." Exhausted by his angry outburst, he began to wheeze painfully.

"I guess I don't," Longarm admitted grimly, leaning close to the dying man. "Tell me. Was Bucker the one you shot for his horse?"

"Yeah," the man gasped. "We needed it to carry the gold. And I'm the one what did it." Patty Wormser closed his eyes then and groaned. He was evidently in great pain. His eyes flicked open. "I'll be meeting Bucker in hell before long . . . ain't no use denying what I done." He began to cough again; this time a thin trickle of blood leaked from the side of his mouth, gleaming darkly in the moonlight. "Tryin' to get away from Trampas . . . spotted smoke from your campfire . . ." He closed his eyes and groaned, rolling his head in agony. "But that rat louse saw the smoke too . . . knew I'd be headin' for it." The man reached up and, with surprising strength, grabbed the lapel of Longarm's coat. "Get him for me, lawman! He's a mean son of a bitch . . . !"

"Where's the gold buried, Patty?"

"Trampas!" the dying man gasped. "Ask Trampas . . . !"

Patty coughed feebly for a moment, then began gasping for breath. Abruptly the gasping and retching ceased, and Wormser stared with sudden intensity up at Longarm's face—or at the moon behind him, Longarm couldn't be sure which it was. But it didn't really matter; Patty Wormser no longer saw a thing except the darkness into which his flawed soul had fallen.

The tracks left by the fleeing Trampas were not difficult to spot. Before the sun was completely above the horizon the next morning, Longarm was on the outlaw's trail. As he rode, he did some grim calculating. At the start, he had been after six men. Then it was five. Now a man called Trampas had whittled that total down to four. His motive, of course, was greed. The fewer he had to share the gold with, the more for himself. And since he was the one who knew where the gold had been buried, it behooved Longarm to capture this Trampas—and keep him alive.

But Trampas was no fool. Aware that the man who had fashioned that stone dummy lying by the fire might pursue him the next day, he took precautions. High in the Rubies, Trampas found a swift-running stream with a gravel bed. Longarm had traveled almost a mile up the stream before he realized he had lost the man's trail, and that though he had watched carefully and with all the skill gained in his years of tracking human quarry, somewhere along the bank of the stream Trampas had found a spot solid enough to allow his horse's hooves to leave no sign, and had left the bed of the stream and ridden off.

Longarm guided his horse up onto the bank and sat the animal awhile, pondering his next move. He had come close—infuriatingly close—to tracking down this band of murdering outlaws. Once he had found himself following a golden trail; after that he had set a snare which had brought two birds close to his grasp. But now here he was, still high in the Rubies, his quarry long gone, more than likely on his way to Ruby Wells to finish the job of whittling down the robber band.

Longarm turned his weary buckskin and started back downstream, taking a heading he judged would bring him back to Ruby Wells, and a bed with clean sheets. He was not unhappy at the prospect of returning to the mean little town. As he had told Marshal Billy Vail often enough, it was the smell of his own bedroll that always drove him back to civilization eventually.

• • •

A day later, having reached the rugged foothills of the Rubies, Longarm—aware suddenly of a horrible stench—topped a gentle rise and pulled up sharply. He was startled and appalled. His buckskin shook its head vigorously. It, too, was offended at what its senses revealed.

A cloud of obscene vultures flapped laboriously into the sky from the enormous, putrefying banquet spread on the flat before him. Beyond the reeking mounds of broken sheep loomed a steep cliffside, topped with a black, jagged crown of pine. From that pine bluff the hundreds of sheep that Carmen had heard Cal Wyatt tell about had been stampeded. Cal had told Carmen the truth; the sheep had been rimrocked.

Taking his handkerchief from his pocket, Longarm held it over his mouth and urged his horse on toward the grisly scene. He would have liked to cut directly away from it, but he was searching for someone, or the remains of someone—the young man Carmen loved, the one who had brought her to Cal Wyatt's room in Ruby Wells.

Longarm's horse balked as it moved in among the fringes of torn and bloodied sheep. The sluggish, overstuffed vultures watched him warily; then, with red-veined eyes and tearing beaks, they went back to gorging themselves. Longarm's mount was fetlock deep in gore when the lawman saw the skeletal remains of a human forearm and shoulder blade in close to the cliff face. The rest of Manuel was buried in among the sheep skeletons picked almost as clean as the forearm. Steadying the big buckskin with soft words, Longarm guided the animal still closer to the sheepherder's remains, then dismounted carefully. Watching where he placed his boots, he moved as close as he could, took the sharp, sun-bleached clavicle in his bare hand, and pulled gently.

The young man's head emerged from the pile of broken bodies, and Longarm saw what had killed the sheepherder. The entire right side of his face had been stove in, undoubtedly the result of the fall. Longarm let go of the man's collarbone and straightened to return to his restive buckskin when his eye caught something dark and rectangular on the ground beside Manuel. By raising the sheepherder, Longarm had uncovered it. Curious, Longarm bent and retrieved it.

He found himself holding a copy of Webster's dictionary. Opening the book, he saw the name *Manuel Alava* written in a painfully accurate script. Longarm shook his head sadly and closed the book. Remounting his horse, he took one more look around, then dropped the dictionary into a saddlebag and headed back through the gore and the feeding vultures to cleaner ground and fresher air.

He would not go back to Ruby Wells, he told himself unhappily. He had something to give Carmen Montalban.

Chapter 4

A few minutes later, with the stench of putrescent flesh still clinging to his nostrils, Longarm rode across a small, grassy meadow to find a line of horsemen emerging from the timber ahead of him. He pulled up and saw another line of horsemen approaching him from his rear. He had ridden neatly into a trap.

In all, there were close to fifteen horsemen, with one man, obviously the leader, riding before the others and pulling to a halt a few feet in front of Longarm, a thin smile on his lean, handsome face. He was blond and darkly tanned, with eyes so blue it was almost as if there were holes in his weathered face. A thin scar ran down the left side of his face, causing a slightly ironic downturn to the corner of the man's mouth. He regarded Longarm coolly, chucking his hatbrim back off his forehead.

"We saw you. In there with the vultures, picking the bones of the dead," the blond man said. "What's the matter with you, mister? You hungry or something?"

Longarm reached into his saddlebag and withdrew the dictionary. "Nothing to get nervous about, old son. All I took from the dead man was his dictionary."

The fellow's eyes narrowed, and Longarm heard a mutter run through the ranks of mounted riders that surrounded him. "Dictionary? Now what the hell you want with that, mister."

"Might be I was fixin' to write some letters home. Might be, but it wasn't."

"Talk plain, mister. What're you tellin' me, that you waded through all that just to steal that there book? So you could write letters?"

"Don't make much sense, does it?" Longarm agreed amiably.

"No it don't, and that's a fact. And here's another fact, mister. We don't take kindly to strangers pickin' the dead over. Lucky for you that was just a no-account sheepherder or we'd string you up."

"You don't like sheepherders, then."

"Hell, no! Dirty no-accounts, that's all they is. They smell worse'n their sheep, and their sheep smell worse'n hell on a holiday. Everything in front of a sheep is eaten and everything behind is killed. Hoofed locusts is what they is, and a sheepherder is no damn different. Besides, this black-faced Spaniard went across the Lazy C deadline. Serves him right. Him and his sheep!"

Longarm studied the man for a moment, then said, "You asked me why I took this dictionary. It belonged to that Basque sheepherder, Manuel Alava. I reckon Manuel was picked up by someone and flung off the bluff after his sheep. A man doesn't run for a dictionary when he's trying to stop men on horseback from rim-rocking his sheep, so I figure whoever did it threw this dictionary over the bluff along with him. You wouldn't happen to have any ideas on who that might be, would you, old son?"

The sharp, accusatory tone caught the blond man off-guard. Longarm was surrounded by hostile, well-armed horsemen; he should have been intimidated. Obviously he wasn't.

"Now just who in hell are you, mister, to ask me that?"

"Deputy U.S. Marshal Custis Long. And who might you be?"

"Hell, why didn't you say you was the law?" the man exploded angrily. He shook his head in exasperation. "I'm Wilt Kincaid, foreman of the Lazy C. And we don't know who stampeded them sheep and kilt that Basque kid. We just come upon it ourselves a week ago. The smell is spookin' our cattle something awful, and Sir Henry is madder'n hell at whoever done it."

"Sir Henry?"

"My boss, the owner of the Lazy C." The man's lean face sobered as he straightened in his saddle and looked beyond Longarm at the timberline to Longarm's right.

Glancing in that direction, Longarm saw a tall horseman approaching. He cut quite a figure, and the horsemen surrounding Longarm and Kincaid quickly pulled their horses aside to make way for this newcomer.

"Who's this man, Kincaid?" the fellow asked as he drew nearer, his voice powerful, his eyes boring like rifle barrels at Longarm.

"He's a lawman, Sir Henry," Kincaid replied, his voice suddenly respectful, his whole bearing more subdued. "His name's Long."

Sir Henry reined in, straightened in his saddle, and fixed Longarm with his powerful gaze. "Is that so, young man?"

"That's so," Longarm replied, impressed by Sir Henry, and not a little amused as well.

Sir Henry wore a white hat, a blue flannel shirt laced at the bosom with yellow silk cord, corduroy trousers and leggings, boots, and California spurs. He was armed like a battleship, carrying two large Colts, what appeared to be a bowie knife, and a double-barreled shotgun that he rested across his pommel. Slung over one shoulder was a leather cartridge belt.

"And what has brought you to my range, may I ask?" Sir Henry demanded.

"Official federal business, Sir Henry. It's a long story."

"Indeed? Well, I'm in the mood for long stories." The fellow was suddenly smiling. "Come to my ranch and join me in supper. I hope, for your sake, young man, that your story is not only a long one, but plausible as well. I must warn you, sir, I do not take kindly to interlopers, federal or private." He glanced then at Kincaid. "Get back to that northern herd, Wilt. Those beef are losing ground on that flat. Push them higher, if need be."

Kincaid nodded and turned his horse. In a moment he and his men were riding swiftly back across the meadow. Sir Henry turned to Longarm. "We have a long ride ahead of us, Mr. Long. You can tell me your story then, if you wish."

Sir Henry set off at a smart trot. Longarm deposited Manuel's dictionary back in his saddlebag and rode after the cattleman.

During the three-hour ride, Longarm told Sir Henry as much as he deemed it necessary for the man to know. Meanwhile, Longarm had ample opportunity to study Sir Henry. He was a handsome man in the prime of his life, obviously an excellent horseman and one who did not lack either courage or enterprise. He was at least six feet tall and built sparely; despite his height, he could not have weighed over a hundred and seventy pounds. The thick coils of hair that curled down from under his huge white hat were a dark, lustrous auburn. His eyes were deep brown, piercing in their intensity as they looked out at the world from under imperious, slightly drooping eyelids. His dark mustache he had waxed to points as sharp as the tip of his bowie.

It was late when Longarm and Sir Henry pulled up on the bank of a swift-running stream. On the far side, situated grandly on a broad tableland, sat a large, many-gabled mansion. Its most impressive aspect was the number of its windows and chimneys. A pillared veranda surrounded the ground floor. The log walls had been covered with adobe, and at that moment the late-afternoon sun bathed the house in a bright, shimmering light.

"Look at that," Sir Henry said, almost reverently. "Is it not a magnificent prospect, Long? It reminds me of the estate of my forbears in a somewhat smaller and, I must say, greener land."

"It's a pretty sight at that, Sir Henry," Longarm acknowledged.

"Indeed, sir, a very pretty sight, if I do say so myself."

With that, Sir Henry led the way downstream to a ford and splashed across the stream ahead of Longarm. Once they had gained the tableland, Longarm was doubly impressed. Sir Henry had a sizable ranch and a veritable maze of corrals and buildings. Working hands were everywhere, and each one was busy. This was no dude outfit; it was a working spread, and Sir Henry was obviously its dynamic heart.

As they rode toward the main ranch house, Longarm heard the rhythmic clangor of a blacksmith's hammer on his right, and on his left the yips of ranch hands watching their bronc peeler gentling an unruly bronco. Behind one of the barns, Longarm glimpsed some very fine-blooded riding stock. A magnificent Appaloosa, he noted, was running with them. As the two men dismounted in front of the big house, Sir Henry glanced quickly, proudly, about him, then led the way up onto the veranda.

Before he could reach the door, it was opened for him by an Indian servant, a woman of tremendous girth and large, black eyes. Sir Henry stepped back to let Longarm precede him into the house. As soon as they were both inside and Sir Henry had rid himself of his cartridge belt and most of his armament, he turned to Longarm, his dark eyes gleaming.

"I hope, sir, that you were suitably impressed. I am a working cattleman, not one of those 'innocents from abroad,' as they say. I came to this land not to rob it of its wealth, but to prosper as a free man and give back as good as I get. I believe, sir, that I have done that. Join me in a drink!"

Sir Henry led the way into the living room and thundered a request to another Indian woman, apparently his housekeeper. "Drinks, woman!" he cried. "Drinks! I'm parched. I've ridden halfway to hell and back!"

Longarm sat down in a leather armchair covered with a buffalo robe. On the floor were spread two immense bear rugs, and over the fireplace—a huge affair that dominated the entire left wall of the living room—were the heads of a pronghorn and an elk, both magnificently displayed, their eyes still fierce as they gazed down at Sir Henry, who had settled into his own huge leather armchair across from Longarm. Though no expense had been spared, apparently, the enormous living room was essentially the reflection of a man's taste. Longarm saw no curtains at the windows, no doilies on the arms of furniture, no knickknack shelves cluttering the corners or hanging on the walls, no candles, no frivolous touches of any kind to mar the stark, simple utility of everything in the room. But every flat surface had been polished to a bright luster, giving Longarm a mental picture of those two Indian women polishing the interior of this home from top to bottom, without rest and without end.

Longarm stretched his feet out, his heels catching for a moment on the thick bear rug at his feet, and took out a cheroot. "Mind if I smoke?" he asked.

"It's a filthy habit," the cattleman replied severely,

"but it is better than chewing tobacco. That I will not abide."

"If you prefer, I'll just chew on the tip. I just about decided to give up on this filthy habit, anyway."

"As you wish, sir. You are my guest."

At that moment, one of the Indian woman entered with a large tray. On it were two cups and saucers, a sugar bowl, a bowl of cream, what looked like tiny pastries, and a pot of tea. The drinks Sir Henry had thundered for had been brought in. It was not what Longarm had expected.

"Ah!" cried Sir Henry. "Wait till you try this tea, Long. A blend I have sent over to me from England."

As the Indian woman poured, Longarm had to admit to himself that the tea's aroma was pleasant. He leaned back and chewed contentedly on the end of his cheroot. He would let his guest continue the initiative. Sir Henry was an expansive Englishman, obviously not one of the remittance type encountered so often throughout the West, but a hard-working, hard-driving fellow who took pride in what he was accomplishing. He was also high-handed, and it could be that he was the one behind the destruction of two large flocks of sheep and the murder of Manuel. More important, since he was not primarily interested in this sheepmen-cattlemen conflict, it was possible that Sir Henry might have information on that train robber, Trampas.

The Indian woman handed Longarm his cup of tea. Without inquiring, she had given him cream and sugar along with it. One of the small pastries was on the saucer with the teacup. Longarm sipped the tea; with a pleased nod, he indicated to the watching cattleman that he did indeed find the tea all that the man had said it was.

As he sipped his own cup, Sir Henry said, "If I could get my ranch hands to become addicted to tea instead of to that abominable whiskey they sell hereabouts, I'd be a good deal better off. And that coffee they drink!" He shook his head in amazement and took another sip of his tea.

Longarm said nothing, he just sipped his tea. He would have preferred his with less cream and sugar.

"I suppose you are here to investigate the death of that Basque," Sir Henry said abruptly, "and the destruction of sheep hereabouts."

"Hereabouts? Have you heard about any other sheep that have been destroyed recently?" Longarm inquired.

But Sir Henry was not to be caught that easily. "Oh, I have heard various tales. It has been difficult to find out the truth. What I do know, Long, is that the nesters and now the sheepherders are moving in on what is and always has been cattle land—open range. But the cattleman was here first, and he intends to defend his right to run cattle on this magnificent land."

"By 'defend his right,' you mean slaughter sheep and kill their herdsmen."

"You are putting words into my mouth, Long."

Longarm smiled. "I was drawing a conclusion, Sir Henry, that's all. Rimrocking sheep is one way to keep them off your range. Killing herders is another."

"I do not approve of such violence. I deplore it, as a matter of fact. But I do understand how some cattlemen might find it difficult to restrain their men, especially when those men see what happens when a flock of those hoofed locusts feeds on their grass—or even crosses it on the way to higher graze."

"You've had some trouble keeping your men on a tether? I must admit, they weren't neighborly when I met them. Fact is, they seemed downright mean." Longarm smiled and finished his tea, placing the empty cup carefully on the large, brilliant silver tray.

"I do *not* have trouble curbing my employees, Deputy," the man said, his face pale at the implication of

Longarm's query. "Others might, but I do not. Wilt Kincaid is a tough man, but he works for me—and he knows that I will not stand for such violence."

"Fine," said Longarm, twirling his cheroot slowly, wishing suddenly that he could light it up. It annoyed Longarm that he found himself pursuing this matter of the sheepherder and his problems in this land, when he was here to find that gold and to apprehend those train robbers. It was Trampas and the others he was after, he reminded himself.

"What you seem not to understand, Long," said Sir Henry, finishing his own tea, "is the damage those sheep do to the land."

Longarm sighed. "I hope you ain't going to recite that worn-out nonsense about sheep destroying the grass," the lawman drawled. "I heard it all before."

"You call that nonsense!"

"I should've thought you would too, Sir Henry. You know sheep and cows have been grazing the same pastures for years, with no harm done to either stock. Sure, the sheep eat right down to the roots, and their sharp hooves do damage the grass, but that's only when they overgraze. Cows and sheep get along together fine when there's enough range for both. Cows prefer grass, and sheep like to browse brush and weeds. I don't suppose either animal smells like a rose, but they don't mind each other's smell as much as your cowboys like to think they do."

Sir Henry was taken aback. He looked with sudden confusion at Longarm. "Well . . . I must admit, Long, that you *are* right, to a degree. The South Downs of England are the result of centuries of intelligent grazing by sheep *and* cattle, dairy cows to be exact, but this is not England, need I remind you. This land is a semidesert area of juniper-pinyon hillsides and sagebrush flats, for the most part. Furthermore, since there is a very poor control on the amount of livestock we can graze on this open range, there is no way to prevent that overgrazing you mention. What we have then is the lesser of two evils. Overgrazing with cattle is infinitely preferable to overgrazing with sheep. I have seen what happens when sheep are allowed to overgraze, especially on low-lying range that only cattle can feed upon. The sheep move on to higher ground and survive, but they leave behind a dry ground laid bare to the sun, which will not put forth new growth until the next year's rains. I have been 'sheeped' in that fashion more than once in the past year, Mr. Long, and I do not intend to allow that to happen again."

Longarm sighed. There was no use in arguing the case for sheepherding with this man, or with any cattleman or cowpuncher. Longarm wouldn't have tried it with Sir Henry if he had not been impressed with the man's obvious intelligence and good sense. "Well, Sir Henry, as I told you, I'm not in these parts because of this range war that's brewing, though I suspicion it might keep me here a mite longer than I want."

"You're after those train robbers."

"Yes. The men who killed that postal clerk. They were holing up in the Rubies. Leastways, that's what I thought."

"You could hide a regiment in those barren peaks, I imagine."

"Maybe so. But that fellow Trampas—the one I mentioned to you on the ride here—has already murdered one of his band, and I have an idea he's on his way to Ruby Wells now. Trouble is, I don't know the man by sight. Have you—or any of your men—heard of such a fellow?"

Sir Henry frowned thoughtfully and shook his head. "Never heard of the man. If you want, I'll call my men to the porch and ask them."

"I would purely appreciate that, Sir Henry."

The man smiled. He seemed considerably more at

ease, now that he knew Longarm was not injecting himself into the range feud. "My friends call me Henry."

"Mine call me Longarm."

"Longarm it is, then," the tall rancher said, getting to his feet. "Come with me, and we will see what we can find out about this Trampas fellow."

"What Trampas fellow, Henry?"

Both men turned. Entering the living room from the hallway was a tall, red-headed woman, obviously related to Sir Henry. She had the same lidded eyes, a similarly lithe figure, the same clean lines in the face. She was dressed in a pale green dress with an apron front, topped with lace tight about her throat. A dark green ribbon had been threaded through the crown of her abundant red hair, the tresses of which reached down her back, well past her shoulders. Despite her dress, she carried a riding crop.

"Ah! Madeline! How nice. I want you to meet Custis Long—Deputy U.S. Marshal Custis Long. And that Trampas fellow is why he finds himself our guest at the moment." Sir Henry turned to Longarm. "May I present, Longarm, my niece, Madeline MacCauley. She has come west to avoid the boredom of London's drawing rooms. I have provided her with a small house on a hill near the river. You might have noticed it as we rode in."

"I guess I missed it," Longarm said, nodding his greeting to the woman.

"But I noticed you riding in with Henry," Madeline said, smiling warmly at Longarm. "We don't have many riders on the Lazy C who hold themselves that straight when they ride, or do it so easily. You ride very well, Mr. Long."

"Madeline is an excellent rider, Longarm. And she prefers to ride astride, Western-style." He frowned unhappily. "I am glad her mother is not here to see it."

Madeline's dark brows shot up mockingly. "Poor, poor Henry. He shocks so easily, I am afraid."

Sir Henry's face darkened in consternation, but he did not repond to the gibe. "Join us," he told Madeline. "Longarm has a question to ask of our riders. And then we will see about dinner."

Madeline looked warmly at Longarm. "Henry is always pleased to have guests that he may impress." She laughed. "And I confess, I enjoy it too. I hope you will be able to stay with us for a while, Mr. Long. A new face is most welcome."

By that time they were stepping out onto the porch. The compound was still alive with the activity of many men, all moving quickly and purposefully about on various errands, despite the lateness of the hour.

Sir Henry's appearance on the porch was instantly noted, however, and a single shout from the man brought activity to a halt. He beckoned to the watching hands, and at once they started toward him. Watching the men gather, Longarm heard Madeline's gasp and turned quickly to face her.

"Look!" she said, pointing to the west.

Longarm, as well as Sir Henry, turned in that direction and saw Wilt Kincaid returning to the Lazy C. Only he wasn't alone. Before his horse trudged two men, Basque sheepherders by the look of them. The two men walked with as much dignity as they could command, considering their situation.

The ranch hands who had already gathered before Sir Henry were now also watching the small party approaching the compound.

"Wilt's got hisself some sheepmen," a puncher commented, the tone of his voice revealing the depth of his contempt for those who would herd woolies.

"I can smell their stink from here," another commented.

There was low laughter at this, and another wondered if they should let Wilt back into their company, since he had allowed himself to get so close to the Basques. Someone suggested dunking the three of them in sheepdip before allowing them any closer. Longarm felt uncomfortable as these remarks were voiced, and a glance at Madeline told him that she, too, did not like the tone of what she heard.

Sir Henry, however, straightened alertly as Wilt and his two captors neared them. "Do you see, Longarm?" he inquired of the tall lawman. "Do you see now the difference between a man astride a fine horse and those two before him, accustomed as they are to trudging through the dust? The sheepmen walk alone—outcasts, each and every one of them. But the cowboy is a different entity entirely. I liken him to the knights of old— a clean, fine man, as brave as a mastiff, a man fit like no other to tame this magnificent land."

"Henry," Madeline said coolly, "you sound like a fool—a romantic fool at that."

"Perhaps," Sir Henry replied, "but I have seen the flush in your face as you rode beside Wilt Kincaid on that Appaloosa of yours."

"It is the Appaloosa, I assure you," Madeline retorted sharply, "that raises the flush on my face. Your foreman is a cold, unfeeling brute. As a 'knight of the West,' he leaves much to be desired, I am afraid."

She had spoken in a soft voice that could only have been heard by her uncle and Longarm, and when she finished, she glanced at Longarm for an instant, as if to say she would challenge him also if he took up Sir Henry's argument. Amused and not a little impressed with Madeline's pluck in standing up to Sir Henry, Longarm looked back at Wilt Kincaid as he herded his two sheepmen toward the porch.

The crowd of men parted to give themselves a wide berth as the sheepherders trudged toward them. One of the Basques was much older than the other, and both were wearing the traditional garb of the Basques, unlike Pablo Montalban. On their heads they wore *boinas,* dark berets that looked feminine and useless when compared to the wide-brimmed hats of the cowboys. They did not wear boots, but prefered rope-soled shoes, or *alpartagas,* and they each carried a combination shepherd's staff and weapon they called the *makhila.* Long ponchos covered their shirts and reached past their knees. What Longarm saw of their pants were covered with patches, with even the patches themselves patched. Their ponchos were dark and unspectacular, as were their sullen faces as they looked neither to the right nor to the left during their march to the ranchhouse.

Abruptly, Wilt pulled up. The two Basques heard the horse being reined in behind them and came to a halt also. Though they could undoubtedly feel the hostile eyes peering at them coldly from all quarters, they paid no attention to this, but simply kept their implacable gaze on Sir Henry.

"What have you got here, Kincaid?" Sir Henry asked.

"Sheepherders," Kincaid responded. "I found them nosing around. And they wouldn't tell me what they was up to. The older one just said he wanted to see you."

"Me?"

"He said he was looking for the Englishman with the big house on the river," Kincaid replied. "I figure that would have to be you, Sir Henry."

Sir Henry nodded and looked at the older Basque. "What do you want with me?" he demanded.

The older Basque gazed for a long moment up into Sir Henry's face, then said, his voice low but powerful, "I want my son."

Sir Henry was startled. "Your son?"

"Yes. My son. Manuel."

Sir Henry glanced at Longarm, then back at the old Basque. He knew where Manuel was, of course, since Longarm had told him. But he was understandably reluctant to tell this man before him of the fate of his son. Even sheepherders have feelings, Sir Henry realized.

"I myself have not seen your son," Sir Henry began cautiously. "Who are you, sir?"

"I am Miguel Alava, and this is my boy Felipe. Together we have searched the Ruby Mountains, following the track of Manuel's flock. It seemed to us we must be close. And then this man, he tell us to leave your range."

"They wouldn't go, Sir Henry," Kincaid said. "They insisted on seeing you."

"I see."

"You do not own this land," Miguel stated flatly. "It is open range. This Mr. Erikson tells us, and he is right. Manuel has brought the sheep of Mr. Erikson to this range, and now he has disappeared. Either you let me search for my son—or take me to him."

There was more than the hint of a threat in the man's voice. The cowboys stirred angrily, and Sir Henry's face darkened. Again he glanced nervously at Longarm. Miguel Alava had put him on the spot, and in a moment Sir Henry was going to have to tell Miguel some very bad news.

Longarm cleared his throat. "I'll tell him, Sir Henry."

The fellow took out a handkerchief and mopped his brow. "I wish you would, Longarm. This is most unfortunate."

Miguel turned his dark, impassive face toward Longarm, his almost black eyes pinning Longarm with an intensity that gave the lawman momentary pause.

"I know you," said the Basque's son. "Carmen told me. You are the U.S. marshal. You saved Carmen from Wyatt. Now you are with these men." Felipe spat on the ground, causing a slight commotion among the ranch hands. They had not expected to see such insolence from a sheepherder.

"Enough, Felipe!" said the boy's father. Then he turned his eyes once again to Longarm and waited impassively.

Longarm glanced at Kincaid. The foreman had a slight smile on his scarred, handsome face. He had known all along that Manuel was the dead sheepherder Longarm had found, but the foreman had been content to say nothing, and to drive the two through the sun of a long afternoon instead. Madeline had called the foreman a brute; it was not strong enough.

"I am not *with* these men, Miguel," Longarm said quietly. "Like you, I have been searching through the Ruby Mountains."

"Yes," acknowledged the Basque. "You search for the train robbers. I understand."

"Well north of here," Longarm resumed unhappily, "close to where Kincaid found you, there is a steep bluff." Longarm paused for a moment and took a deep breath. "At the foot of that bluff are the sheep your son was herding. And with those dead sheep—what is left of them—I found the body of your son Manuel."

"It is as Cal Wyatt says!" whispered Felipe, horrorstruck.

Miguel's dark eyes regarded Longarm for a moment longer, then he lowered them. A shudder appeared to pass over the squat man's frame. When he looked up again, his face had aged and a pallor had crept into it. He looked at Sir Henry.

"Why did you do this thing?" Miguel asked softly. "All say that you are fair, that you do not wish violence, even though you hate the sheep and those who tend them."

Before Sir Henry could respond to the sudden accusation, Miguel pulled a long knife from under his poncho and started for Sir Henry, his movements so swift that he was on the porch almost before Longarm could react. As Miguel raised his hand to drive the point of his knife into Sir Henry's heart, Longarm drew his Colt in one fluid motion and clubbed the knife from Miguel's hand. As the knife tumbled from the man's grasp, Wilt Kincaid drew his revolver and leveled it at the Basque.

He would have pumped lead into Miguel's back if Felipe had not swung his *makhila* with ferocious accuracy up at the foreman, clubbing him solidly and sending the blond foreman tumbling back over his horse's rear end, his revolver discharging harmlessly into the air. Instantly the ranch hands closed upon Felipe, ripping the shepherd's staff from his hand and flinging him to the ground.

Longarm coolly fired two shots over their heads. The two shots slowed the men some, and a third shot —this one a little lower—got their complete attention. "Get back away from that boy!" Longarm commanded.

A groggy Kincaid looked furiously at Longarm. "Whose side are you on, lawman! These two sheepers tried to kill me and Sir Henry!"

"I'm on no one's side, Kincaid. Except the law's side. I keep the peace is what I do, and right now it ain't very peaceable around here. So you stay right where you are, and tell your men to let that boy go."

Sir Henry, still shaken, spoke up then. "You heard him, Kincaid. Do as he says!"

Longarm glanced at Miguel. The man was down on one knee, holding the hand Longarm had struck with his revolver. "Sorry, Miguel," Longarm said, "but you didn't leave me much choice. I sympathize with you about your son, but I don't suspicion Sir Henry had a thing to do with it."

Miguel looked up bleakly at Longarm. "It is his foreman, then. This Englishman does not always know what his men do. He does not want to know, I think."

Madeline bent and took the older Basque's right hand. "Come inside," she told him, "and let me look at that hand. Your son too."

The Basque got slowly back up onto his two feet, looking with surprise into Madeline's face. She glanced swiftly at Sir Henry. "Surely you can understand the man's grief. His reaction was normal when you consider what he and his people have been going through because of you and the rest of the cattlemen in this territory."

Wearily, still quite shaken by the episode, Sir Henry nodded. "As you wish, Madeline," he told her.

But Miguel Alava would have none of it. He pulled his hand quickly out of Madeline's grasp. "No," he said. "I will not go inside." He looked coldly, impassively about him at the ranks of equally cold, equally unrelenting faces. "Come, Felipe," he said to his son. "We will leave this place of pestilence."

"Wait," said Longarm, as gently as he could. "Do you want help in recovering your son's body?"

"Where is the place?" the old man demanded, turning to face Longarm squarely.

Longarm glanced at Sir Henry. "Kincaid knows the place. He could show him."

"Yes, of course," Sir Henry said.

"You goin' to make me take that sheepherder back up into the Rubies?" Kincaid exploded. "I been ridin' all day!"

"You took him *from* there, even though you must have had a pretty good idea what he and his son were looking for—and you found him near that ridge, didn't you?"

Red-faced, furious, Sir Henry's foreman nodded curtly.

"Then you can take him back," Sir Henry snapped.

"And see that no harm comes to either of them," said Madeline, "and do whatever you can to help them in their trial. This man is going to bury his son. Whether he herds sheep or not, he has a heart and he grieves, like all of us. Or is that too difficult for you to understand, Kincaid?"

"Madeline!" Sir Henry said. "That was uncalled for!"

Stung, Wilt Kincaid turned on Madeline. But his anger died when he saw the cold fury in her face. She was at that moment impossibly beautiful—and unattainable. And Wilt Kincaid was very much in love. Watching the two of them facing each other in that instant, Longarm recalled Madeline's words concerning Kincaid earlier, and wondered which of the two was the more unfeeling.

Kincaid swung away and started for his horse. As he did so, Sir Henry called for the hands to provide horses for both of the sheepherders, then turned and moved back into the house, choosing to ignore the muttered outrage his order had generated in the ranks of his loyal ranch hands.

Sitting back down in the armchair he had occupied earlier, Longarm felt the need of something stronger than tea. "Do you have any liquor, Sir Henry?"

Preoccupied, the cattleman looked at Longarm questioningly. He wasn't sure what Longarm was asking until Madeline, coiling herself on a divan beside Longarm, chuckled and said to her uncle, "He would like something stronger than tea, Henry." Then she looked at Longarm. "My uncle is an abstainer, Mr. Long. Tea is his drink, I am afraid."

"I am sorry," said Sir Henry, taking a deep breath. "After something like that, I suppose I can understand the wish for strong drink. I could almost wish for one myself."

"That's easily remedied," Madeline said.

She called in the Indian housekeeper and told her to bring the whiskey from her place. The instructions alarmed the Indian woman, and she looked with apprehension at Sir Henry. With a wave of his hand, he dismissed her misgivings.

"Do it," he said wearily. "Do it. Go get the whiskey. We'll have it before dinner."

Madeline smiled at her uncle as the massive Indian woman padded hastily from the room. "You're getting human, finally," she told the man.

"Perhaps," Sir Henry said wearily. "It is this damnable conflict between the cattlemen and the sheepmen. I have tried to see it as a simple case of land management. But just now I saw it in terms of two quite human and quite pathetic human beings."

"I wouldn't underestimate the Basques," said Longarm.

"Oh, after the way that man came after me, I fear there is no chance of my doing that. None at all. They are most fierce. Now I see why Erikson is bringing them in to herd his sheep." Sir Henry shook his head wearily. "I am sure I do not know where this is all going to lead."

"It will lead to more bloodshed," Madeline snapped. "As long as you and your silly cowboys continue thinking this is your country to run as you please." She glanced swiftly at Longarm. "Is that not so, Marshal Long?"

"I wouldn't like to comment, ma'am," Longarm said hastily, unwilling to be brought into this debate. He could see at once that this was an old conflict between Madeline and her uncle, and it was one that Sir Henry probably never got to win. Longarm didn't want to jump in on Madeline's side and make the odds even worse, even though he did see a good deal of sense in Madeline's position.

"You don't think this fighting over grazing land will

lead to more bloodshed?" Madeline insisted. She had the bit in her teeth and wasn't going to let go, it seemed.

"Perhaps cooler heads will prevail," Longarm managed, feeling strangely uncomfortable under the heat of the woman's concern. He glanced at Sir Henry. "And I think maybe Sir Henry is the man to see that that comes about. How do you see it, Sir Henry?"

"Well, of course. Of course, Longarm. You are quite right. Quite right. There is to be a meeting of the Cattlemen's Association next Monday, and I intend to raise my voice on that occasion and plead for moderation. I am thinking of offering a reward for any information leading to the capture of the person or persons unknown who rimrocked Erikson's sheep and killed that young man. I am certain the rest of the members will be only too anxious to join me in that endeavor. We should be able to offer a quite sizable amount."

Madeline laughed. "Henry, do you really expect Bide Hanson and Waggoner and all those other cattlemen to join you in that? You are *such* a romantic! Really! I have little doubt that it was Bide or perhaps Mitchell of the Rocking 7 who rimrocked those sheep."

Sir Henry frowned and looked away from Madeline at Longarm. "Perhaps Madeline is right, Longarm. I can't be sure she is mistaken. To hear those men talk, you would think any crime would be acceptable if it rids the open range of these sheepherders and their sheep."

"I didn't tell you," Longarm said, "of the death of Mooreland, did I?"

"Old Mooreland?" the man exclaimed. "The sheep rancher? He's been in this country for years. What happened?"

Longarm told the cattleman. With Madeline listening as well, he described what had happened to Mooreland's sheep, and then told of Mooreland's suicide with as much delicacy as he could manage.

When he had finished, Sir Henry was staring straight ahead, his face fierce with a simmering anger. Madeline, too, was silent, her face drawn. Longarm found himself moved by their silent outrage. It was more eloquent than words would have been, no matter how well chosen—and it convinced Longarm that he no longer need suspect the cattleman of having anything to do with either abomination.

Perhaps now Sir Henry would be angry enough to convince the cattlemen in the Association to bring those who were guilty of these crimes to justice. Longarm sincerely hoped so. He was after train robbers, and he did not want to get any more involved in this unpleasant business. It was far too difficult to tell the honest fellows from the sidewinders in this kind of a conflict.

"That's terrible," Sir Henry muttered at last, shaking his head slowly. "I knew how he loved that dog. But to kill himself . . ."

"I used to ride over to Mooreland's ranch," Madeline said softly.

The bottle of whiskey arrived from Madeline's place at that moment—just in time. Madeline fixed them all a drink, and Longarm was astonished at the size of the drink Sir Henry took. Then it was time for supper. As they entered the dining room, Sir Henry paused in the entry and shook Longarm's hand warmly.

"I didn't thank you," the man said. "You saved my life back there. That was quick thinking. I'm afraid I was too astonished to defend myself."

"He saved you *and* the Basques," Madeline remarked to her uncle as they sat down. She looked across the table at Longarm, through the blazing candelabrum that had been placed between them. "We must have a nightcap later this evening, Longarm. Perhaps at my place. I'm afraid my nerves won't allow me to sleep otherwise."

Perfectly aware of what her niece was proposing, Sir Henry diplomatically busied himself with forking an enormous steak onto his plate as Longarm smiled back at Madeline and inclined his head in acceptance of the woman's invitation. But sleep, Longarm knew, was the last thing either of them were thinking of at that moment.

Sir Henry passed Longarm the platter of steaks, and Longarm took it from him with enthusiasm. He realized suddenly that he was ravenous.

Chapter 5

"You must think me a shameless hussy," Madeline said, as she put her drink down and moved closer.

"Right now, ma'am," replied Longarm, "I'm not thinking much at all."

She smiled wickedly. "I know. You're just looking."

She was right, of course. And Longarm had no excuses to offer. Madeline had been wearing only a long, filmy nightgown by the time he reached her place for that nightcap she had promised him. Then, after the second drink, she had uncoiled herself from the small sofa where she had been sitting, turned her back to him, ducked her head, pulled the nightgown over her head, and flung it into a corner. The drink still in her hand, she had turned to face him.

He felt surprise and a curious tightening in the chest —or maybe a little lower down.

Madeline was still moving closer. Her red hair was loose, and it cascaded down her back and coiled about the erect nipples of her firm, upthrust breasts. Her pubic hair was darker than he would have expected, an exciting contrast to the milky whiteness of her belly and thighs.

He put down his own drink—just in time. She laughed softly and took his face in her hands, leaned still closer to him, and kissed him on the mouth. She moaned provocatively as her lips probed his and opened. As her tongue found his, she flung her arms around his neck and ground her naked body against him.

Longarm responded. He brought his hands up to cup her warm breasts. His rough fingertips caressed the nipples. He heard her groan, her arms still about his neck, her tongue still probing deliciously. He could smell her. It was the aroma of a woman without the taint of soap or perfume. The smell of her filled his nostrils, arousing him to an even keener pitch.

He broke the kiss and took one of her nipples in his mouth. It swelled even larger and grew as hard as a bullet as his tongue flicked it expertly. Madeline leaned back, moaning softly, then snatched at his hand and ran ahead of him into the next room, her bedroom. In an instant she had flung herself on the bed, pulling Longarm down beside her. She opened her legs hungrily, and Longarm's probing fingers thrust themselves deep into her crotch, then past her moist, pliant lips. She began to moan as she moved closer to him.

But Longarm was still dressed. With a frantic, fumbling grab she worked at the buttons of his fly and tried to slip her hand in. But Longarm's britches were just too tight. "Damn!" she muttered, as she tugged furiously and pulled Longarm's britches down over his narrow hips, freeing him at last.

"Now!" she pleaded huskily, as she felt his solid readiness under her fingers. "I'm ready!"

"I reckon so," Longarm replied.

With his big hands, he thrust her buttocks under him as he moved between her legs. He went in full and deep. Madeline moaned and flung her head back, brought her legs up, and locked her ankles around the back of his neck.

"Deeper, Longarm!" she commanded.

It was a familiar cry and Longarm did his best to oblige. He pulled away from her, leaving just the tip of his erection within her, then plunged deliberately, powerfully, deeper than he had been able to go before.

Madeline uttered a sharp, guttural cry that was wrung from the deepest part of her. The woman's ankles tightened convulsively around his neck as he continued to thrust. Madeline cried out in pleasure and pain, "Oh, that's it! Keep going! Faster!"

After a dozen deep thrusts, Longarm felt her juices begin to flow. Her cries of excitement increased. With each shattering plunge her ecstasy mounted, her cries grew more intense, and it all had its effect on Longarm. He was also moving toward orgasm. He pounded harder, bringing sharp, deep yelps from Madeline. Abruptly she became rigid under him. Her ankles tightened. Her inner muscles squeezed about his erection, and he pressed hard for the instant before both of them came to a sudden, overwhelming outpouring.

Longarm fell forward upon her glistening body, aware that he was still large within her. She panted softly and straightened her legs out upon the bed and began to stroke his hair.

"Mmm," she said. "That was so good. Do you know how long it has been, Longarm? In this damn land of cowboys?"

"Long enough, I imagine."

"You can't imagine. It's filled with men, all right. Grass-chewing, ponderous, 'yes, ma'am' and 'no, ma'am' cowboys who are either too dirty or too shy to know what a woman wants and needs. They understand it in animals, and in themselves—but not in a woman! You don't know how glad I was to see you riding in with Sir Henry today. I knew from the way you rode that here was a man who knew about women, who knew about life—who understood!"

"I didn't know it showed," he said. "But if we keep

talking like this, we're going to lose what I still got going."

She smiled. "I can feel him! He's a wonder. They say it's not important, the size of a man. But don't you believe it, Longarm."

"I won't, if you tell me not to."

With him still inside, she swung out from under him smoothly and mounted him from the top, falling forward heavily, gasping with pleasure as she felt him going in deeper and deeper. Soon their bodies were locked together and there was no room left for him to probe. Squeezing delightedly with the muscles in her buttocks, she began rotating her hips very slowly.

Longarm lay back and let Madeline enjoy herself. She knew precisely how to do it, prolonging it as much as was humanly possible, pausing in her hip-rotations more and more often, for shorter and shorter periods, as she succumbed to her own mounting pleasure. Abruptly, her long red hair streaming down over Longarm's face and shoulders, she began rocking herself back and forth until at last, with a deep groan of joy, she poured her juices down over him in a hot, delicious explosion that sent her falling forward upon his chest, limp and trembling.

Longarm had held himself back, intent only on her pleasure. Now he pulled her higher on the bed, then rolled over on top of her.

"Oh!" she cried. "Again! So soon! I don't know if I can!"

"Sure you can. Just lay back and let it happen, woman!"

He was already thrusting with full, slow, even strokes. He was determined not to hurry, and used only a part of his weight and strength. He had told her to lie back and relax, and that is just what she did for the first few minutes. She was still panting from her own wild ride of a few moments before, but gradually she came to life under him. Longarm felt her inner muscles responding to his measured, metronomic thrusts. She began to meet his thrusts, to move faster, to drive up at him still harder. Tiny cries of delight began to escape from her. She kept her eyes shut tightly and began to snap her head back and forth.

Longarm himself was on his own now, building to the final moment. It had been a long time coming, for both of them, but by this time their bodies had taken over, and with a mounting fierceness, they slammed at each other recklessly. He pounded with fast, repeated drives until he could hear Madeline's tough, short grunts. Her body pulsed under him, then withdrew, drawing him into her. Then she arched, crying out in a kind of sob. Longarm could hold back no longer. He felt himself pulsing out of control, emptying, throbbing, until he was drained completely.

He dropped finally upon her, his face resting in the cloud of red hair beside her cheek, spent utterly. When their breathing had quieted, Madeline said softly, her fingers running idly through his hair, "That was nice, Longarm. So very nice. You have no idea how long I've waited for something like this to happen to me . . . again."

Longarm shifted his weight off her, but she turned and snuggled close to him. He put his arms around her shoulder and drew her still closer. "It's been a long time for me too, Madeline. In my line of work, a man doesn't have the company of a woman as regular as some other men do."

"You'll stay the night here with me, then?"

"I don't reckon that's wise. Your uncle might not understand."

She chuckled huskily. "Oh, he'd understand, all right. That's just the trouble."

"And I reckon some of your ranch hands saw me walking up here after supper."

"Yes, of course." She sighed, then brightened and leaned closer to him and took a quick nip out of his ear. "But you don't have to go right now."

"Don't reckon I do," he said, pulling her closer and kissing her on the lips.

She had seemed to Longarm to be a hard, perhaps even cruel, woman when she had confronted Kincaid earlier. But there was no cruelty in her now, he was certain, just a warmth and passion that appealed to him. It made him wonder at the ability people had to draw the best—or the worst—out of others.

Madeline began to run her index finger down his chest. As the finger plowed through the thick mat of dark hair on his chest, she said, "Whose side are you on, Longarm? The cattlemen or the sheepmen?"

Longarm was startled by her question. He took her hand in his, halting its unnerving progress past his navel. "Neither, Madeline."

"I see. It's that man Trampas you're after, and that's all you care about?"

"That's not *all* I care about, Madeline. But him and his gang are why I was sent here. They murdered a postal employee when they robbed that train."

She nodded, as if she had heard all this before, and said, "I think the cattlemen are insufferable. And poor Uncle Henry is helpless when it comes to curbing men like Bide Hanson and the other cattlemen. I don't like Wilt Kincaid, either. I don't trust him. I wouldn't put anything past him. Maybe that Basque was right when he accused Kincaid of stampeding those sheep and killing his son."

"Maybe," Longarm said, without too much conviction. He was finding himself disturbed once again by the controlled ferocity in Madeline's tone when she referred to the Lazy C foreman.

"I gather you don't like Kincaid—not at all."

"He presumed to take liberties with me, Longarm. I won't have that."

"Not unless you want them."

"Exactly."

"When was this, Madeline?"

"As soon as I got here, less than a month ago."

"I thought you'd been out here longer."

"I've been in the West for years. My last permanent stop was San Francisco. I got bored there and wrote Uncle Henry."

"He seems to think you just came West."

"The poor dear. He's a romantic, Longarm. He believes about people what he wants to believe."

"Is there more to you than Uncle Henry suspicions?"

She laughed wickedly and pulled Longarm closer. Just before she kissed him on the lips, she said softly, "Now what do *you* think, Longarm?"

The next morning, Sir Henry called his hands together a second time so that Longarm could ask them about Trampas. Wilt Kincaid was back, and as the other hands tramped across the compound toward the veranda, Longarm looked them over. They were all sizes and shapes, but one characteristic was common to each of them: the squint and rolling gait of the working cowboy. They were men who belonged on horses, and once astride one, they gained a power and grace that escaped them completely when afoot. Longarm wondered if this could be part of the reason these cowboys hated the sheepherders so readily. They saw in those who had to trudge on foot about this big land a reminder of what they might become without the horse—or without the need for one.

There was one hand, however, who was not of their stamp—who was a singular contrast to his dusty, leathery companions. Though he was among the last to stroll across the compound to the veranda, the other hands gave way to him without murmur, instinctively, the way one gives a wide berth to something moving in the grass. He came to a halt close to the veranda alongside Wilt Kincaid, his arms folded, his cold eyes resting speculatively on Longarm, and then on Madeline, who was standing beside the tall lawman.

As Sir Henry spoke up to acquaint his men with Longarm's mission in the area, the marshal looked over the fellow standing beside Kincaid. He was wearing a blue shirt, a dark, buttoned vest, and well-tailored pants, the cuffs of which were neatly tucked into his high cordovan boots. A black silk bandanna was knotted neatly at his neck. On his head he wore a gray fedora, but it did not look at all comical or out of place. The man's guns were not the guns of a working cowboy; they were the efficient tools of a hired gunman. They gleamed in the bright morning sunshine, and there were two of them, worn butts-out and holstered low.

In the company of hard-working, no-nonsense cowhands, this gunman might have appeared incongruous, ridiculous even. But Longarm was not laughing. It was the cold, heavily lidded eyes that kept the man from being a joke. It was always the eyes, Longarm realized, that told a man what he needed to know about another; this one was a killer.

"What's this feller supposed to look like?" one of the hands asked Sir Henry, in response to Sir Henry's request for information.

Sir Henry turned to Longarm, indicating that Longarm should perhaps be the one to reply.

"I don't know what he looks like," Longarm admitted. "All I know is, that's his name. Maybe you've heard of someone called by that name."

The fellow who had asked the question shrugged. "Never heard of anyone called himself Trampas."

"What's he *smell* like, Marshal?" the gunslick asked, his lean face creasing into a cold smile, his eyes alight with the mischief of his question.

"About like you, I'd imagine," replied Longarm slowly, deliberately, appraising the man coolly.

The fellow's expression did not change, just the eyes. They went cold. Longarm had felt such eyes on him before, when he crouched on a trail, his Colt in his hand, a coiled rattler in the shade of a boulder before him.

"Now that wasn't called for," said Wilt Kincaid angrily.

Longarm turned to Sir Henry. "You've got a gunslick on your payroll, Sir Henry. What is his name?"

"Name's Frank Tully, Marshal," said the gunslick, his voice sharp, meticulous. "Perhaps my question was out of line, but there was no need for you to get nasty about it. All I meant was that if you don't know what this fellow looks like, you're going to have a difficult time tracking him down." He smiled then. The man's teeth were clean and bright in his tanned face.

"I hired Frank myself," said Sir Henry. "Frank came to my assistance during a poker game last week at the Drover's Palace. I caught a man cheating. He was about to cut me down with his belly-gun when Frank, who had been sitting beside me, cut him down. I, for one, am quite willing to have a man who can draw and shoot as well as that on my side. With this trouble brewing, I offered him a job on the Lazy C."

"Town life was beginning to pall on me, Marshal," spoke up Frank Tully at that point, his eyes no longer cold, his quick smile doing its best to erase all menace from his appearance.

Longarm shrugged, then looked around at the other ranch hands. They stared back at him impassively. They knew nothing about any Trampas, obviously. But even if they did know something, it was just as obvious to Longarm that they would keep their mouths shut and let Longarm flush his own quarry.

Turning to Sir Henry, he shook the Englishman's hand. "Thank you for your hospitality, Sir Henry. I guess I'll be on my way. I won't catch Trampas or any of his band standing around on this veranda."

"Good luck to you, sir," said Sir Henry warmly.

As Longarm started for his horse, he glanced once in Madeline's direction. She was watching him, but she was smart enough to let her eyes reveal nothing more than a friendly interest. He touched the brim of his hat to her as he swung into his saddle. Madeline smiled briefly, mischievously.

As Longarm pulled the buckskin around, he thought he caught a glint of pure, unadulterated hatred in Kincaid's eyes. It had flared to life the instant Kincaid caught Madeline's mischievous smile.

With a wave at Sir Henry and Madeline, Longarm rode out of the compound, an oppressive sense of disaster following after him. There were too many eyes on him, he realized, and too many who knew his business. But then, he knew what he was about, didn't he? He had made himself a target deliberately. There was no one else handy he could use as bait. The trouble was, there sometimes wasn't all that difference between a cleverly baited trap and a fool victim with a bullet in his back.

Chapter 6

Longarm was almost pleased when, less than a few miles from Montalban's sheep ranch, he caught the glint of sunlight on metal in among the rimrocks above the trail directly ahead of him. The suspense was over, and since he was not yet within rifle range, he had some time to plan his response.

He kept going until he reckoned he was almost within range, then reined in cautiously, dismounted, and proceeded to examine the right front foreleg of his buckskin. He took his time, found nothing amiss, of course, then let the leg go and patted the horse's flank comfortingly. Still without revealing any great sense of urgency, Longarm led the horse slowly, gently off the trail and in among the rocks until he was certain he was out of sight of the varmint watching from the rimrocks. Then, looping the reins about a juniper branch, he snaked his Winchester out of its saddle scabbard and moved up into the rocks.

Once he judged himself high enough and close enough, he slipped off his spurs and continued along the narrow ledge that led around behind the rimrocks. As he ran swiftly, silently along, he appreciated the low-heeled army stovepipes he was wearing. Longarm spent crucial moments like this afoot, and he could run with surprising speed for a man his size in the skintight boots. Slowing up some, he crouched down behind a slablike boulder, and kept going until he was just beyond it. He had guessed correctly. Below him, not more than twenty feet away, Wilt Kincaid was lying prone on a flat shelf of rock that jutted out over the trail below. It was an excellent spot and gave him command of the trail for hundreds of yards in either direction.

Kincaid was getting just a mite impatient, however. He sat up abruptly, bringing his rifle in and setting it down carefully beside him. Then he stood up and peered out over the trail. The man was trying to get a look at Longarm's horse—and Longarm. Having seen nothing, the man returned to his rifle and was in the act of reaching down for it when Longarm spoke up.

"Leave the Winchester right there, Kincaid."

Kincaid jerked his hand away from the rifle and stared up in shocked surprise at Longarm. Longarm waggled his rifle. Kincaid raised his hands above his head. Longarm smiled.

"With the sun at my back, mister, you should have figured that sun reflecting off the rifle barrel. Slowly now, unbuckle that gunbelt and drop it down there beside the rifle."

As Kincaid's hands dropped to his gunbelt, he said, "Okay, mister, you got me cold this time, but there'll be other times when you won't be so lucky."

"What have you got against me, Kincaid? Don't tell me that escorting that Basque to his son's body has turned you into a bushwhacker."

The man's gunbelt dropped with a thump on the stone ledge. Kincaid took an angry step toward Longarm. "That ain't it and you know it."

"It's Madeline, then."

"Yes, damn your hide. I want that woman! But I don't want her soiled by the likes of you. I saw you goin' to her place last night. And so did a few others! You compromised her openly, you son of a bitch!" The fellow's face was so red it was almost in flames as he finished his denunciation, and Longarm realized with a sudden deep sense of frustration that his elaborate trap with himself as the bait had netted him only a lovesick—though admittedly dangerous—suitor. He decided to speak reasonably to the man.

"The woman's not married, Kincaid. And she's over twenty-one. I figure what she figures. She's old enough to choose her own friends. Seems to me she's not at all anxious to make friends with you. You're fishing in an empty stream where that woman is concerned."

The man was trembling by this time. It didn't matter that Longarm was telling him something he undoubtedly already knew. In fact that probably made it considerably worse. All he knew was that standing before him was the only available target for his frustration. Without a weapon in his hand or on his person, he started across the ledge, obviously intent upon climbing up to where Longarm stood. "Put down that rifle, Marshal," he said furiously, "and I'll take you apart, bolt by bolt."

The situation was so incongruous that Longarm tilted his head back to laugh at the onrushing foreman. Kincaid pulled up abruptly, a look of surprise flashing across his countenance. That was when the mountainside behind Longarm reverberated thunderously. The blast seemed to fill the universe, and in that instant Longarm felt his skull blown apart by a terrific impact on the back of his head. In the fraction of a second before the world distintegrated around him, he saw Kincaid's angry features begin to soften into something like a smile . . .

When he drifted back into light, he found the vacant blue sky, unblinking, uncaring, peering down at him. Specks floated casually across the wide blue eye, like cinders caught in a chimney's updraft. Vultures. He wasn't dead yet, then. They were still up there, waiting for all the vital signs to fade away, for the immobility of death to manifest itself. Longarm moved his head slightly, and all the hammers in hell rained down upon his skull. He winced and screwed his eyes shut and hung on as the ground tipped sickeningly under him. But he was patient, secure in the knowledge that nothing lasts forever, and at last the pounding subsided.

He opened his eyes and found himself staring into Wilt Kincaid's smiling face. Only it was a frozen smile, a grimace really, made more terrible by the long scar that ran down his cheek. His face was so close to Longarm's that if the blond foreman had been breathing, Longarm would have felt every sour exhalation; but Longarm felt nothing. A dead man doesn't have to breathe anymore.

Longarm smelled, adrift in the midday heat, the stench of fecal matter. It seemed to come from Kincaid. Longarm tried to move his left arm, but it was under his body, which was wedged down between two boulders. His right arm responded, however, though he had the odd sensation that it was not entirely his arm, that it was someone else's and was moving only on a whim. Directing it as much with his eyes as his sense of touch and distance, he reached out and thrust Kincaid's face to one side. He wished he hadn't when he saw what lay on the other side of Kincaid's rigid smile.

Kincaid had been shot in the throat, just above the Adam's apple. The bullet had ranged upward and exited, tumbling, from the rear of the skull, leaving a gaping, messy hole. It reminded Longarm of the sick heaviness in the back of his own head. Cautiously he reached back and felt of his skull. It felt very bad. All caked and torn meat. Stickiness. The area seemed numb, however. The thudding pain he experienced was deep inside his skull. Gingerly he probed for pieces of shattered skullbone, for the site of entry. He wasn't careful enough, and a dagger of pain sliced through his entire skull.

As he closed his eyes and waited for the pain to ease, he felt a bitter elation. The bullet had not penetrated his skull. It had ripped a deep furrow through scalp and hair, but then it had glanced off. He had a thick skull, it seemed, thicker even than Billy Vail realized.

The killer had dragged Kincaid up beside Longarm and flung him down to make it look as if the two had killed each other in a confrontation. Anyone with sense would be able to see, however, that a man with the back of his head blown out is not going to be capable of aiming a rifle and shooting another man while that fellow is moving toward him.

Still, no one would likely question it—certainly not after the vultures got through cleaning the skeletons.

Since he couldn't move his left arm, he used his right arm to push himself up out of the narrow space into which he was wedged. The effort caused a hammering pain in the base of his skull. But Longarm simply closed his eyes, clenched his teeth, and continued to push. He was no longer resting his entire weight on his left arm, and feeling began to flow back into it. Pins and needles came first. The sensation was excruciating. He tried moving his fingers. They felt rubbery. He knew they were moving, but he couldn't *feel* them moving. And when he tried to use his left arm to support his weight and help push him upright, it was no good at all.

So he hung there, inches above the ground, his right hand supporting him, an enormous crippled bug frying in the sun. At last the pins and needles subsided. Now the arm just ached. Again he tried to use the arm, and this time he was successful. Grabbing hold of the boulder on his right side, he hauled himself up out of his narrow prison and found himself looking down at Wilt Kincaid.

The odor that came from him was much stronger now. The death spasm had opened his bowels, and whoever had done this thing had had the pleasant job of dragging his befouled corpse up off the ledge and then dropping it down beside Longarm. Longarm felt his stomach begin to rebel—and found the sensation curiously comforting. It meant that he was unquestionably alive.

He wasn't so sure by the time he reached his horse. He had passed out twice as he labored down the rocks to where he had left the animal, his rifle serving as a crutch at times. He began to expect the blackouts and to sense their imminence. With his rifle as an aid, he would quickly slump down, then hang on as he spun out of consciousness. But each time he would come to and find himself clutching his rifle firmly, the trail below just that much closer.

Focusing his eyes well enough to drop the Winchester into its scabbard was difficult enough, but even more difficult—impossible it seemed, at one point—was untying the reins from the juniper. He managed it at last, and then turned stiffly around to survey the horse—and his next problem, mounting up. The animal regarded him warily, his ears laid back almost flat, his head low.

Longarm kept a firm grip on the reins and, moving close to the animal, leaned heavily on the buckskin's quivering flank. Presently he thought he might have the strength he needed to pull himself into the saddle. He lifted his left foot and somehow fumbled it into the stirrup. He tried then to pull himself up and got about halfway before he slid down again. He waited and rested a minute, his head leaning against the buckskin's flank, then tried again. The third time he made it and dragged his right foot across the cantle. Once secure, he urged his horse on down the trail. He had not been far from the Mantalban ranch when his bait had been taken, he reminded himself ironically, and he was hoping he could make it to the ranch without any further blackouts.

He rode sagged over the animal's neck, the buckskin keeping a steady pace. He measured time by the slow passage of boulders and the slipping past of islands of juniper and pine. The ground became less rocky and barren. He was riding alongside a stream, the sound of its water a pleasant, enticing music. His mind wandered. He was no longer making a conscious effort to direct the horse. He would not have known in which direction to go even if he had been able to do so. He just clung to the saddle, the universe whirling sickeningly around him . . .

Abruptly the horse quickened its pace to a lope. Frantic to stop it, Longarm tried to pull up. Instead, he pitched sideways off the buckskin and found himself staring dazedly up at a darkening sky. The cool grass held him with a tender, soft gentleness he had never known before. The horse pulled away from him, blowing nervously. But he paid no attention. The earth was a gently rocking cradle lulling him into a delicious sleep . . .

When he awoke, he was inside a cool room, the sounds of morning drifting over him. He heard a chicken clucking. He opened his eyes. Carmen was bent over him, her eyes sad. They widened with surprise and pleasure, however, as she saw him looking up at her.

"Ah! Mr. Longarm! You have a terrible wound in your head, but you will be all right now! I know that! You are *not* dead!"

"If I am dead," Longarm replied, smiling, "at least

I've gone to heaven. Where's your father, Carmen? I have a few things to tell him."

Her eyes grew sad again. "I cannot get my father. I will get Pedro."

Before he could get her to explain the absence of her father—which seemed to have ominous implications—she vanished out the door. Longarm turned his head slightly and saw a window framing a bright blue patch of morning sky. He had been unconscious for how long, he wondered. A night? A few days, maybe?

Pedro, a tough, wiry young man who looked about twenty, returned with Carmen, his dark face grim. He looked down solemnly at the lawman. "Carmen say you fine now. Is that right?"

Longarm started to sit up. At once Carmen was beside the bed, assisting him. Longarm put his right hand up to his head and found it swathed tightly in bandages. He fingered the area of the wound carefully, but this time felt no sudden bolt of pain. He smiled up at Carmen. "That your bandage?"

She nodded, pleased.

"How long have I been here?"

"A week and a day, Mr. Long," said Pedro. "How do you feel? Can you ride?"

"More than a *week*!" Longarm exclaimed, surprised.

He flipped back the blanket that was covering him, and sat up on the bed. He was wearing his longjohns. His shirt, coat, pants, and stockings were folded neatly on the dresser beside the small bed. The room tipped slightly as he stood up to walk over to the dresser. He almost lost his balance, but again Carmen was at his side, steadying him.

"I'm fine, Pedro," Longarm told the boy. "Just fine. A mite unsteady on my feet, but nothing that won't pass, I reckon, thanks to you people. And I won't soon forget this."

"Good," Pedro replied. "Can you ride, Mr. Long?"

This time, Longarm noticed, Pedro's concern was quite noticeable. Longarm looked into the boy's dark, frightened eyes. "What is it, Pedro? What's wrong?"

"It's father!" Carmen cried. Her eyes, also, revealed the terrible tension she was under.

"What about your father? What happened to him?"

Pedro spoke up then. "When we found you, you were babbling like a man gone mad. Soon we learned of the death of another—Wilt Kincaid, the Lazy C's foreman. This we found when we listened carefully to the wild things you say when Carmen try to clean your head wound." He smiled thinly at the memory. "You thought we were vultures picking the flesh from your bones and you told us to go after Kincaid instead. You said he was still back there, grinning."

Longarm sat back down on the bed, a frown on his face, and looked at Carmen. The girl nodded unhappily to confirm her brother's words. It did not please Longarm to realize he had babbled like that, but he had heard that head wounds could sometimes make a man do that. He wondered bleakly what else he had talked about—his recent indiscretions with Madeline, maybe?

"My father took your horse and went back along your trail," Pedro continued. "He found Kincaid. I told him to bury the man, but my father would not do such a thing. Even a man such as this, he tell us, deserves a decent burial. So he rode to the Lazy C with Kincaid's body."

"But they held him there, Mr. Long!" Carmen cried anxiously, breaking impatiently into Pedro's account. "Marshal Toady rode out and brought him to Ruby Wells. He is in jail now."

"He has already been tried, Marshal Long," Pedro said. "He is to be hung in two days."

"Jesus!" Longarm muttered, getting to his feet. "You two get out of here while I dress."

90

When they hesitated, he waved them out with an impatient gesture. As they left the room, he reached hastily for his shirt, his mind racing. It was obvious that the town marshal was acting in accordance with the local cattlemen's wishes. Wilt Kincaid's death was just a handy pretext to get Pablo Montalban. It had not been planned that way, but Sir Henry was obviously willing to go along. He was astonished at Sir Henry's apparent willingness to comply with something like this, but he told himself he should not be surprised at anything a cattleman does if it means getting rid of a sheepherder.

As Longarm finished dressing, he noticed that Pablo had retrieved his hat for him, most likely when he had gone back for Kincaid's body. He tried to wear it in his accustomed manner, but found that the bandage made this impossible. He left the room, calling to Carmen, asking her to remove the bandage if she could.

He sat down at the kitchen table and put his head down on his forearms as Carmen and her mother carefully removed the bandage, then the dressing. They decided that a much smaller, less bulky bandage would suffice, but as Carmen wrapped this second bandage about Longarm's head, she cautioned him about letting dirt get into the wound, even though it had pretty well scabbed over. He raised himself up, his head feeling a mite lighter, and saw the impatient Pedro, arms folded, waiting in the doorway. The young Basque evidently intended to ride into Ruby Wells with him.

"Stay here, Pedro," Longarm told him. "I don't want Carmen or your mother left alone. Not with the feeling against the sheep ranchers running this high. They need you. I'll ride in and bring your father back with me. I am a federal officer. I have jurisdiction in this territory. My word ought to be enough to get your father out of jail."

"I told them you were here when I was at the trial. I told them you would tell them what happened. But the judge rode out here and said you were out of your head, that it was likely that Papa had shot both you and Kincaid. He said you would die soon."

"Some judge."

"He does not like sheepherders. And he is a judge only because that is what he calls himself."

Longarm nodded. He knew the type; the West had doctors with the same qualifications. "Well, I won't look dead when I ride in, Pedro." He smiled then, and looked at Carmen. "Unless I don't get fed soon. I'm as hungry as a bear in the springtime, and as weak as a calf without its mama. I figure a good meal, maybe some of that lamb stew you got simmering on the stove, would set me up real good and proper."

The two women almost flew to the stove. Longarm left the cabin and returned a few moments later with Manuel Alava's dictionary. Examining it on the way in, he had assured himself that there were no bloodstains on its cover or pages. He sat back down and placed it silently on the table. When Pedro saw it, he recognized it at once. His slight intake of breath brought Carmen around. One look and she reached for the volume, her eyes flooding.

As she clasped it to her bosom, Longarm said, "I figured you might want to have it."

Unable to speak, she nodded, then fled to the privacy of her room. Longarm took a deep breath as Theresa Montalban returned to the stew. Pedro turned and left the cabin, leaving Longarm to his thoughts. It was more than a day's ride to Ruby Wells. To be on the safe side, he had better get there soon. They were supposed to hang Pablo legally, but lynching a murdering sheepherder would be a perfect way for a cow town like Ruby Wells to spend an evening.

• • •

Longarm had not ridden more than a few miles before he realized that there were still a few nuts and bolts loose topside. Gritting his teeth, he attempted to treat his pain as he heard the ancient Greeks had done—with contempt. But by the time he reached a ridge overlooking Ruby Wells the next afternoon, he was looking for someone to bite.

As he started down the slope, he heard the click of horseshoes on stone behind him. He turned to see six well-armed riders moving off the ridge after him. He was about to be surrounded. He shrugged, turned back around in his saddle, and gave his horse the lead as it picked its way down the slope. When he reached the meadow, he did not bother to turn around a second time, and soon enough the horsemen behind him had pulled abreast of him.

Turning slowly, Longarm saw himself peering at a young man with long, stringy, prematurely white hair. His face was dark and gaunt. Gleaming eyes peered out at Longarm from dark hollows. He wore a battered black hat, the rim of which flopped loosely down over his forehead and neck. A dark poncho covered his shoulders and upper torso, and he wore the rope-soled shoes of the Basque instead of riding boots. Riding behind this white-haired apparition, Longarm saw Miguel Alava and his son, Felipe. The three other riders closing in on Longarm from the other side were cut from rougher cloth. Slovenly, bewhiskered, their pants torn, their boots worn, the only thing clean or efficient about them were the well-oiled Colt revolvers slung at their hips.

As Longarm pulled up, the white-haired one smiled. His teeth were not nearly as white as his hair. "I just couldn't believe it," the man drawled, in a friendly enough tone. "Miguel here says you are the deputy U.S. marshal that stopped him from killing Sir Henry.

But Judge Barclay told Pablo's jury that you was practically dead already. You dead, mister?"

"I ain't dead, not quite. Now who the hell are you? I got business in Ruby Wells."

The fellow yanked his horse cruelly to bring him closer to Longarm, then heartily shook Longarm's hand. "I'm Kyle Erikson, and right glad to meet you. You already met Miguel and Felipe. The gents on the other side have decided to throw in with us sheepmen. It don't matter how they smell, just so they aim straight and keep their powder dry. That lean, mean-lookin' one's Peter, the other two's Luke and Bigger. You'll know which is Bigger if you look close enough."

The three men nodded sullenly at Longarm. It was clear they did not feel at all easy, riding up to a lawman. Longarm returned their nod, making no effort to lessen their evident nervousness. If there was one thing the sheepmen around here did not need to give the cattlemen at this time, it was the kind of excuse that the presence of these three imported gunslicks would almost inevitably provide.

"While we're sitting here on our sweaty horses," Longarm reminded Erikson, "an innocent man is sitting in jail, waiting to be hanged for a crime he knows he didn't commit. So if you'll pardon me, I got some riding to do!"

As Longarm urged his horse forward, Erikson called out, "Maybe you heard? There's been some talk of a lynching! That's why we're ridin' in with you!"

As the six riders stayed with him, Longarm flinched. He had been afraid of a lynching and had ridden hard to reach Ruby Wells before dark. He was certain that his appearance and his testimony alone would free Pablo Montalban from an imprisonment that even the jurors must have known was unjustified. But this sad little army at his back was likely only to make matters worse.

"Erikson," he snapped, "you and your friends keep out of this until I make my play! You got that straight? Now move off! I dont want us entering town together!"

The sheepherder grinned. "Good idea!" he said. "We'll back your play! Don't you worry!"

With that, he waved to Longarm, then peeled his horse around with a vicious yank on the reins and rode off toward the north of Ruby Wells, the five members of his army following raggedly after.

Longarm rode into Ruby Wells and down its main street and up to the hitch rail in front of Town Marshal Willis Toady's office without a single surprised glance in his direction. Longarm guessed it was because he had already been pronounced dead by that Judge Barclay. He was a ghost, and that made him invisible.

He dismounted carefully, unwilling to rattle the loose marbles in his head too violently, then pushed his way through the sparse crowd keeping vigil in front of the marshal's office. They looked into his face as he brushed angrily past them, but did not recognize him. Wills Toady did, however. He almost swallowed the toothpick he was chewing on.

"Gawdamighty, Marshal Long! Where's you come from?" he howled, jumping to his feet and upsetting his chair in the process. "I thought you was dead—along with poor Kincaid!"

"Never mind that! Release Pablo Montalban!"

"Hey, now! Just a moment! You can't come in here like that and tell me what to do! That man was tried by a jury, and . . ."

He didn't finish because Longarm had him by the front of his shirt and was lifting him off the floor, despite the man's awesome girth. "Do as I say, doughface! Pablo didn't kill anyone! The same person who shot me, shot Kincaid. And I don't know who that was! Yet!"

Longarm didn't release the marshal, he flung him toward the rear cells. Even as Toady hit the floor, he was scrambling frantically for his key ring. "I . . . I don't like this, Marshal! But . . . if you're a witness like you say . . ."

"It's like I say! Now open up!" Longarm's head was pounding something fierce by this time, and he attributed his lack of patience with a fellow lawman to that fact. Indeed, it was not pleasant to see the fat man's pudgy fingers trembling as he attempted to select the proper key.

At that moment the outer door swung open and Sir Henry stalked in, with Frank Tully and two others behind him. The man was astonished and undoubtedly delighted to see Longarm standing there.

"Longarm!" the man cried. "I thought you had been killed along with Kincaid! Why, this is astounding! Simply astounding!"

"Never send a judge on a doctor's errand," Longarm replied, smiling carefully. "I think I'm alive. Not kicking much, but alive."

"He . . . he wants me to release Montalban!" the town marshal bleated. He sounded anxious to have Sir Henry countermand Longarm's orders. Again Longarm found it difficult to comprehend the depth of these people's contempt for sheepherders.

"What's this?" asked Sir Henry, turning with a frown to Longarm. "Pablo Montalban killed Kincaid!"

"You know that for a fact, do you?"

"He was convicted! In a court of law!"

"And by a judge who has probably never seen the inside of a Blackstone. And who pronounced me dead. You know, Sir Henry, if Pablo had left Kincaid to the vultures, none of this would have happened to him. Because he felt Kincaid deserved a decent burial and hauled his corpse all the way to your place, he finds himself waiting to be hung!"

Sir Henry took a deep breath. "Tell me, Longarm. What happened?"

Longarm told him as much as he remembered, and when he had finished, Sir Henry looked at the town marshal and nodded to him. At once, Toady turned and went to release Pablo.

"And you don't know who shot you—or Kincaid?" Sir Henry asked.

"I don't reckon I do."

"Any clue at all?"

"Nope. My back was to the buzzard, whoever he was."

"Was it you the murderer was after—or Kincaid?"

"I just don't know, Sir Henry. All I *do* know is he got us both. And that judge wasn't far wrong, I reckon. I was near dead, and the firebells are still going off in my head while I'm standing here jawing with you." Longarm glanced at the cattlemen standing beside the big rancher. "I know Frank Tully, Sir Henry. Who are these two other gentlemen with you?"

"Oh, excuse me, Longarm," Sir Henry said. "Let me introduce you."

The one closest to Sir Henry was Bide Hanson, the owner of the Bar H, a man Longarm had already heard mention of—a tough-looking, heavyset fellow. He shook Longarm's hand quickly and nervously. But his grasp was powerful, and his dark, glowering eyes regarded Longarm without fear, and with perhaps a touch of truculence. There was a bitter, seething undercurrent in his manner, as if he had long since lost all faith in anything except his willingness to fight.

The second cattleman shook Longarm's hand easily, with a kind of shy friendliness that reminded Longarm of a big, flop-eared Labrador a friend of his had once owned. His hair was gray and his face had the flushed puffiness of a man who turns too often to the bottle for consolation, though why such an obviously good-natured fellow should need consolation was beyond Longarm. His name was Wally Waggoner, and he was the owner of the Diamond A.

"Right glad we got this nasty business straightened away, Marshal," Waggoner said, running his hand through his gray hair. "Yessir, could have been a terrible miscarriage of justice."

Bide Hanson wasn't so sure. He shifted his feet in frustration. "The way I look at it, one way or the other, them Basques are due for a hanging if they don't take their damn sheep off this range!"

Longarm looked at him. "In other words, Hanson—any excuse."

Bide's hard eyes fastened their gaze on Longarm's without flinching. "Yes. Any excuse, Marshal."

Longarm turned to Sir Henry. "And you, Sir Henry. Is that how you feel?"

"That may be a rather extreme viewpoint, I admit, Longarm," replied Sir Henry uneasily. "But it captures the sentiments of many cattlemen in this land, I am afraid."

"I asked how *you* felt."

"Don't drive him into a corner like that, Marshal Long," said Frank Tully, his voice quiet, but loaded with menace.

"Now, Frank," protested Sir Henry. "There's no need for you to step in like that. Longarm and I are good friends. More than that. He saved my life."

"That's right," said Bide Hanson. "Saved your life from one of them black Spaniards." As he said this, he looked beyond Longarm at someone standing in front of the open doorway that led to the cells.

Longarm turned to see Pablo, a free man, standing there. He looked for a long moment at Bide Hanson; then his face softened almost imperceptibly and he looked at Longarm. "I knew you come in time," the man said. "It takes more than a single bullet in the head to stop you, I think." His smile was wintry, but genuine.

"Thanks to Carmen and your wife. They must have taken good care of me."

Pablo nodded curtly, as if to acknowledge the indisputable proof of that assertion, then started past Longarm. "I go home now."

"Better wait for me," Longarm said. "There's a crowd out there. I don't think they are going to hold still for long when they see you free."

The Basque stopped and turned around. "I am a free man. I did nothing. You have told these men."

"At least let me go out with you and explain." Longarm looked at Sir Henry. "It would help, Sir Henry, if you added your voice to mine."

"Consider it done, Longarm," Sir Henry said, without hesitation.

"Might be dangerous," muttered Frank Tully.

"What is this, Sir Henry? Is Frank Tully your conscience now?"

"Not at all," protested Sir Henry, flustered. "But after what almost happened when that Basque, Miguel, attacked me, and then the death of my foreman, I feel that Frank could prove . . . useful."

"You know," said Bide, "we still don't know who shot Kincaid. It could have been one of these black Spaniards, the same one that threatened Kincaid."

"You mean Miguel."

"That's just who I mean. It could have been him." Bide was onto something now, and he wasn't about to let it go. The man fairly glowed with the thought that maybe he could pin the murder of Kincaid on a Basque, after all.

"I don't think so," said Longarm.

"But how do you *know*?"

"I saw something . . . just before Kincaid was shot."

"What, damn it!"

"I'm not going to spill my guts here in the middle of this fine company. What I saw is my business. All you need to know, Bide, is that from what I saw, there is no possibility that the murderer of Kincaid was a Basque."

"I am ready to leave now," said Pablo. He was, for good reason, impatient to leave the jailhouse.

"Let's go, Sir Henry," said Longarm.

The crowd outside the marshal's office had grown considerably since Longarm came in. Undoubtedly it was the news that Sir Henry and two other local cattlemen had rushed into the office soon after that had brought the additional curiosity-seekers. It was an anxious crowd. Quite a few were undoubtedly fearful that they might be robbed of a hanging—or even better, a lynching.

It was with a deep groan of rage and frustration, therefore, that the men crowding close upon the office porch greeted the sight of Pablo Montalban. As Longarm came to a stop beside Pablo, he saw Erikson and his three hired guns across the street. Miguel and Felipe were not in sight, and for that Longarm breathed a sigh of relief. He tried to catch Erikson's eye and warn him away with a glance. The man meant well, but Erikson's provocative presence could only do harm at this time. In this atmosphere, the sight of the man who was bringing sheep onto this range would be like a lighted match thrown into a keg of gunpowder.

But Erikson stayed where he was, his three hired hands straightening alertly as Pablo came to a halt between Longarm and Sir Henry.

"Maybe you better explain Pablo's release, Sir Henry," said Longarm, as the crowd's sense that something was wrong increased, and a few of its more drunken members surged closer to Pablo.

Sir Henry held up his hand. "This man is innocent!" he yelled over the murmur of the unhappy crowd. "Marshal Custis Long here was a witness to the killing of Wilt Kincaid! Marshal Long was also injured, as you know. But he has recovered, and he assures me and the town marshal that Pablo Montalban is innocent!"

"Aw, hell!" cried someone in the back of the crowd. "Let's hang the son of a bitch anyway!"

There was an embarrassed ripple of laughter at that, and a few faces immediately looked away from Longarm and Sir Henry. People walked away, disappointed perhaps, but relieved, as well. The bloodthirsty comment by one of their number had actually helped Pablo by underscoring the essential bloodthirstiness of the entire business. Longarm turned to Pablo.

"I guess you can go now. Take my horse, the buckskin. The sooner you get out of here, the easier I'll feel —and the happier you'll make all your friends."

"There's no need to worry, Longarm," said Sir Henry. "Frank and I shall escort Pablo from this town and see that no harm comes to him. Indeed, sir," he said, with a sudden rush of feeling, "now that it is all over, I am most glad you arrived on the scene. As Wally said, it would have been a terrible miscarriage of justice." Sir Henry glanced sharply at Frank Tully, then. "Don't you agree, Frank?"

"I certainly do," snapped Tully.

"Fine!"

Sir Henry shook Longarm's hand firmly. Despite the ache in his head, Longarm felt a growing warmth toward the Englishman, including his preposterous cartridge belt and big white hat.

He watched with Wally Waggoner and Bide Hanson as Sir Henry and Tully rode out of town with Pablo, then glanced across the street to find that Erikson and his three buddies had quietly vanished. He took a deep breath. Good. Now maybe he could get something for his pounding head. He sure as hell needed it.

Chapter 7

Longarm asked both Bide Hanson and Waggoner if they would care to join him in a drink at Slade Barnstable's saloon, the Drover's Palace, but both declined —Bide sullenly and without grace, and Waggoner nervously, as if it were now poor politics for him to be seen in public with the tall lawman.

With a shrug, Longarm strode away from the two cattlemen and down the street to the Palace, musing on the irony of his situation. He had just prevented the cattlemen from doing a foolish thing that would have brought discredit and dishonor upon them from all sides. Yet, somehow, he had to be regarded by them as a dangerous and unwanted meddler, an apologist for sheepmen. There was only one thing worse than being wrong, it seemed, and that was being right.

Fortunately, Sir Henry still had style. Longarm wondered, though, how long the tall Englishman would be able to keep it, with that slick gunman at his elbow.

As he pushed his way through the batwings and paused inside the saloon to let the street glare fade from his eyes, he became aware of a sudden silence, along with the smell of stale liquor and of men who had lived long, careless hours between baths. The silence lasted only a few moments. Then the click of poker chips and the low, rough buzz of men's conversation filled the place. Unwilling to stand at the bar, considering the condition of his head, Longarm sought out a table along the far wall, well out of the glaring rectangle of sunlight slanting in above the batwings. It was a golden, late-afternoon sun, and dust motes swam in its light. He would have welcomed its light and warmth if it were not for the dull, persistent ache in his head.

Longarm peered around at the place as he waited for one of the girls to come over to his table. It was obviously the biggest saloon in town, but that wasn't saying much. There were plenty of bottles and a lot of glass behind the long, mahogany bar. Two kerosene lamps hung down from the shellacked ceiling. A few portraits of bosomy, half-naked dancing girls—or sirens, he couldn't tell which—adorned the walls, which were resplendent in a red-and-white-striped wallpaper. The floor was covered with sawdust that was far from fresh. The gaming and poker tables were at the rear, and girls in short skirts, red ones mostly, were wheedling cowboys into buying them drinks or taking them for a short walk to the curtained cribs at the rear of the room. As Longarm took it all in, including the smell, he wondered what made those who ran cattle and rode horses feel that they were so much better than those who trudged behind flocks of sheep. They both smelled the same, drank the same, and lusted the same, for all of their supposed differences.

He was getting restless, wondering why the waitress hadn't come over to his table, when he saw Slade Barnstable approaching him, two glasses and a bottle of whiskey in his hand, a broad smile on his face.

"I told the girl to let me serve you," the man told Longarm. "I would deem it a pleasure if you would join me in a drink—on the house, of course."

"What's the occasion?" Longarm asked.

"You are a modest man, sir," Slade said, sitting down and pouring the whiskey deftly into the two glasses. His skill was that of an ex-barkeep, and the man obviously took great satisfaction in it. He pushed

Longarm's drink to him and raised his own glass in salute. As Longarm lifted his glass, Slade said, "First you rescue Carmen Montalban from my loyal but intemperate friend, then you ride in to save her father from the rope. I would say both heroics deserve a salute. I salute you, sir."

Longarm was too weary to do anything more than nod to the man and down his drink. Slade's heavy sarcasm was not lost on him, but he was in no condition at the moment to call the man on it. He would let the man play cat-and-mouse if it amused him. Besides, the drinks were on the house.

Longarm smiled. "This is fine whiskey."

Slade acted as if he were offended. "But you do not believe me. You think I am, perhaps, sarcastic. You do not think I mean what I say?"

Longarm pushed his empty glass toward the man. "As long as the drinks are on the house, Slade, who am I to find fault?"

Slade smiled and poured. "I like a man with your sense of priorities. Yes, indeed."

"Down the hatch," Longarm said, raising the whiskey to his lips a second time.

Slade emptied his glass, then pushed his black, flat-crowned Stetson back off his forehead and peered at Longarm. His sardonic, narrow face appeared to be filled with concern. "You don't look good, Marshal, and that's a fact. I see your head is bandaged."

"That's right."

"I assume the person or persons responsible for that outrage have been suitably punished."

"Not on your life. Never did see the son of a bitch."

The man frowned. "A shame! That *is* a shame. Though I thought I heard differently."

"Word gets around in this town. Even when it's wrong."

Slade smiled placatingly. "It is a small town, really.

Lost in the foothills of the Rubies. It isn't often that someone as direct and uncompromising as yourself rides in. Since you saw Wilt Kincaid shot, it is logical to assume you saw the one who was responsible."

"Logical, maybe—but that ain't necessarily how it came about."

"Interesting."

"Ain't it?" agreed Longarm amiably. The good whiskey was quieting the clamor in the back of his head somewhat.

The trouble was, Longarm was trying to remember something, something important. And it wasn't all that easy with Slade peering at him and the business of the saloon going on full blast on all sides of him. He had told Bide Hanson he was certain it was not a Basque who had shot Kincaid and bushwhacked him. And he *was* certain. But *why?* What was it that he knew? It was in there somewhere, an elusive but absolute certainty, tantalizingly out of reach.

The fact that he couldn't reach it angered Longarm and set him on edge. He looked with sudden truculence across at Slade. "What's your interest in all this, Slade? You figuring on making a fortune selling whiskey to the survivors?"

"The survivors?"

"Of this here war that's shaping up. Cattlemen against the sheepherders."

"Well, as a matter of fact, I do own a substantial interest in the Humboldt River Cattle Company. I don't suppose it's any secret that my sympathies lie with the cattlemen in this area."

"Where's your ranch, Slade?"

"South of here. The Bar B."

"And your foreman is Cal Wyatt."

"That's right."

"He don't seem to spend much time on the ranch tending to business."

Slade smiled thinly. "You don't see him in here this evening, do you? I assure you, Marshal, since that business with Carmen Montalban, I have kept a tight leash on Cal."

"This Humboldt River Cattle Company—it's a syndicate?"

"That's right. The other backers are in Chicago. I am the principal stockholder, however."

"Isn't that nice?"

"Not really. It is quite a responsibility. The range is getting overcrowded, Marshal. And with Erikson bringing in these sheep and importing Spaniards to herd them, we're heading for conflict. It is unfortunate, but true."

Longarm leaned back in his chair. No matter what he did, it seemed, he found himself dealing, one way or another, in this mess that Slade had just referred to. And that was not his job.

He was after the remnants of that gang that had robbed the train and killed the postal employee. And that meant he was looking for a man called Trampas. He really *must* keep that in mind, he told himself fervently.

Slade smiled. "Would you like another drink, Marshal?"

Longarm pushed his empty glass toward Slade.

As he poured, Slade said, "You seem to be under some duress."

"The back of my head is falling out. Otherwise, I'm in fine shape." Longarm looked at Slade through narrowed eyes. "You notice any strangers riding into town recently?"

"They've been coming in steadily these past weeks. Are you looking for any man in particular?"

"Yes. He calls himself Trampas."

"Is that all you know about him?"

"That's all."

"If I hear of such a man, I will let you know at once."

Longarm nodded wearily. He had no faith whatsoever that Slade Barnstable would let him know anything, at once or ever. The man would probably warn Trampas if he happened to stumble on the fellow. Barnstable didn't like Longarm, and Longarm didn't like him. Longarm had been a fool, most likely, to even mention Trampas to the saloon owner. But he was feeling giddy with the whiskey and irritable because of the constant, nagging discomfort in the back of his head. He had the odd feeling that if he put his hand back there, he would find that half his brains were hanging out.

Longarm became aware that a tall, elderly fellow dressed in a black suit, with a black string tie contrasting with his white broadcloth shirt, was standing over him, peering at him out of pale, watery blue eyes. The man wore no hat and was as bald as a cue ball.

As Longarm met his gaze, the man took an involuntary step backward, his lean, cadaverous face registering shocked surprise. "It is true," he cried, his soft voice quavering. "You are alive!"

Slade chuckled. "Marshal, let me introduce you to Judge Alvin Barclay."

The judge stuck out a long, thin hand. It wavered slightly, and as Longarm took it, he had the impression that all he could feel were bones, brittle bones, with no skin at all holding them together. He shook the judge's hand carefully.

"Sit down, Judge," Slade said. "You might as well get to know the man you pronounced dead not too long ago."

The cadaverous fellow pulled out a chair and slumped into it. Slade snapped his fingers to one of the girls, indicating that he needed another glass. Judge

Barclay moistened his large, pendulous lower lip and looked with some concern at Longarm.

"You must forgive me, Marshal. I was a bit premature in my pronouncement, it seems. But you have no idea how close to the brink you looked when I peeked in at you. Your face was the color of the underside of a dead fish, and I could barely detect any pulse. I must admit, I did not stay long in that Basque's *jacale*. It stank of sheep." He glanced at Slade, his long, bony nose wrinkling in disgust. "Furthermore," he went on, "I was constantly aware of Montalban's son behind me. At any moment I expected a knife blade to bury itself in my unprotected back. It was a most unpleasant business, I assure you. Weeping women, a black devil of a young man, and your . . . corpselike attitude. I left the place as soon as I could. Perhaps too soon, I can see now. But to me, there seemed no doubt about it at all. You were dead. There was no possibility that you could corroborate Pablo's most unlikely story."

"That's all right," Longarm told the man. "I understand perfectly, Judge. You knew which side your bread was buttered on and took no pains to look too closely. By the way, where did you get your legal training?"

The man pulled himself up to his full height. "I am self-taught, Marshal. A credit to independent initiative. I know the law because I know life. Tooth and claw, sir. That's life. To the victor belong the spoils. The survival of the fittest."

Slade leaned suddenly closer to Longarm. "And cattle are the fittest, Marshal, as are those men who drive them. This is no place for woolies, or the black men who live in their stench. They will not survive!"

The glass arrived for the judge, and as Slade poured for the old man, Longarm felt himself growing very weary. He watched as the judge's shaking hand reached for the full glass of whiskey, then he sighed and looked away. He was suddenly embarrassed to see what steely concentration it took for the man to lift the glass and bring it to his lips without spilling the drink over his shirt front.

What he saw entering the saloon wearied him even more.

With an arrogance that could only be described as foolhardy, Kyle Erikson and his three imported mercenaries were striding toward Longarm's table through a tense, growing, electric silence. Following Longarm's gaze, Slade turned in his seat to find himself staring up at Erikson.

Erikson halted before them, the other three stopping behind him. Longarm was grateful for small favors; the two Basques were still not in sight. The tall lawman's head was pounding vigorously, however, by this time.

Ignoring Slade, Erikson addressed Longarm. "You saved Pablo, like you said you would, Marshal. But now you're in here drinking with this rumdum of a judge and Slade Barnstable. Whose side are you on, anyway?"

Longarm moistened his lips. The question and its implications infuriated him. But he told himself that it would do good to let his temper get the better of him, especially with the back of his head leaking brains. In as calm a voice as he could manage under the circumstances, he said, "I ain't on any side that I know of, Erikson. I'm here on other business."

"*Other* business! Hell, we got business aplenty for a lawman what ain't afraid to show his badge. Mooreland is dead. More than half his sheep was dynamited and the rest is scattered to hell-and-gone. And now Manuel Alava's dead, and better than a thousand of my sheep he was tendin' was rimrocked. Food for vultures, they is now! If that ain't business worthy of a lawman, I'd purely like to know what is!"

Longarm closed his eyes. His head was exploding

in all directions, but he kept his voice as level and unperturbed as ever. "What do you suggest I do, Erikson? I got no clues yet as to who might have committed those crimes. You have some kind of proof you'd like to show me?"

"Proof? You saw what these cattlemen almost did to an innocent man! You saw how quickly they were ready to hang Pablo Montalban. What more proof do you need?"

"I see," Longarm replied wearily, surprised at his own forbearance. "I see. What you'd like is for me to lock up every cattleman in the territory. Is that it, Erikson? Look. I understand you're purely frustrated, but there's nothing I can do right now. I suggest you go back to your sheep ranch and keep a sharp lookout. Storming at me isn't going to help you worth mention."

The lean man straightened, his dark face hardening. "Go back to my sheep and keep a sharp lookout, is it?"

"Yes, Erikson. For now."

"Damn you," Erikson said, obviously lulled into a dangerous recklessness by Longarm's patience. "I know now what your purpose was in helping Pablo—and why you stopped Cal Wyatt. It's that woman! Carmen! You're after her! You're after beddin' down with that black morsel!"

The sudden, shocked silence that greeted that assertion alerted Erikson to the enormity of his blunder. He looked swiftly around him, then back at Longarm, a smile flickering hopefully over his gaunt face. Longarm got slowly, carefully to his feet. He moved his chair out from behind him. He did not want it to get in his way. His head, he found to his delight, no longer resounded painfully with each inhalation. Instead, Longarm felt only a rush of giddy pleasure. He had been looking for someone to bite, and now this slandering fool had presented himself.

Reaching out swiftly, Longarm grabbed the front of

Erikson's poncho. Hauling the man close, he slapped him across the face with his right hand. Erikson's head snapped around. Longarm backhanded him. Erikson's head snapped back again. Longarm repeated the chastisement once more, and then a third time, after which he flung Erikson to the floor. The sheepherder overturned a chair as he went down.

Erikson's three bodyguards were in the fact of drawing their weapons, but Longarm simply laughed and indicated the crowd of cattlemen that had moved close behind them. Each one had his own sixgun out. The three dropped their own weapons back into their holsters. Erikson, cradling his jaw with both hands, climbed back up onto his feet. Tears of rage and humiliation sparkled in his eyes.

"Better get on out of here, Erikson," Slade told him. "And take those three jokers along with you."

As the four left the place, Longarm slumped back into his chair. The elation he had felt was gone; the pounding in his head was back, fourfold. Slade, a wide grin on his face, poured Longarm another drink.

"Looks like you finally chose the right side, Marshal."

"I didn't choose any side, Slade. Not yours, not Erikson's." Turning his head, he squinted at the judge. "Just tell me. Do you know anyone around here calls himself Trampas?"

The man shook his head quickly, nervously. "Nope. Never. Never heard the name. And that's one I'd remember." His hand trembling, he pushed his empty glass toward Slade.

Slade glanced at him. "That's all, Judge. You can leave now."

Without a word, the old man got to his feet and was gone. If ever a fellow knew his place, Longarm mused, Judge Barclay was such a man. Barclay was in Slade's pocket, which gave Longarm some indication as to the source of justice in Ruby Wells.

Slade peered at Longarm. "You look all done in."

"That misunderstanding with Erikson took the starch out of me, and that's a fact."

"Have another drink."

"I've had enough. Slade, I'm looking for this man who calls himself Trampas. He likely hit Ruby Wells a week back." Longarm reached in his pants pocket and took out a bright, freshly minted double eagle and slapped it down on the table. "And I'm looking for anyone passing these a little too freely. You give me a line on either, and I'll be out of your hair. Unless, of course, you or your friends try to hang any more innocent Basques or rimrock any more sheep."

The man considered this for a moment, then nodded. "All right, Long. I'll ask around, and tell my girls to keep their eyes open."

Longarm pocketed the coin, one of the many he had picked up in the mountains. "And now, Slade, I'd like one of your girls, one you can trust. My head's about coming off, and I guess that whiskey didn't help as much as I thought it would."

Slade got to his feet. "I'll get Rose. She won't go with just anyone anymore. She is a very independent woman." He smiled. "She owns a half-interest in the Palace. You be nice to her and she'll be nice to you."

Longarm nodded. "Get her."

Rose's full name was Rose Sharon O'Riley, and she was indeed independent. Only when Longarm explained that he was in no physical condition for play did she consent to go with him to his hotel room. Even so, she was wary, and Longarm understood why. Men had likely told her before that they weren't interested, that all they wanted was someone to talk to, then found it was a vow they could not keep.

As she closed the door behind them, Longarm lit the lamp on the dresser and then carefully pulled down the shades. Then he turned to look at Rose. She was standing by the door, her back to it, watching him through narrowed eyes.

"You know what I said," she told him. "I ain't in the mood tonight. I ain't been in the mood for a good many nights. Even for a lawman. So now let's see just how straight you are."

Longarm winced as he slumped down onto the edge of the bed. "Don't shout, Rose. I told you, I'm in no condition. But I need help, and that's why I'm turning to you. Like I said, I'll pay."

Rose's voice softened as she said, "It's your head, huh?"

"That's right."

As Longarm started to pull off his boots, Rose moved closer and took off his hat. She placed it on the bed beside him and examined the bandage. "You want I should take this off and have a look at it?"

"If you do it careful. And maybe you could wash it."

Rose brightened. "Sure," she said. "I could do that. I wouldn't mind doing that at all."

"Well, I'd sure appreciate it."

"You just take it easy and I'll go get some soap and water and some fresh bandages."

"That's fine, Rose. I'll take it easy."

He finished undressing while she was gone, and was sitting up in the bed when she returned with a white enamel pan filled with warm water, bandages, and something for a dressing. She was even humming softly to herself as she kicked the door shut behind her. It dawned on Longarm that this was probably the first time in a long time that Rose had been asked to help a man out by ministering to his medical rather than his carnal needs.

She was a big woman and she smelled good to Longarm as she bent close to him and worked. Her hair was a rich auburn, and as she glanced at him from time to time, he noted how big and expressive were her rich brown eyes. Her complexion was very fair, with a light sprinkling of freckles over the top of her cheeks and the bridge of her nose. They did not detract at all from her robust beauty. Her lips were full and provocative, and he liked the way she talked, with just a touch of the Old Country in her voice.

"Where you from?" he asked.

"County Cork."

"I could tell."

"Could you now? Keep your head still or I'll be after giving you a crack where you'll feel it the most. It needs cleaning, but its healing, I'd say. The trouble you got is inside. That was a nasty crack. What did it?"

"A bullet."

"Jesus," she said softly, reverently. "You are a lucky man, and that's no lie."

"That's no lie."

She was as gentle as she could be while she washed out the wound and applied a fresh dressing. Her fingers were as light as feathers as she wound the bandage around his head. When she had finished, he thanked her and lay carefully back. It seemed to him that the throbbing was not so bad. But then, he had been deceived before into thinking he was going to be without pain.

"Thank you, Rose. You did that very nicely, and I sure do appreciate it. You should have been a nurse."

"Yes," she said shortly, her face reddening slightly as she picked up the bandage and ointment. "Perhaps I should have been."

"I didn't mean anything by that, Rose. I'm sorry, I haven't been thinking very clearly of late."

"With such a blow to the noggin, I wouldn't think so." She smiled at him. "You are forgiven. I guess it's difficult for a man to talk to a whore. She takes everything the wrong way, if she's in a foul mood." She started for the door. "I'll be back," she said, and was gone.

Longarm was feeling a bit guilty. Once again he was setting himself way out on a limb in hopes that someone—in this case, Slade—would try to saw it off. Only this time he was not alone on that exposed branch. Perhaps he should tell Rose to leave.

He pulled out the derringer he had unclipped from his watch chain and placed under his pillow. Satisfied that it was in good working order, he was putting it back under his pillow when he heard Rose at the door.

She entered, smiling. "All tucked in nicely, I see." She sat down on the bed and looked at him closely. "You look much better, I'm pleased to say."

"Rose, the reason I wanted you in here with me tonight is I want someone to stand guard while I sleep for a few hours—four at the most. I am pretty well done in, but I got the feeling that trouble is on its way, and I want to be ready for it when it gets here. You understand?"

"Perfectly."

"But I decided it would be too dangerous. You might get hurt if my hunch is a good one. I wouldn't like that."

"Glory be, the man cares what happens to me!"

Longarm laughed. "Of course I do, Rose. But you see my point. I don't want you to get hurt. And usually it is the innocent bystanders that get it in the neck, if you know what I mean."

"I know what you mean."

"So . . . you can go now, Rose. And thank you."

"Mind if I stay for a little bit?"

Longarm frowned. "Well, of course not . . . but you understand, you'll be taking a chance as long as you're in this room."

"I've taken worse chances, and besides, I like you, Mr. Long. You're concerned about someone else besides yourself. Do you know how rare that is?"

"Maybe it's not so rare as all that, Rose."

She leaned over and kissed him on the lips. "I think it is, Mr. Long."

"Call me Longarm," he said, smiling in surprise and pushing himself up a little higher on his pillow. He really was not in any condition for play, so he decided he had better change the topic. "Slade tells me you're a capitalist already, Rose."

"What do you mean?"

"You own a half-interest in the Drover's Palace."

"Sure and that man is a bigger liar than I am. I don't own no half-interest in the Drover's Palace, Longarm. I own three-quarters! He's a minority, he is, and the poor man knows it."

"How come?"

"Too much cows, that's the trouble. He got way in over his head with that syndicate. Them fellows've got the money, but not poor Slade. He has to keep up with them, he does. So it's me he has to come to when he needs it."

"You?"

She smiled and nodded her head slyly. "Oh yes. The work I do is very well paid, Mr. Longarm. It is very much in demand, it is. And besides that, I like to gamble now and then—but only when I'm lucky, you see."

"Yes," Longarm said, smiling at the woman. "I see."

"Now lean back. You need comfort, I'm thinking. If my sainted mother knew what I did to keep myself fed and clothed, she'd have a fit, she would. But she'd have a bigger fit if I didn't do it right. So you just rest your head back on that pillow and let me comfort you."

While she spoke to him, her voice growing softer, more caressing, she took off her clothes swiftly and slipped into the bed beside him. She had not been wearing a corset, so the action had been almost one single continuous motion, and now he could feel the heavy warmth of her pressing close upon him. Despite his condition, he felt himself responding.

"Now you just lie quiet and let me pleasure you. You're a big man—a nice big man—but you've been knocked around some," she said, kissing him lightly on the forehead while her hands moved slowly down his flank.

Then she was lightly kissing one of his breasts, her teeth gently teasing the nipple, after which her lips, warm and moist, moved slowly, very slowly down his torso, while her hands continued to caress him. Occasionally her fingers would pinch him, ever so lightly, and the result, he found, was astounding. He began to glow. It was as if his whole body had become one single, throbbing entity. He started to move, to reach out for her—but she slapped him, sharply, with the flat of her hand, and he knew she meant it. He was to lie still, to do nothing.

He leaned back and closed his eyes, allowing her free rein over his body. His head spun deliciously with the pleasure of it. Then her fingers closed above his erection. After a few moments of gentle—maddeningly gentle—ministrations, he felt the warm tangle of her hair as it fell about his naked hips. Her lips opened and sent her darting tongue over the hollow between his thigh and groin. It set him on fire. He strained toward her. She chuckled deeply, and her flaming tongue and then her warm, devouring mouth answered his need at last . . .

He opened his eyes and smiled at her. She was astride him now; she had brought him back with extraordinarily gentle skill and had mounted him almost imperceptibly, until now her insistent yet gentle contractions were causing him to writhe slowly under her.

"How's your head now?" she whispered softly.

"It's not my head I'm thinking of," he told her huskily.

"Just don't you go getting anxious, now. Just lean back. You been doing just fine, I'm thinking. You'll be asleep soon after."

All the while she spoke to him, she was continuing her gentle yet insistent contractions until Longarm was no longer interested in her words—or sleep. He felt himself arching incredibly under her, rising to meet each of her soft thrusts. He felt her hands flat on his chest, and grabbed them, arching still higher—and then exploded up into her in a long, incredibly sustained orgasm that left him limp, his head throbbing gently, but not painfully.

She rolled off him swiftly and pulled the covers up over him. He looked at her through a fog of sweet drowsiness. "You'll need a shave and a bath tomorrow," she advised him softly, as she bent to kiss his rough cheek.

"Wake me in four hours," he managed. "That's all I need. Four hours."

She straightened as she nodded her head in agreement. He turned his head slightly and was asleep almost at once.

He had slept too long. He could sense it even as he struggled up out of the depths of his dream and fought himself awake. A gray suggestion of light was filtering in through the window. It was dawn, no later. He swung his head. Rose, a wooden chair behind her, was opening the door and peering out.

He saw a bright stripe of gaslight from the hallway fall across her full, freckled face, and then the alarm that transformed it. He plunged his hand in under his pillow for the derringer as Rose tried to slam the door. But it was thrust roughly, powerfully back on her. She was thrown against the chair she had been sitting on all that night just as an enormous blast thundered in the narrow hallway outside the door. A dark stain appeared on Rose's cheek, just under her left eye, and something raw and wet and clinging was flung against the wall behind her. She collapsed upon the wooden chair, but did not remain in it long before she slid off its seat and sprawled on the floor.

The killer tried to open the door wider, but her body wedged itself against it. As Longarm leaped across the room, he heard the killer curse futilely. He grabbed the door and yanked viciously in an effort to get at the man. But it didn't help, and he heard him turn and start swiftly down the hall, his riding boots clumping heavily. Longarm wedged himself through the doorway and caught a glimpse of someone rounding the corner, heading for the stairwell.

Doors all down the hallway were flung open. A burly man next door reached out to grab Longarm as he started after the killer. Longarm knocked the man viciously back into his room as he fought past him, but then someone else farther down the corridor stepped out to block his progress. Longarm still had his derringer. He could have shot the fool, but of course that was out of the question.

From behind him, he heard a cry of outrage. A voice called, "Stop that man! He's murdered a woman in here!"

The fellow coming for Longarm stopped then, alarmed at what he had heard. And then he saw the derringer in Longarm's hand, turned, and dove into his own room, slamming the door after him. Longarm raced past to the turn in the corridor and was in time to see a torn pants leg and a worn riding boot with scuffed heels disappear out a window. An arm circled around his neck and tried to pull him down. Longarm stepped back swiftly, buried his elbow in someone's gut, then flung the man off him and continued down the corridor to the window.

He was too late. No one was on the narrow roof,

and Longarm could hear the swiftly fading gallop of a horse riding out.

Longarm whirled. The hallway behind him was crowded with uncertain men, all of them dressed in long, flowing nightshirts, all of them breathing heavily, each one frightened, yet anxious to do the courageous thing. They saw a murderer standing in front of them, and he was armed. Somehow they had to take him and not get themselves killed in the process.

Longarm raised the derringer and strode angrily toward them. "Get out of my way. If you want to do some good, wake up the town marshal and get him up here. Someone has just shot and killed Rose O'Riley."

The crowd pushed back, uncertain.

"You heard me, damn you!" Longarm cried, his fury at Rose's death making him dangerous. "Get the town marshal!"

The crowd broke. Two men turned and fled down the stairwell, and the others backed up and then turned and fled into their rooms. One chunky fellow with a red face and wild blue eyes was still poised in the doorway to Longarm's room, peering down at the crumpled body.

Longarm brushed past him and said, "Help me get her onto the bed!"

"Me?" The man had been in a kind of stupor. He backed hastily away from Longarm.

Longarm reached out, took him by the nightshirt, and hauled him into the room after him. "You heard me," he said. "Take her legs. I'll take her under the arms."

The man did as he was told. As soon as Rose was on the bed, he turned—clapping his hand over his mouth—and fled the room. Longarm kicked the door shut after him, then turned and looked over at the dead woman.

Then he glanced at the chair by the door. Instead of

waking him as she had promised, she had decided to stand watch over him while he got a good night's sleep. She had evidently liked him. She had been impressed by the fact that he could care about someone besides himself, and had wanted to demonstrate to him that she could care too.

And for that she was dead.

The town marshal decided there had to be an inquest. He found a skinny young doctor to pronounce Rose dead and announce to the world that it was a gunshot wound that had killed her. Judge Barclay, still sober at that early hour, dealt very patiently with the witnesses that Longarm had had to stumble over as he raced after the killer; and it was Barclay's decision that Rose O'Riley had been shot by a person or persons unknown.

Longarm got directions to Erikson's sheep ranch and left Ruby Wells, not having seen Slade since the man had come to take Rose's body from Longarm's room. Everyone said Slade was quite broken up by Rose's death.

It was noon when Longarm reached Erikson's ranch. The sheepman emerged from a long, low, unpainted frame ranch house to greet Longarm as he rode in. The smell of sheep was heavy on the wind, and the ranch was a maze of low sheds and wooden fences, some of which were in very bad repair. A small flock of sheep huddled mindlessly in one corner of a lot behind the largest of the sheds.

"You heard about it, huh?" Erikson said nervously, stopping some distance from Longarm's horse. He did not intend, it seemed, to ask Longarm to light. "I ain't armed," he added hastily, as he saw the grim look in Longarm's eyes.

"Heard about what?"

"What Bide Hanson and his men did to me last night."

"Never heard a thing. What'd he do?"

"Rode in here and shot up the place, that's what. Look around you. See any windows that ain't broke? Lookit them fences over there! See how they're trampled! And those sheep I got in the back lot are the only ones still left of them that was here. Bigger and the boys been busy all morning, buryin' the ones Bide killed. Shot some of them, he did. Others he clubbed. They went at it until they was too tired to kill any more; then they rode off, yellin' and threatenin'."

"Your three gunmen weren't much help, I take it."

"Nope. Damn them, they was off somewheres."

"All of them?"

"That's right."

"When did they get back?"

Erikson smiled then, a sardonic yellow smile. "When all the trouble was done. This mornin' sometime."

"All together?"

"I don't remember. I was inside and I heard them outside. They said they'd been back awhile—looking over the damage, they said."

"I'll bet they were all broken up about it."

"Well, now it'll be our turn, Marshal, if you won't bring no law to this territory yourself. We ain't afraid of Hanson or any of them. You can tell them that."

"You want me to turn right around and ride over to Bide Hanson's place and tell him that, do you?"

Wearily, Erikson shook his head. Then he looked up at Longarm and tipped his head. "If you didn't come out here 'cause you heard about this, why did you ride out? You still sore at me for what I said in the Palace? Hell, you took it out on me real smart-like. I guess you got my number, all right. I learned my lesson, sure enough."

"You ain't so tough. Is that it?"

"I know when I've met my match, let's just put it that way."

Longarm had liked the man better when he was an arrogant fool. This sudden contrition was enough to make Longarm throw up. That was the thing about Erikson; there was nothing about him solid or predictable. He seeemed to be playing a role; but it was a role he kept changing.

"I want to speak to your three helpers—the ones with the guns who don't wash all that often."

"Sure. No harm in that, I suppose. Why don't you light and come inside?"

Longarm nodded and dismounted, then followed Erikson to his ranch house, tying his horse up at the hitch rail in front.

"I'll go find them," Erikson said. "You could just go on in. I got some hot coffee on the stove."

"That's all right, Erikson. I'll go with you."

In his new role of meek helper, Erikson made no protest to that, and the two set out toward a clump of pine on the ridge back of the ranch. When they reached it, the three men were standing in the pines, waiting for them. Two of them had shovels in their hands. The one with the torn pants leg and the scuffed boots did not. Two Basques were standing just behind the three men. Both carried shovels.

The fellow without the shovel took a nervous step away from his companions. He looked as if he were maneuvering for more room, and he kept his right hand over the grips of his big Colt. Longarm smiled and addressed the fellow.

"What's your name again? I believe Erikson introduced us earlier, but I plumb forgot it."

The fellow glanced nervously at his companions, then spoke up, "Name's Luke. Luke Twitchell. What you want from me, Marshal?"

"I see you got a torn pants leg, and those ain't the newest boots in the world. You got the heel of that left one pretty well wore down. I noticed before how poorly you and your pals were dressed. Figured Erikson wasn't payin' you enough."

"You fixin' to buy me a new pair of pants, is you?"

Longarm had heard Rose's killer curse in angry frustration through the door. He knew he would recognize that harsh voice again anywhere. He looked coldly at Luke. "I'd like for you to curse at me, Luke. Think you can do that?"

Erikson, standing nervously to one side, called out, "Now don't you be shy, Luke. You can curse as good as the next one!"

But Luke was confused. He frowned at Longarm. "What the hell, Marshal? Why should I swear at you?"

"Because maybe I've come to bring you in for killing Rose O'Riley."

The man's face registered first surprise, then resignation as he backed up and clawed for his sixgun, swearing suddenly with bleak vehemence. As Longarm drew his own Colt, he ducked low and crabbed to his left, a grim smile lighting his face. Yes, he recognized that loud curse. It told him all he knew it would: Luke Twitchell *had* been on the other side of that door.

Luke's first shot went wild. Still crabbing to his left, Longarm snapped off a shot and caught the man high on the left shoulder, slamming him back against a pine. Propped up by the tree, Luke managed a second shot. This one cut uncomfortably close to Longarm's right ear. Longarm threw himself flat and aimed carefully, with both hands steadying the .44, and squeezed off a second shot. This slug hit Luke in the chest, fourth shirt button down. Longarm's third shot spanked a puff of dust from Luke's vest and made a small hole about where the man's heart should be. Luke sagged down the pine, then spilled forward onto the ground.

Longarm swung his sixgun around swiftly, covering Luke's two buddies. Both men had dropped their hands to the butts of their revolvers, but neither had drawn them. Now they slowly raised their hands over their heads.

Longarm got up and holstered his weapon. "You two can relax," he said. "I only heard one horse riding away this morning."

As the two men slowly lowered their hands, Longarm turned to Erikson. "Now, what time did Luke ride in this morning? And this time I want the truth."

Erikson moistened his suddenly dry lips. "Guess maybe I didn't tell it right, Marshal. He rode in about ten o'clock. Later than the others. Said something about . . . a girl."

Longarm nodded curtly. "Bury the son of a bitch with those dead sheep. And then I want you to tell me how to get to Waggoner's place. If Bide's acting up as bad as you say, he won't be much help in quieting things down. But Waggoner seems a reasonable sort."

"He's a lush."

"And you're a liar. It don't look like I got much to work with, does it?"

Erikson nodded to Bigger and Pete. The two men advanced on their dead companion with bloody shovels. Longarm started back to the ranch with Erikson, while the sheep rancher gave him directions to Waggoner's spread. By the time they had reached the rabbit warren of sheds and fences, Longarm saw that the burial of Rose's killer was proceeding apace. The ridge behind the ranch was empty.

"Take me to Luke's bunk," Longarm told Erikson. "I want to look through his possibles."

Erikson quickly led Longarm into the bunkhouse, and a moment later Longarm was pouring fresh, gleaming double eagles into his palm from Luke's deerskin pouch. He dropped the coins back into the pouch carefully, then put the pouch back in with the rest of Luke's belongings and looked closely at Erikson.

"Think maybe you can tell me the truth, first time running?"

"Damn you, Marshal, you can make a man pretty mad when you put your mind to it."

Longarm smiled thinly. "Seems to me you're no slouch at that, either. Did those three gunslicks of yours come together in the same package—or did you pluck each of them from the gutter one by one?"

"I hired each man separate. But I don't know if they knew each other before I signed them up, if that's what you mean."

"Show me the other two's bunks."

Erikson did, and after a quick, thorough search, Longarm found no more golden coins. This didn't mean much, however. Luke could have been holding the wealth for all of them. Or maybe Trampas had given his boys orders not to show any of the gold, to let him bury it all until the heat was off, only Luke had simply disobeyed.

As Erikson left the bunkhouse with Longarm, the sheepman was sweating. Longarm let him sweat until he reached his horse and mounted up. Gathering in his reins, he looked down at Erikson. "I don't know for sure, but it looks like you're harboring fugitives, Erikson."

"Fugitives?"

"That's right. Fugitives from the federal government —train robbers and killers."

Erikson looked sick.

"Thing is, you don't want to let on you know that. They've already killed one man for sure, a postal employee, and this morning Luke killed Rose O'Riley when he was trying to get at me. You'll make a nice cover for them out here, I figure, as long as you don't give them any cause for suspicion. If you tell them what I just told you, they'll come after me, I reckon. But more'n likely, they'll take care of you first."

The man swallowed.

Longarm waved as he turned his horse. "Keep them well fed, Erikson."

When Longarm glanced back at the sheep ranch a quarter of a mile behind him, he saw Erikson still standing where he had left him. The poor man seemed rooted to the spot.

Chapter 8

As Longarm rode on through the afternoon on his way to Waggoner's Diamond A, he went over in his mind the violent and unsettling events of the past few hours. It was not a pleasant thing to do, but he had to take stock. He had been foolish to brace Luke that way; cornering a rat is never a wise policy. Longarm could still feel that slug snicking past his right earlobe.

But he was satisfied he had made Erikson cautious enough not to force the issue with his two remaining gunmen. Longarm was almost certain they were all that was left—not counting Trampas—of the gang that had heisted the coin shipment. They were using Erikson's employment as a cover while they waited for the heat to die down—and for Trampas to show up. Longarm was pretty sure that neither Pete nor Bigger was Trampas.

Meanwhile, Longarm would also wait for Trampas to show. He would keep an eye on Erikson and his two gunslicks. When a third gunman appeared, Longarm would have Trampas. Of course, nothing ever worked out exactly as planned, at least not as Longarm planned. Much could go awry with his scheme; but it was the best he could come up with at the moment. He would let those two remaining train robbers bait his trap for Trampas. Longarm decided it was time he stopped using himself for bait. His head was still pounding from the first attempt, and now Rose O'Riley was dead.

Longarm would, instead, get himself involved in this

damned war between the cattlemen and the sheepherders. Though he had shown Erikson no sympathy at Bide Hanson's depredations of the night before, there was no doubt that this sort of thing could not be allowed to go unchallenged. Undoubtedly Bide had heard of Longarm's fracas with Erikson and had concluded —as had Slade—that Longarm was now throwing his weight behind the cattleman. He had not waited long to take advantage of the situation.

That was why Longarm was now heading for Waggoner's ranch. Wally seemed the least pigheaded of all the cattlemen Longarm had met so far, and just maybe he'd have something stronger than tea to offer Longarm when he invited him in.

Erikson had called Waggoner a lush. And Longarm had noticed that Waggoner looked as if he drank too much. As Longarm sat his horse in the sun and waited while Waggoner's wife sent a long-legged youngster running for her pa, he thought he had the answer.

Standing alongside the woman on her right were two hulking sons with blond hair that fell down over their eyes. On her left side squirmed a tall, gangly, thatch-topped girl of twenty or more. She was thin enough to take her Saturday-night bath inside a rifle barrel. She wore what looked like a flour sack for a dress. She had freckles and peered at him carefully through her blowing hair. She scratched her elbows a lot.

The two boys were easily as tall as their father. They wore torn shirts and faded Levi's and boots that were held together with strips of cloth wound tightly around them. They were tanned almost black and had dark, glowering eyes. Dogs guarding an Indian encampment had a more pleasant aspect, Longarm mused.

And Waggoner's wife was standing with a loaded shotgun trained on Longarm. Her bony face was feral in its singleminded distrust of him. Her hair was as long as her daughter's, but it was graying. She had no discernable breasts; her arms were as bony as her daughter's, perhaps even a bit more scrawny, and her dress had even less appeal than the flour sack the girl was wearing.

Longarm shifted slightly in his saddle, and the shotgun, which had been wavering slightly, steadied quickly. The back of Longarm's head began to pound slightly as he peered into the shotgun's awesome bores.

At last the swift young girl who had been sent after Waggoner came loping back, her face bright with excitement. She skidded to a dusty halt, barefoot, beside her older sister and nudged her eagerly, then said something that made the older one giggle. Waggoner was on his way from a large horse barn on the other side of the compound. He was not hurrying and twice he stopped to say something to a hand who was out of sight back inside the barn.

When he saw Longarm, he hurried his pace a little, and by the time he reached the front of his house, his face was beet red. "Put down the shotgun, Melody!" he yelled at his wife. "Damn! Don't you know no manners a-tall?"

As Melody reluctantly lowered the double-barreled shotgun, Waggoner snatched it from her with such force that Longarm was afraid it might go off. Then he turned on his offspring. "Ain't you got nothin' better to do than to gawk when a man comes ridin' to see me!" As he spoke, he ran his hand affectionately through the young girl's hair.

The older girl vanished inside after her mother and the two boys headed for the corral on the other side of the barn. Wally Waggoner, his right hand still resting on his young daughter's head, smiled up at Longarm.

"Why don't you light and rest a spell, Marshal? Right glad I am to see you! You can tell me about that terrible shootin' this mornin'. I understand poor Rose O'Riley was kilt!"

Wearily, Longarm dismounted. "I guess maybe I could do that, Waggoner. Do you think one of your boys could take care of this horse for me?"

Waggoner turned and yelled at one of the two boys. The boy turned sulkily and started back. "He's fine, just fine, with horses," Waggoner said hopefully.

Longarm nodded and followed the rancher inside. Waggoner led Longarm through a large room that obviously served as the family room. It had a huge fireplace at one end and looked as if a Mexican revolution had culminated within its confines. As he passed through it, Longarm looked furtively for dead bodies in under the debris. There was no other way he could account for the smell. Smiling, Waggoner led him into the kitchen.

The kitchen was worse.

Waggoner cleared off two places at the table with a wide, sweeping brush of his forearm. Dishes, bottles, tinware, and glasses crashed to the floor. "Damn it, Melody!" Waggoner cried. "You knowed I was bringing someone inside! Least you could do was clear off the table. You had all morning, and all day yesterday too!"

"Been busy," she said tersely, peering at him out of dark hollows, her pinched face working. "You know I been busy!"

"What doing, for Christ's sake? You're *always* busy, for Christ's sake! But I never see you do anything."

"Get the Indian!"

Waggoner sighed and looked apologetically at Longarm. "I know this ain't pleasant for you, Marshal."

"I said get the Indian!" Melody repeated.

Waggoner turned to the youngest girl. She had followed him in, keeping as close to him as a cat. "Charity, go fetch Three Toes. Tell her she'll have to stay awhile, and that I'll have plenty of tobacco for her."

Charity flung herself out the kitchen door. Her running footsteps faded rapidly.

Waggoner smiled over at Longarm. "It's five miles to Three Toes' lodge, but you'll see how long it takes for her to bring back that Injun. She's a good worker, Three Toes. She'll have this place a'gleamin' like new silver in no time."

While Waggoner had been telling Charity to go after the Indian woman, Melody Waggoner had started from the kitchen, her older daughter following along behind her. As the tall, leggy girl moved past Longarm, he felt a quick, bony hand reach out and grab him in the crotch. It so startled him that he almost cried out. He had glanced quickly around, but by then the girl had vanished from the kitchen with her mother.

"What's . . . what's the older girl's name, Waggoner?"

"Patience," Waggoner said, "but she ain't, though. Not a bit of it."

And Melody, Longarm realized, wasn't at all melodic. He had never before seen a man's wife so close to the edge. And Longarm was uneasily convinced that her fury a moment earlier in the kitchen had been caused by her frustration at not being allowed to pull the trigger of that double-barreled cannon she had been holding on Longarm outside.

He looked carefully around the kitchen at the shambles. He had the uneasy sense that he was surrounded by surly, threatening residues of Melody's person, and that they would soon renew the attack in her absence. A butter churn was sitting in a huge wooden bucket half-filled with water on the floor by the sink. The sink itself was hidden completely by an incredible mountain of dishes and pans. Another wooden bucket was overturned on the floor beside the sink. It must have been filled with milk at one time, but most of the milk had spilled out, leaving a damp whitish stain on the floorboards. A huge tiger cat with one ear completely gone was nervously finishing up what was left. Blankets, mattresses, and sacks of grain, flour, and corn meal were heaped in the far corner. The corn meal had spilled out of a hole in the side of the sack to mix with the spilled grain and flour. White, ghostly footprints emanated from the flour sacks to cover most of the kitchen floor. Flies were everywhere, feeding on the particles of food remaining on the floor and sideboards. A thick swarm had found an opened keg of molasses in one corner. The long-handled ladle that stuck up out of the keg was black with molasses and flies. Under Longarm's boots, spilled sugar and salt grated like sand, and throughout the kitchen, a damp, clinging, rancid smell hung like another presence.

"There ain't no sense in waiting till Three Toes gets here for a cup of coffee," said Waggoner. "I'll make it myself."

He began rummaging through the pile of pots and pans he had so unceremoniously brushed onto the floor a moment before. As he hauled up a battered gray enameled coffeepot, Longarm slapped at a persistent swarm of flies that seemed drawn by the bandage on the back of his head.

"I'd like something a little stronger, Waggoner," said Longarm. "If you've got any around, that is."

The man looked with joy upon Longarm. "You are not a Methodist, Marshal!"

"Nope."

"My wife's a Methodist, heaven help us both." He dropped the coffeepot back down upon the frying pan and cannisters and dishes at his feet, causing the one-eared cat to wince pitifully. "We'll go outside," he told Longarm, "where a man might have the privacy to indulge in a small nip. How's that?"

"Fine," said Longarm, getting up.

What he had meant was, Thank God.

• • •

In the far corner of the horse stable, a ladder led to a lower loft. Waggoner led Longarm up it with great nimbleness. His eagerness to share a drink seemed to have taken years off his life. What Longarm found, after Waggoner had pulled back four loose wall boards, was a completely stocked bar.

"You wouldn't happen to have any Maryland rye, would you?" Longarm asked.

"Of course I would, Marshal. Glad to drink with a man who knows his liquor. I'll join you."

He blew loose grains of grass seed out of two tumblers, unstoppered the rye, and poured them both generous drinks. Longarm drank his half down at once, then leaned back in the hay. He felt like a kid playing hooky from school.

"And now, Marshal, what can I do for you?" Waggoner asked, downing his drink as if it were a glass of water.

"Bide Hanson shot up Erikson's place last night."

"He's a tough one, Bide is. He has perhaps gone too far this time, do you think?"

"If he had anything to do with what happened to Manuel Alava or the dynamiting of Mooreland's sheep, then I'd say he's already gone too far."

"Don't know about poor Manuel," Waggoner said, pouring himself another drink, "but on the night Mooreland's sheep was dynamited, Bide was in town with me. He was with me most of that day too. He couldn't have had anything to do with what happened to Mooreland. Another thing, we all liked Mooreland. He'd been here as long as most of us, and he never caused no trouble. He'd always keep his sheep where they belonged and if they used the same water hole as our cattle, he'd keep them well back until our cattle was done. He was a man who knew his place. And he shore did love that border collie." He gulped half his drink. "Yes he did."

"You don't think Bide had anything to do with that?"

"I know he didn't, Marshal."

"What about Slade?"

"Hell, Slade was up to his ears pouring drinks for us. We had us some poker game going on at the Palace, and Sir Henry was losing again!"

"I take it Sir Henry loses a lot."

Waggoner grinned. "He likes to fancy himself a cardsharp, poor innocent Englishman. But his losin's have kept me and Bide and a few others hereabouts in business long after good sense would tell us we should quit."

"But you think Bide or someone else could have been responsible for the rimrocking of Erikson's sheep and the death of Manuel."

"Erikson has a talent for antagonizing cattlemen. You know that. I heard what you done to him yesterday in the Palace. Way I heard it, the man made himself about as welcome as a skunk at a lawn party."

"He sure doesn't know how to back off gracefully," Longarm allowed. "I probably shouldn't have lost my temper. The man was quite subdued when I saw him a little while ago."

"That's a change, for that one. So maybe you should have lost your temper." He shook his head. "I wish I could. I tried it once with my wife. Never try *that* again!"

"Methodists are tough," Longarm said, trying to be agreeable.

"This one sure as hell is. And a slob to boot. I just had to adjust is all, Marshal."

"And call in the Indian."

"That's right. Call in Three Toes. She'll wash out that kitchen in no time, bury most of the dishes she can't clean, and haul away the rest. She sells most of it, I understand. Has a regular hardware store outside of where her people live. A Shoshoni, she is. Used to live in a wickiup made of sapplings and army blankets and anything else she could steal. Now she's got herself a fine frame house."

"Furnished with what she took from here?"

The man nodded agreeably and winked at Longarm. "Sometimes I go fetch her myself, if you know what I mean."

"Takes you a while to get her here, does it?" Longarm held his glass out for another libation.

"It does that, Marshal," the man said, pouring. "Like I said, I just had to adjust."

"You can call me Longarm."

"You can call me Wally."

"Wally, we're going to have a full-scale war on our hands if Bide gets to thinking he can shoot up a sheepherder's ranch whenever he feels like it. I was hoping you could help me gather the rest of the cattlemen in the area, the small ranchers like yourself, and sort of get our plans straight."

"Plans?"

"Maybe help keep the big ranchers like Hanson, Slade, and Sir Henry from running away with the bit in their teeth, if you get my meaning."

"I get you. When would you want this meeting to take place?"

"As soon as possible."

"Tonight, then. Soon's Three Toes cleans out the kitchen. I'll even get her to clean the other rooms downstairs. We'll have a nice fire in the fireplace and plenty of coffee, and maybe a few drinks for them that ain't Methodists." He winked broadly at Longarm and reached for the Maryland rye.

That same afternoon, Wally Waggoner sent his two boys, Josh and Perry, after the three other small ranchers in the neighborhood: Stiff Mitchell of the

Rocking 7, Pete Kitchen of the X Bar, and Dick Greer of the Circle D.

By the time the three arrived, Three Toes had done wonders. She had arrived in a battered farm wagon pulled by two mules. In no time flat, the wagon was piled high with what appeared to be junk, then parked out behind the ranch house. For the next hour or so, all she seemed to do was lug in buckets of water from the pump in the front yard. After that, she remained inside. Longarm, lurking near the barn with Wally, heard a few startled yelps from the women inside, and caught a glimpse of the tiger cat shooting out one window like a bolt of furry lightning.

When, past dusk, Three Toes drove off with her loot and Longarm and Waggoner ventured into the ranch house, Longarm was astonished. The place was as clean as a garter snake's belly and just as slick. There was enough furniture—tables and chairs and end pieces—to handle the cattlemen Waggoner had sent for, but little else. The kichen was a wonder. Dishes were clean and piled neatly in cupboards; pots and pans were hanging from hooks over the stove, which was now gleaming. The bags of grain, flour, and corn had been removed, with their contents, Longarm assumed, placed in cannisters in the huge closet he now saw off the kitchen. The mattresses were gone, as well as the sour stench that had hung in the place.

At the stove a quiet, reasonably content Melody Waggoner and her daughter were busy with supper and refreshments for the guests. Patience stole a quick, excited glance at Longarm, who noted that the flour sack she was wearing had ribbons on it about the neck and sleeves. Longarm made a mental note to be careful around her. Very careful.

Soon after, the cattlemen arrived. First came Dick Greer. He was an excitable, thin fellow with a shock of hair the color of freshly peeled carrot. His lean, freckled face was leathery, his eyes frank and clear, and he shook Longarm's hand warmly and wandered into the room with the fireplace, looking about the place in wonderment.

Stiff Mitchell and Pete Kitchen rode in together. Stiff was a tall man who walked as if he had once broken every bone in his body, with the result that every move cost him actual, physical pain. Watching him dismount and approach the ranch house, Longarm decided the back of his head was no longer hurting him. Stiff's eyes looked shrewdly at Longarm as he shook the marshal's hand, and his smile was thin and cautious while Waggoner told him who Longarm was.

"Heard he was around," Stiff said, nodding curtly and moving past him into the house where Longarm heard him greeting Dick Greer heartily.

Pete Kitchen was a chunky fellow in a deerskin jacket with plenty of fringe. He wore a large black plainsman's hat, shoved well back of his forehead. He had a pleasant face and he smiled easily. Longarm did not think he was the type to stampede sheep off cliffs.

"Pleased to meet you, Marshal," he said, shaking Longarm's hand heartily as Waggoner introduced them. "Hope you can bring some sanity into this territory. We near got a war on our hands and them damn woolies are like to destroy all our pasture. We should rimrock every last one of them, I'm thinking."

Longarm followed Pete Kitchen into the house, chastened. The man's honest Christian face had fooled him completely.

"Hey! What happened in here?" asked Dick, turning to face Waggoner. "Where's that nice leather couch you used to have against that wall?"

"It got dirty."

Dick looked quickly around at the others and then the three of them broke into laughter, right on cue. The three men had known what the question would be—as well as the answer. Waggoner laughed right along with them as he led them into the transformed kitchen.

The meal was an excellent one, with enough courses to satisfy a French chef, and when it was done the five men retired to the living room to belch and smoke cigars. Longarm was generous with his cheroots and they settled down around coffee and a huge platter of doughnuts as Waggoner explained to the three cattlemen why Longarm had called for the meeting. When he finished, he leaned back in his chair and nodded to Longarm.

Longarm cleared his throat and said, "I am not accusing anyone here of anything illegal concerning the sheepherders. I don't think any of you—" and here his gaze rested for a moment on Dick Greer— "would do anything to hurt a sheepherder or his livestock. I understand that. But my worry at the moment is that things might get out of hand and someone besides Manuel and Mooreland might get hurt."

"Don't forget Wilt Kincaid," said Stiff Mitchell, stiffly. "There's some talk that Basque, Miguel, killed him."

"I don't think so," said Longarm, aware once again of that faint, nudging certainty he couldn't quite get a handle on. Whatever it was, it was crucial, and he was afraid he was losing it.

"That's just it," said Waggoner. "We're all too suspicious of the Basques, and they're suspicious of us."

"They got reason to be suspicious of cattlemen," said Pete Kitchen. "Not many cattlemen go out of their way to help a Basque shepherd."

"Why should we?" demanded Dick Greer.

"Just sayin' what's true," persisted Kitchen. "Only the other day, one of them fellows did me a good turn."

"How so?" asked Waggoner.

"My Ellie Mae was thrown from her horse about three miles from the ranch. She hurt her ankle some and couldn't walk. A Basque fellow twice her age picked her up in his arms and carried her all the way to my place. I tried to invite him in to thank him, but he just plumb turned and walked away, without a word. Ellie Mae said he was as silent as a rock while he carried her. Never said a word to her."

"A silent, strange band. Remind me of gypsies," said Stiff. He slowly, painfully took his cheroot from his mouth and tapped its ashes into a saucer.

"He didn't want to accept your offer to come in because if he did and you fed him, he would feel under an obligation to you," Longarm explained.

"An obligation?" Kitchen said, confused.

"I know these people," Longarm went on, "from the few times I've run across them in the Southwest. The thing is, if he broke bread with you, Kitchen, he would not be able to take a stand against you if you joined forces against him and the other Basques. Once a Basque has offered his hospitality to you or accepted yours, you have a man whose loyalty is almost unquestioned."

Kitchen nodded. "I see. And he could not be sure I would not one day be his enemy, since I am a cattleman."

"That's about it. He may also have been very worried about leaving his sheep untended. Don't forget, it was probably just him and his sheepdog looking after that flock."

"But he left his sheep to take my Ellie May home."

"Yes he did, Kitchen."

Longarm let that sink in. For a moment or two there was a profound silence about the table. Then Stiff looked at Longarm. "What else can you tell us about these gypsies, Marshal?"

"Well, first of all, they ain't gypsies."

"I know that, man. Just used the term. It appeals to me." The man's lean face slowly cracked into a smile.

"These Basques are from Spain, it looks like. Their language is a total disaster and not related to any European language. There's a joke that Basques are honest because when the devil came to tempt them, he wasn't able to use their lingo. Anyway, the Basques all speak either Spanish or French, so there's no real problem. That boy, Manuel Alava, had a dictionary, a Webster's he was reading when he was killed. The fellow was teaching himself English that way. They read a lot, sheepherders. Ain't much else for them to do. It is a lonely job, mighty lonely."

"They is ruining the grass, though," said Dick Greer, shaking his had. "We got to stop them somehow."

"You can stop them," Longarm said.

"How?" asked Pete Kitchen.

Every eye was on Longarm now, more than anxious to hear how they could get rid of the pesky woolies and their Basque shepherds.

"Shoot them. Get your men together and ride out and shoot every Basque or Indian shepherd you see. And keep shooting at any that come over the horizon. Then dynamite all the sheep. Rimrock them. Poison them with blue vitriol or saltpeter, or lace some grain with strychnine and spread it near the sheep's bed ground at night so the hungry sheep will eat it as they move out in the morning. Fire is something else you could try. Drive them into the corner of a corral and touch one off. Soon you'll have the entire flock blazing." Longarm paused a moment to look around at the faces of the men. They were appalled. "Thing is," Longarm said, finishing up, "you'd best assign a regular army of sheep killers to keep up with the job. Because sheep have been around since mankind first began, and I got a hunch they're going to keep right on coming."

"My God, Longarm," said Waggoner, "we couldn't do that!"

"That so?" Longarm looked around at the others, and stopped at Dick Greer. "What about you, Greer?"

"I . . . I don't think I could do that, either."

"Stiff? Pete?"

Both men shook their heads firmly.

"All right, then. You can't slaughter sheep and you aren't murderers, which means, I reckon, that you'll just have to learn to live with the Basques and Erikson and all their sheep."

"But how?" asked Greer. "They'll ruin our grazing."

"Not if you keep their numbers down, and that goes for cattle too. Overgrazing is your problem, not sheep. Seems to me the local range manager is issuing too many range permits. Maybe you men should deputize one of your number to go see the man. The way he's going, the range won't be fit for any animals *but* sheep. They can crop closer then cattle, and they've got herders to drive them to any forage that's left. On a depleted range, sheep are the last survivors. Hell, you keep overgrazing and pretty soon you'll be herdin' sheep yourself."

The four men were aghast. With white, shocked faces they peered at Longarm. "You can't be serious," said Stiff Mitchell.

"Well, then, I suggest you go the land office and find out what's going on."

"That's easier said than done," said Pete Kitchen, reasonably. "Do you think those big outfits like the Lazy C and Hanson's Bar H are going to pay any attention to what some range manager in a land office tells them? They'll run as much stock as they can get on a range, and then ship in more. The market's gettin' better all the time, Long."

"Seems to me if you gents can get together with the sheepherders—for your own good, mind you—why, you might be able to talk some sense into Sir Henry and

Bide. Even Slade. He can't fatten beef for that syndicate he's fronting for if there ain't any grass left."

"How do you suggest we join up with them Basques —and that fool, Erikson?" Kitchen asked. "The Basques won't talk to us, and Erikson's hired himself three gunslicks."

"He's only got two left," spoke up Waggoner.

"How come?"

"It's a story I'll let Longarm tell you."

"You still ain't answered me, Longarm," said Kitchen.

"A wingding. A festival or something. Basques love to have parties. Any excuse. I'll talk to Pablo Montalban and Erikson. And you'll all be invited. I'll see to it that Sir Henry, Slade, and Bide Hanson are invited as well. Once you see them as human beings just as ornery as yourselves, you'll find it a lot easier to leave them alone, maybe even help them. Those Basques are a long way from home, and this is a big, lonely country. Some of you men must remember what that's like."

"I do," said Stiff Mitchell softly. "I surely do."

Waggoner looked quickly around the table. "Well then, gentlemen, I see that we are agreed that Marshal Long will attempt to arrange a get-together of some kind with the Basque sheepherders. It surely can't hurt."

The three cattlemen nodded, not too eagerly. But they were willing, and that was all Longarm could hope for at this stage.

Waggoner got up. He was smiling conspiratorily at Longarm. "The little woman and the rest of the kin are off in bed," he told Longarm. "Will you entertain our guests while I go see to the refreshments?"

Longarm grinned. "Just don't forget that Maryland rye."

• • •

It was late, and Longarm was having difficulty getting to sleep. He was thinking over what he had accomplished and he kept remembering Waggoner's statement: *It surely can't hurt.* But nothing was ever as simple as it appeared, and perhaps this warfare between the cattlemen and the sheepherders wasn't so simple either. At the heart of Longarm's uncertainty was Erikson. There was something about that man that did not ring true, that never had from the moment Longarm first laid eyes on him. He had brought in five Basques in the past months, according to Waggoner, but the man's flocks never seemed to amount to anything. With the loss of those sheep that had been rimrocked, the man's flocks should have been down to nothing, yet he continued in business. Even the Basques wondered about him, since the flocks he gave them to tend were so small, at least in comparison with the number of sheep they had been used to herding in the Southwest. . . .

Longarm became aware of a scraping noise at the door, a soft, persistent sound. He was sleeping in a small storeroom on the first floor on a cot Waggoner had brought in for him. Remembering the glances Patience had been sending his way all during the supper that night, Longarm had rolled a large barrel of salt against the door. The sound he heard was the barrel rocking gently back and forth as the door behind it was persistently pushed. Swiftly, silently Longarm left the cot and crouched beside the barrel.

Faintly, ever so faintly, he heard Patience calling his name: "Mr. Longarm! I've come to visit! Mr. Longarm . . . !"

Longarm did not respond. Instead he sat down on the floor and braced his back against the barrel. It began to rock once more. Longarm slowly moved it back the few inches that the girl's patient efforts had gained. He sat there for almost fifteen minutes while the barrel rocked futilely behind him.

At last the rocking ceased. Listening carefully, he heard the girl's naked feet padding away down the hallway. A moment later there was a tiny squeak as a door opened and closed. Longarm stayed with his back braced against the barrel for a few minutes longer, then carefully, wearily rolled two more heavy barrels against the door. After that he climbed back onto the cot.

This time he slept almost immediately.

Chapter 9

The fandango had been a greater success than Longarm had hoped for, and the only disappointment for him was the absence of Sir Henry. Every other cattleman in the neighborhood had shown up, including a wary and watchful Bide Hanson. He stuck close to Slade, and both of them tried not to enjoy the lamb shishkabob, but Longarm saw them furtively licking their fingers on more than one occasion, and the wine the Basques had provided was soon flowing freely.

It was getting late now, and Longarm was standing with Waggoner with his back to a cottonwood, watching a traditional Basque dance, the dance of arches, or *vztai dantza*. Carmen had tried to get Longarm to join in, but he had refused, and Felipe Alava had eagerly stepped forward to offer himself as her partner the moment Longarm had declined. The dance was in full swing now, and both Waggoner and Longarm were engrossed. The girls held hoops of wood out before them, while the male dancers tried to spear the hoops with their *makhilas*.

The tempo was increasing as the drums and stringed instruments, mostly guitars, were struck faster and faster. A kind of joyous frenzy prevailed, and as the young Basque males increased the tempo of their thrusting staffs, the excitement on the faces of the Basque maidens left no doubt in Longarm's mind that both partners in this wild dance knew precisely what universal activity they were aping.

"It's almost indecent," said Waggoner to Longarm, chuckling.

A shrill scream filled the night. A male scream. Carmen froze and Felipe thrust his *makhila* through Carmen's hoop, after which he, like everyone else—the musicians, the other dancers, the drinkers standing by the barrels—froze also. The scream had come from behind Longarm. Close behind. Before he could turn, a hand was clamped down onto his left shoulder, followed by a gurgling sound even closer.

Turning, Longarm was almost dragged to the ground as the fellow who had grabbed his shoulder sank forward, the dark handle of a knife protruding from his back. When he struck the ground, the knife in his hand broke away from his fist and clattered ahead of him on the hard-packed surface. Longarm nudged him slightly with the toe of his boot, turning him enough to see his face.

It was Slade's foreman and lieutenant, Cal Wyatt.

His brains still rattling from the scream, Longarm hunkered down beside Wyatt and placed his hand on the man's neck. There was no pulse, none at all.

He straightened, and in that instant the horrified silence broke.

The party was over. Most of the guests had gone, some of the women in shock, a great many of the men muttering to each other, angry. Slade took the body of his lieutenant without a word to Longarm or anyone else. Within the past few days Slade had lost first Rose and now Wyatt, and everyone stood back and respected his obvious grief. But the cold look on his face as he rode off indicated that he did not intend to let the matter end here.

Longarm and Waggoner and Stiff Mitchell had remained behind at Pablo's ranch, and now sat together at a table under the stars near the cottonwoods. They had drinks in their hands and had been sitting silently for a long while. Longarm could hear Pablo and his family in the house behind him. And he thought he could hear someone—it might have been Carmen—crying softly.

Waggoner looked at Longarm, took a deep breath, and shook his head. "And I said it surely couldn't hurt. I guess I was wrong."

"Dead wrong," said Stiff, carefully lifting his drink to his mouth.

"Don't go blaming yourself," Longarm told him. "If you want to blame someone, blame Slade. I warned him he shouldn't bring Wyatt along, and he assured me he had no intention of doing so. He knew there was bad blood between us—and also between Pablo and Wyatt for what he tried to do to Carmen. I don't think Carmen would have left her house if she had known Cal was out here."

"I think it's pretty clear what happened," said Stiff Mitchell. "Cal came uninvited."

Longarm didn't comment. None of the cattlemen or their wives and guests had any doubt that it was a Basque knife that had been buried between Cal Wyatt's shoulder blades. It was also obvious to many, if not to everyone, what Cal was doing that close behind Longarm with a knife in his hand. What few, if any, knew was which hand was it that had plunged that blade into Cal's back.

Longarm did not have the slightest doubt. Later, when these two men were gone, he was going to have to go inside and thank Pablo Montalban for saving his life.

Longarm had seen Carmen's face when she looked down and saw, gleaming in the firelight, the black knife handle protruding from the dead man. With a shudder she had moved quickly back, her eyes searching for her father. When, a moment later, he stepped out of the darkness beyond the glow of the large bonfire, she caught his gleaming eyes, and in that instant their communication was complete. He had managed a barely perceptible nod and his eyes had narrowed in warning. Carmen had spun about then and fled into the house, where she had stayed. Pablo's wife and his son had remained with him as the Basque dealt with the awesome unpleasantness that remained.

"I suppose this is going to make matters a lot worse," said Mitchell, slowly straightening his back as he put down his empty glass. He had been drinking steadily, but Longarm could not detect much effect on the man; He just held himself a little straighter. "At least between Slade and the Basques."

"I don't see why it changes anything for me," said Waggoner, "or for you, either, Stiff. We still know we got to live with these people."

"I suppose so," agreed Stiff cautiously.

"Besides," Waggoner went on, "the death of Cal Wyatt's no real calamity, especially when you consider what he was up to."

Waggoner glanced significantly at Longarm. Neither man, out of a fine sense of delicacy, had yet admitted openly that he knew Cal Wyatt had been about to kill Longarm when he was struck down.

"That ain't about to make Slade go any easier," said Longarm. "Or Bide Hanson. What happened here can still be used as an excuse—and it will be. It don't really matter who was to blame. The convenient thing will be just to remember it happened. I reckon you fellows better keep those warm sentiments about living peaceably with the Basques to yourselves for a while. But it sure would be nice if you *acted* like that was how you felt. Might be that kind of an example would be a real help."

By this time the bonfire had become only a bed of

snapping coals, and Longarm had been aware for the past few minutes that the crying inside the ranch house had ceased. Now he heard a door open, turned his head, and saw Theresa Montalban and Carmen leaving the ranch house and heading for the long table where Longarm and Mitchell and Waggoner were sitting. It was a mess of plates, glasses, tin mugs, and bottles. They had come out to clean up.

Longarm stood politely as the two women approached. Stiff Mitchell and Waggoner got up also. The two men shook Longarm's hand, then said goodnight to the women and left for their horses. As they rode off, Longarm entered the ranch house to thank Pablo Montalban and to shake his hand as well.

Two hours later, under the stars, Longarm was still not asleep. He had refused, as gently and as politely as he could, Pablo's offer of a bed for the night for two reasons, though he had given Pablo only one of them.

He had told the man he was afraid now that some fool of a cowhand from Slade's ranch might get liquored up and ride over to cause trouble for Pablo and his family while they slept. For that reason he felt it would be a good idea for him to sleep away from the ranch house so he could nip any such action in the bud.

Pablo had thanked him for his concern and let him ride out to make a cold camp under the stars.

The other reason Longarm did not want to sleep under Pablo's roof was the presence in the ranch house of so much tension and sadness. He felt—whenever he looked at Theresa or Carmen or tried to catch the wary, troubled eyes of Pedro—the heavy burden of their concern and fear. Pablo himself was deeply troubled, though when Longarm had thanked him, the tough little man had straightened and said shortly, "I do it for both of us." And Longarm had known at once that Pablo was thinking of Wyatt's shameful attempt to take his daughter in that hotel room in Ruby Wells.

But now that he had escaped the tension of the Montalban household and was pretty certain no cowboys would be riding over now to destroy the Montalban's sleep, he still found himself unable to relax, as jumpy as a flea heading for a sheep dip.

He was not upset to realize that Pablo had not just found himself behind Cal Wyatt. The Basque had obviously caught sight of Cal when he slipped into the cottonwoods and had decided to avenge, in his own way, the dishonor Wyatt had brought upon the Montalban name. The fact that he had saved Longarm's life in the process was almost beside the point. Pablo had as much as admitted this to Longarm when the marshal had thanked him.

But it was not this that kept nudging fitfully at the tall lawman. It was something else. Sir Henry and Erikson, both of whom had been invited days before, had not shown up at the festivities, even though Slade Barnstable and Bide Hanson had been able to make it. Waggoner said he had talked to Madeline personally and had been told that Sir Henry would be delighted to come. Dick Greer, stuffing his nose with cotton first, had ridden onto Erikson's place and, without dismounting, had told Erikson that he and his men, all of them, were welcome. He had received a surly but definite indication that Erikson would show up.

So where were they? Why hadn't they shown? Longarm had been looking forward to the big, bluff, preposterous Englishman, even with that gun-toting gambler at his side. And Madeline. That Erikson and his men had not shown did not trouble Longarm personally; he just did not like Erikson that much. But his absence troubled Longarm, especially coupled with the absence of Sir Henry.

With his soogan's flap tied securely, he lay still, reasonably pleased that he had found a spot overlooking the Montalban ranch that did not have a hidden root or boulder waiting to jab him as soon as he crawled into the bedroll. He looked up at the sky. There was a thin sliver of a moon and it was too low to give the sky much light, which gave the stars an excuse to gleam shamelessly. He looked up at the extravagant display and told himself to relax and go to sleep . . .

The ground trembled under him. He sat up. The sound of rapid hoofbeats was carried faintly up to him on the knoll. He peered through the night. It seemed to be coming from across the broad stream on the other side of the cottonwoods behind Pablo's ranch house. For just an instant he thought he saw something pale moving rapidly out of sight beyond the cottonwoods. He unflapped his soogan and rose to his feet to get a better view.

But he could see nothing now—only the dark stream running through the lighter meadow, the indistinct smudge of the cottonwoods, the slumbering ranch house just below. And there was no sound of pounding hooves.

He stood for a while longer, peering into the night. The stars, bright though they were, and plentiful, were no help. At last he got back into his soogan, told himself angrily that he had better forget all this nonsense and get some sleep, and almost immediately dropped off.

Theresa Montalban had just provided him with a magnificent breakfast and Longarm was standing at the hitch rail in front of the Montalban's front porch, gathering the reins of his buckskin, when Madeline and Frank Tully topped a rise this side of the cottonwoods. Four Lazy C hands were riding behind them. Something in the way they rode warned Longarm. He decided not to mount up just yet.

Tully was riding a big chestnut, Madeline her Appaloosa. They both rode very straight in the saddle and cut fine figures in the morning sun. Tully still wore his fedora. Madeline's dark red hair was caught back in a tight bun, emphasizing her high cheekbones. She looked stunning. No wonder poor Kincaid had wanted to kill Longarm for her.

They reined to a halt before Longarm and Pablo, who had moved off the low porch to stand beside Longarm. Theresa, Carmen, and Pedro had stepped out onto the porch.

"Where's Sir Henry?" Frank Tully asked Longarm.

The four other riders had reined in just behind the two. Their faces were grim, their eyes watchful. They were new hands to the Lazy C, Longarm realized. Sir Henry, it seemed, had been dipping into the same trough as Erikson, only his gunslicks were a mite cleaner.

Longarm ignored Tully, a frown on his face, and looked at Madeline. "I was about to ask you the same thing, Madeline. Where *is* Sir Henry? We expected him —and you as well—last night."

"We don't know where he is," Madeline said tightly. "Frank thinks . . ." She couldn't finish. She glanced quickly over at Tully.

"You can talk to me, Longarm," Tully said. "I'm the Lazy C's foreman now." He said this with just a touch of anger. He had not liked it when Longarm had ignored him and spoken directly to Madeline instead.

"All right, Frank," Longarm said. "What do you think?"

"I think something happened to him."

"Go on."

"Something serious."

"Very serious, Longarm," Madeline said. Her face showed the concern she felt.

"All right, so it's serious. What do you want me to

do? I'll help any way I can. But maybe we just better eat this apple one bite at a time. I gather he's missing, and you don't have any idea where he is. Why aren't you out searching for him?"

"We are, Longarm," said Tully.

"That's why we're here," Madeline explained.

Tully smiled coldly. "He rode over alone to this celebration late yesterday afternoon. Only he never rode back."

"But his horse did," finished Madeline.

"It was in front of the horse barn this morning," Tully said, "still saddled, stamping and pawing at the ground."

"He never got here," said Longarm, a sense of foreboding falling over him as he spoke.

"You didn't see him?" Madeline asked.

"Like I told you, Madeline, Sir Henry never showed up here. I wondered where he was. You say he rode over alone? Why was that? You and Tully were invited."

"I . . . I was not feeling at all well last night. I knew the ride would be too much for me," said Madeline. "I'm still not a hundred percent, but . . ." She couldn't go on.

"I had better things to do," said Tully, "than visit a sheeper's ranch."

Longarm nodded. "Well, my offer still stands. I'll do what I can. I suggest we search the trail between here and the Lazy C." He swung up into his saddle. "Why don't you lead the way, Tully?"

"I think we should search this spread first," Tully said coldly, his eyes on Pablo.

Longarm glanced quickly back at the Basque. He saw how the man had taken that; he had been offended, gravely. But he did not say a thing. "Of course we can start around here," Longarm assured Tully and Madeline. "He might have ridden up in the dark and been thrown within sight of the fire. In the darkness no one would have seen a thing. There was a lot of music and shouting, so nobody would have heard anything either. I suggest we look through the cottonwoods first, and then we can follow the stream all the way to the ridge."

He looked back at Pablo. "Why don't you join us, Pablo?"

"We don't need that sheeper!" Tully snapped.

Longarm looked back at Tully, smoldering. "He knows this land about here. He can help. Or don't you want that?"

"Please, Frank," said Madeline. "Let Montalban come. Longarm is right, he knows his land. Sir Henry might be around here right now, needing us."

Nodding sullenly, Tully pulled his mount around so quickly that Madeline had to spur her animal to keep up with them. As Longarm waited for Pablo to saddle up, he watched the two of them riding back through their escort.

He didn't like to see it, but it was obvious that Madeline and Frank Tully were now a very close team. Longarm wondered how Sir Henry had taken that.

As luck would have it, Pablo was the one who found Sir Henry's body.

Tully and Madeline, with the four riders flared out behind them, had skirted a large flock of sheep and continued on upstream toward the ridge beyond the cottonwoods, but Pablo had spotted something on the other side of the stream, closer to the ranch house. He had guided his horse across the shallow stream without saying anything to Tully or Madeline. By the time he had reached the crumpled body lying in the shallow water, he had had to shout loudly across the stream to get their attention.

It was Longarm who heard him. Looking closely at Pablo, Longarm caught a glimpse of what he was standing over in the shallows, took out his Colt, and fired a single shot into the sky. Tully and Madeline, on the ridge, pulled up and glanced back over their shoulders. Longarm waved once, then turned his horse around and crossed the stream and dismounted beside Pablo.

Pablo kept his distance from the body, as if he were afraid it would jump up and threaten him. In a way, that was what very well might happen, Longarm thought as he leaned down over the silent form to examine it. The Englishman had been dressed expensively in a dark frock coat, with faun-colored trousers tucked meticulously into the top of his expensive California boots. His big white hat had probably been immaculate as well.

It wasn't anymore. And Longarm knew Sir Henry was dead because the man's head was completely underwater, his hat crushed under his face, and what looked like a deep laceration on the back of his head.

As Longarm waded into the shallow water and leaned down to lift Sir Henry out of the water, Pablo moved closer and bent to help him. Between the two of them, they were able to carry the big man from the water and let him down on the shore of the stream. Longarm went back for Sir Henry's hat, feeling pretty bad as he lifted the high-crowned Stetson from the water and returned with it to place it over the dead man's pale face and white, staring eyes. The man had been dead for some time, Longarm realized. His limbs were unnaturally stiff as he lay on the short grass at their feet.

Longarm heard horses splashing recklessly through the shallow stream. He turned and stepped away from Sir Henry's body as Madeline galloped up. Without completely stopping, she flung herself from her horse with a tiny cry, and knelt by Sir Henry's body, Tully dismounted quickly and, moving close behind her, placed both his hands on her shoulder.

"Easy now, Madeline," he told her. "Easy."

"He's dead!" she cried, staring wildly up at Longarm.

Longarm nodded. "Might've fallen from his horse in the darkness. Got lost, maybe. Struck his head on a hidden rock, passed out, drowned."

"Sir Henry!" she cried. "He was a superb horseman! He *couldn't* have got lost!"

"It was dark. The horse might've stumbled as it tried to cross the stream."

Tully straightened. "That's it, Marshal. Make excuses for your Basque friends. But you know what happened, just like I do. Look at the back of Sir Henry's head."

"I know. There's a laceration, all right."

"So he fell from his horse and struck the *back* of his head!"

"It's possible," Longarm insisted unhappily. "But this is not the time to discuss it, not in Madeline's presence."

"No," he said, helping Madeline to her horse. The woman was sobbing now, her face buried in Tully's chest. "But we'll have time to discuss it later, and then you won't be able to get the Basque off!"

"You're excited now, Tully, and your blood's up. You're apt to make wild charges. I can understand that. And I am sure Pablo can too. But I would advise you to keep that kind of talk to yourself for now. You got a very unhappy, near-hysterical woman there who needs looking after. I think maybe it'd be a fine notion for you to take her on home where she belongs."

"You can think a lot of things, Marshal," Tully said meanly, "but that don't make no difference to me." He looked significantly around at his new hired guns. They had pulled up in a roughly defined circle around the four of them.

"Frank," Madeline cried. "Please! Take me away from here. Do as Longarm says. I want to go home!"

Reluctantly, Tully patted her on the back and then helped her up into her saddle.

"Pablo and I'll take care of the body," Longarm told Madeline.

She nodded dully at him through her tears.

"We'll take him into Ruby Wells, to the undertaker."

"All right, Longarm," she managed.

Madeline pulled her horse blindly around and galloped off upstream, then charged straight across it recklessly, the water geysering wildly up on all sides of her. Tully mounted up swiftly and, without a backward glance at Longarm, raced after her. The four riders followed them, leaving Longarm and Pablo standing over the dead Sir Henry.

First Cal Wyatt and now Sir Henry. As Longarm reached for his horse's reins and swung up into his saddle to ride back for Pancho's farm wagon, he found himself wondering about Kyle Erikson, the other missing guest.

Chapter 10

Two days later, Longarm found he need no longer concern himself about Kyle Erikson. His two gunslicks had not murdered him. Less than an hour after the funeral for Sir Henry, Erikson rode into Ruby Wells, the two possible train robbers still at his side and four Basques riding behind. Erikson dismounted in front of the Drover's Palace, where a considerable crush of mourners had gathered for the solace only strong drink and the comradeship of one's fellows can bring at a time such as this.

Watching from a corner window, Longarm was relieved to see that the four Basques were remaining outside as Erikson and his two friends strode up onto the boardwalk and shouldered their way through the batwings. As the man paused and stood there in the doorway, noting brazenly the cold silence that greeted his entrance, Longarm realized that the sheep rancher had no idea what had happened in the past few days to Cal Wyatt and Sir Henry.

Longarm was sitting in a corner, nursing a beer, watching it all. Bide Hanson and Wally Waggoner were together at the bar, the other ranchers ranged on either side of them. Slade was moving from group to group, listening, nodding, commiserating. It had been astonishing to Longarm how many people in the area seemed to know and love the tall Englishman who rode about dressed like a Mexican general, but who had always been a voice for moderation. It was this fact more than any other that Longarm heard mentioned by the ranchers and townsmen who circulated about the room.

And it was that quality of Sir Henry's that was most needed now as Erikson stood arrogantly in front of the batwings with his two gunslicks, surveying the room. "Place is sure crowded," he said aloud to his companions, his voice cutting through the icy silence that had fallen over the place. "And with ranchers and townsfolk too. But that won't stop a sheepman from getting served. Not today, it won't."

"What's so special about today?" rasped Bide Hanson, turning to face Erikson.

Erikson lost a little of his belligerence at the awesome hostility generated by the hard eyes and implacable faces of so many men. But only a little. "That's what I'd like to know. With all you fellows gussied up, looks like a wake. Maybe some cowboy got run over by a cow lookin' for its calf?"

Infinity, Longarm realized, could only be understood in terms of Erikson's brazen stupidity.

"Goddamn!" Bide whispered hoarsely.

Almost involuntarily, every rancher and cattleman took a small step toward Erikson. The danger of his situation finally percolated through his thick skull. He glanced quickly around, caught Slade's eye. But Slade only shook his head. Erikson moistened suddenly dry lips. "All right," he said, his voice no longer strident. "What's wrong? What happened, anyway? I been gone for a while."

Slade spoke out then, his voice bitterly harsh: "Some Basque killed Cal Wyatt."

"And maybe the same one killed Sir Henry," said Bide Hanson, his voice breaking with sincere outrage. "It's time, Erikson, to run you and your black Spaniards out of this country. A good place to start would be right here and now!"

161

As Bide spoke, he slapped his shotglass down on the bar and took a step toward Erikson, Wally Waggoner moving right along with him.

"Now hold it right there!" snapped Longarm from where he was sitting. "Think a minute. Erikson had nothing to do with either Sir Henry's death or Cal Wyatt's. He was nowhere around. And both you men know that."

"He's a sheepman, damn him! And he's a fool!"

"I won't argue either point," Longarm drawled. "But your anger at the death of Sir Henry is no excuse to go after Erikson and the other Basques. And we don't know enough yet about Sir Henry's death to accuse anybody, including Pablo Montalban."

"Damn it!" Bide snapped furiously, turning his full fury on Longarm. "Sir Henry was found on Pablo's property, the back of his head bashed in!"

"He was also found lying facedown in the water. He could have got that blow on the head when he toppled back off his horse. Unconscious, he couldn't pull himself out of the water and drowned."

"It was all an accident, huh?" Bide taunted. "You know that for sure, do you, Marshal?"

"I don't know anything for sure. And neither do you."

"I know for sure that Pablo killed Cal Wyatt."

"I hope you also know why, Bide."

"All right. So I know why. The fact is, that Basque didn't hesitate none at all. I know how heavy those staffs them shepherds carry is. They've got a real heavy knob on them. Would've been no trick at all for one of them Basques to knock Sir Henry off his horse with it."

"And why would he want to do a thing like that?"

"'Cause he's a sheeper and Sir Henry was a cattleman—a big cattleman who didn't take no nonsense from sheephers." Bide looked quickly around him, then.

"And maybe because it was Sir Henry who rimrocked them sheep and killed that Basque."

"You don't know that for a fact, do you, Bide?" Longarm asked carefully.

"Hell no, I don't. But it don't matter what I think. All that matters is what some crazy Basque thinks."

"So now you know what's going on in the mind of Pablo Montalban."

"Don't you twist my words, Marshal!" Bide said heavily, his head lowered like a bull getting ready to charge. "You know my meaning. I'm tellin' you what's likely!"

Longarm took a deep breath and decided to let things stand as they were for the time being. Bide had been drinking heavily and was not entirely responsible. Wally Waggoner sensed this as well, and placed a hand gently on Bide's arm and pulled him slowly back toward the bar. For a moment it looked as if Bide would shake off Waggoner's hand, but then he relaxed, straightened, and backed toward the bar with Waggoner.

Longarm looked at Erikson. "I suggest you find yourself another watering hole, Erikson. Don't seem like you'll have much fun tickling your tonsils in here. Not today, anyway. And try not to take it personal."

Incredibly, Erikson refused Longarm's suggestion. He had blundered into a seething cauldron of anger and resentment—all of it directed at sheep ranchers and Basques—and had almost caused Bide and Waggoner to draw on him because of his witless effrontery, but instead of leaving the place so that tempers could cool, he lifted his shoulders arrogantly and, with his two gunslicks at his side, marched toward the bar.

"There ain't no reason why I can't drink here, Marshal," he said. "This here's a free country, and we ain't afraid of Bide or any of you."

Bigger was on one side of Erikson and Pete on the other side as the three men crowded up to the bar.

They were none too gentle as they elbowed Waggoner and Dick Greer to one side.

"Whiskey!" said Erikson, "for the three of us."

The barkeep looked for guidance to Slade, who was standing across the room. Longarm saw the owner shrug, leaving it up to the barkeep. The man reached back for glasses and a bottle.

Bide spoke up: "Don't serve him, Willy. I don't care what Slade says. Or anyone else."

As Bide spoke, he pushed himself away from the bar. At once everyone gave him room. Waggoner and Bigger peeled away from the bar at the same time, with Erikson and Pete moving back also. Dick Greer scampered out of the line of fire and didn't come to a halt until he was crouching close to Longarm's table. The sound of scrambling boots and overturned chairs ceased, and it was obvious that Bide and Waggoner were outgunned.

Longarm jumped to his feet, but his sudden movement acted as a signal to Erikson and Bigger. Both men slapped at their thighs, as did Bide and Waggoner. There was a shattering series of detonations, at least four of them, and all coming so close upon each other that it was like a single titanic blast. The walls of the place appeared to flex outward, and the floor under Longarm's feet bucked. Wincing, Longarm feared he had been deafened.

When the smoke cleared, Longarm could see Erikson and his two gunmen backing hastily toward the door as Bide and Waggoner slowly crumpled forward to the floor. At once the crowd surged toward Erikson and his men, but the sheep rancher fired another shot into the ceiling, halting them. His eyes glaring wildly out of deep hollows, he cried, "First one out that door after us will get a faceful of hot lead! I ain't foolin' neither! And we'll still be shootin' in self-defense! Now stay back, all of you!" As he spoke, he and his two companions backed out through the batwings.

A moment later the sound of their horses galloping down the street and out of town came through the doors. At that moment half the saloon's occupants rushed to Bide and Waggoner's side, while the other half fled from the saloon. Wills Toady had been in the back of the saloon during all this and had kept himself as quiet as a mouse throughout. Now, as Longarm hurried outside, the town marshal grabbed his elbow.

"Longarm! What'll we do? Shall we send a posse?"

"What for?" Longarm asked.

"Why, they're murderers! You saw what they done!"

"They were threatened because they wanted to buy a drink in the Palace—and because they were sheepmen. They tried to buy a drink anyway and were refused. Then Bide Hanson braced them. When the dust cleared, they were on their way out of town. Where's the crime?"

Toady was aghast. "You mean you're sidin' with *them*?"

"Toady," Longarm explained patiently, "I ain't siding with either side! There's no question Erikson was pushing and pushing hard, spoiling for trouble. But you can't hang a man for that. You just settle down and don't go forming any posse yet, not until things calm down some."

"You mean *you're* gonna handle this, Longarm?" The fellow was obviously aching for Longarm to do just that. He was still trembling from the tension inside the Palace a moment before.

Longarm sighed and reached for a cheroot. "It looks like I might have to," he admitted wearily, shaking his head.

With the unlighted cheroot in his mouth, Longarm turned away from the town marshal and started back to the Drover's Palace to see how badly Waggoner and Bide were hurt. He was hoping there was more smoke than fire to the exchange. He liked waggoner a lot. He shook his head again as he pushed through the batwings.

Here he was, sent to track a stolen gold shipment and capture the train robbers responsible, only he was caught instead smack dab in the middle of a range war. He wondered if Billy Vail had planned it that way.

Waggoner was sitting up on the floor, a surprised grin on his face, hugging his left arm with his right. Longarm could see the makeshift bandage that had been wound around the man's arm and realized with relief that Waggoner had received only a flesh wound. Bide was on his feet, leaning against the bar, swearing softly to himself. He was being helped to stay upright by one of his punchers while the bartender wrapped a tight bandage, fashioned from a bar rag, around his thigh. It did not look too serious.

Longarm glanced at Slade, who was overseeing the medical activities as best he could. Some of his girls were crowding close, but none of them dared offer to help. Their eyes were wide and Longarm could hear their excited whispers behind him. "They going to live?" Longarm asked Slade.

"Looks like it. They were lucky, sure as snakes live in holes. Both bullets went right on through. They both lost a lot of blood, though."

Abruptly, the saloon owner turned to the girls crowding behind him. "Get some water and some buckets," he told them. "I want Samuel in here too. We've got to wash this floor down!"

The girls stopped giggling and hurried off.

Longarm bent close to Waggoner. The fellow looked up at Longarm, the weak grin still on his face. "Damn it, Longarm!" the man cried. "That fool Erikson is doing everything in his power to make us hate him and his sheepherders!"

Longarm reached down and gave Waggoner a hand. Waggoner took it and pulled himself up onto his feet.

He was a bit woozy. The scared smile was on his face again. Longarm could tell that the man was positively amazed to find himself still alive. Amazed and pleased and filled with the wonder of it.

Longarm glanced at Bide. Bide was not amazed. He was furious.

"You all right, Bide?" Longarm asked.

"I lost a lot of blood, God damn it! You going to get that man? If you don't, I will, and that's a promise."

"Sit tight," Longarm replied. "I guess I'm in this thing now. Just let me handle it."

"Does that mean we're going to go to more Basque shindigs?"

Longarm shrugged. "Maybe. When all this fuss is over."

Bide's foreman hurried into the saloon and proceeded to help the man out. "Don't you bet on it!" Bide called back as he limped out the saloon door.

Slade spoke up then: "I don't know what side you're on, Longarm, but one thing's certain—if you don't get that son of a bitch, I will."

"No you won't, Slade," Longarm said softly. "I got other plans for you."

"Now what the hell's that supposed to mean?"

Longarm took Waggoner by the arm and walked with him out of the saloon. When he passed through the batwings, he glanced back. The baffled and troubled saloon owner was staring after him, waiting for Longarm's explanation.

But Longarm gave him none and left the saloon with Waggoner. There was little he could tell Slade now, anyway. The plans he had for the man were only just beginning to form. He wanted to work on them for a while longer before he shared them with Slade.

It was a very sore, very weak Waggoner who rode up to his ranch late that same day with Longarm. Waggoner's wife came out of the ranch house with her double-barreled shotgun, her two hulking sons, and her two daughters, and stood stolidly on the sagging veranda as Longarm helped Waggoner down from his saddle.

Longarm glanced at Josh, the oldest boy. "How about a hand here, Josh?" he called. "Your pa's been wounded."

The boy glanced at his mother. The gaunt woman nodded slightly. Josh left the veranda quickly and between Longarm and the boy, Waggoner was able to make it inside. Waggoner's wife didn't try to make a place for her husband to lie down or sit down. She just followed the three of them into the ranch house, the shotgun still cradled menacingly in the crook of her arm.

The place was a shambles already. Longarm felt a sudden exasperation that was close to despair. He looked over at the youngest girl. "Charity," he said. "Get Three Toes."

Charity glanced at her father. Weakly but firmly, he nodded to his girl. "Yes," he rasped. "Get the Indian. Tell her I'm hurt."

As Charity raced out to the barn for a horse, Longarm led Waggoner into what he supposed was the couple's bedroom. He couldn't believe what he saw. The bedclothes were ripped, and soiled piles of clothing had been piled on the bare mattress. A slops jar had spilled, sending its noisome contents halfway across the floor. The place smelled like an ill-ventilated outhouse. He pulled the door shut quickly, backed up, and helped Waggoner to sit down in a chair he cleared off.

"At least, Longarm," the man said, "the bastard didn't kill me." He smiled weakly. "That was the first gunfight I was ever in."

"That so?" Longarm said, doing his best to clear off the table so Waggoner could rest his head on it.

"Yeah. But you know what?" Waggoner rested his head on the table.

"What?"

"It's going to be the last."

Longarm chuckled, swept some debris off a chair, and sat down. He looked around. The two boys had vanished outside. Patience was standing in the kitchen doorway, looking at Longarm hungrily. Melody was in the kitchen, making a fearsome racket with pots and pans. She had not greeted Longarm or her wounded husband, nor had she inquired about the nature or the extent of his wound.

Longarm got the distinct impression that Waggoner and his wife did not get along.

Three Toes, a broad-beamed woman with liquid eyes and braided hair, arrived just before dark and immediately went to work cleaning out the bedroom. She spoke to Waggoner in Shoshoni, which Waggoner seemed to understand pretty well.

Once the bedroom was cleaned out and some fresh air let in and new sheets placed over the mattress, Three Toes brought Waggoner into the bedroom with considerable gentleness, then made some evil-smelling concoction out of bark and mold and applied it liberally to Waggoner's wound, which had begun to fester already. Only Charity seemed interested in how her father was doing, and it was she who helped Three Toes as she ministered to her father.

It was close to midnight when Three Toes drove off, her wagon not as full as the last time. Longarm, carrying a lantern, walked into the bedroom and nudged Waggoner gently. The fellow opened his eyes at once.

"Can't sleep," he said. "Need something to drink." He winked at Longarm. "You know where the liquor cabinet is, I trust."

"I'll bring some later, Wally. But I have a few questions."

"What about?"

"What can you tell me about Erikson?"

Waggoner grinned. "He's a lousy shot."

"How often do you run across his sheep? I mean, just how big an operation do you reckon he has, anyhow?"

Waggoner frowned for a moment as he considered Longarm's question. Then he shrugged lightly and said, "Well, that's hard to say. He's always bringing in large flocks with them Basques. Brings them up from the Southwest and California, but things keep happening to them."

"Like being rimrocked."

"Yeah, that's right."

"What else?"

Again the man pondered Longarm's question. "Well, I can't say offhand. But there's been trouble, off and on. I've heard of things."

"Have you?"

"Sure."

"From who?"

"Well, now that you mention it, from Erikson. That's why the man is so ornery, I suppose. He's always rushing into town to blame us all for what some of us have done. He's getting pretty fed up, I'm thinking." Waggoner rubbed his wounded arm ironically.

"Can you tell me about anything in particular that you heard about from someone else *besides* Erikson?"

"Well, sure. Didn't you tell me that Bide Hanson had shot up Erikson's camp, that he only had a few sheep left, and them huddlin' in one corner of a lot?"

"That's right, I did. But I did not see Bide or his men do it. I was taking Erikson's word."

"Well, why would he lie about a thing like that? And it ain't only happening to him. Don't forget what happened to Mooreland."

Longarm nodded and reached for the lamp. "All right, Wally. Go to sleep. I'll sleep in that storeroom tonight. If you need me, just holler."

"Thanks, Longarm. I sure do appreciate your help."

"You still need that drink?"

He smiled weakly. "Don't reckon I do, after all."

"Goodnight, Wally."

As Longarm turned and walked from the room, he glanced back at Waggoner. Wally's eyes were already closed. The man was justifiably exhausted, and Longarm wondered where his wife Melody was sleeping at that moment.

And Patience.

A voice, close under his chin, asked coldly, "You finished with him?"

Longarm looked down, then lifted the lantern quickly. It was Melody in a ragged nightdress. "Yes, Mrs. Waggoner, I'm finished."

"Is he asleep?"

"I guess maybe he is, ma'am."

"Good," she snapped, and slipped past him into the room, closing the door firmly behind her.

Longarm lit his way to the rear storeroom where he had slept the last time, and into which he had already lugged his bedroll and gear. He was trying to sort out in his mind what little information Waggoner had been able to give him. He hadn't expected that Waggoner would know much, but maybe just help confirm what Longarm was beginning to put together. The next person he should see, he realized now, was Pablo Montalban, and after that—if he could get the man's cooperation—Bide Hanson. It was an unlikely turn his thoughts were taking, but there was no help for it. He would just have to drift with it and see where it took him.

This time Longarm had rolled two heavy barrels against the door, so when he first heard the sound, he couldn't quite believe it. He sat up in his bedroll, glancing quickly about him, trying to pierce the stygian darkness of the room.

He flinched. Cold fingers were brushing his naked shoulder. Patience's voice came in a soft whisper just behind him: "I was a-waitin', Mr. Long, all this time."

"My God," Longarm groaned. "Patience! Is that you?"

It was a stupid question and he knew it as soon as he asked it. But damn it, he had rolled two barrels against the door and had been certain that—like the last time —there would be no successful breach of his defenses. How the hell had she gotten in here?

"I was hidin' in the corner, and you didn't even see me," she whispered, giggling. He felt the flap of his soogan being lifted as her cool, nude body slipped in beside him.

The corner? Where all those sacks of grain and corn and flour had been placed by Three Toes? He could hardly believe it. The girl must have been coiled up inside one of those sacks all this time!

She flattened her small, firm breasts against him, then held her face against his chest while her hands swiftly explored the length of his long body. Longarm tried to pull away.

"Patience," he demanded, "are you a virgin?"

"Yes, damn it!" she said. He could feel her anger and frustration at the fact. "But I don't wanna be! And my two fool brothers, they don't want to help me none a-tall!"

Longarm tried to get out of the soogan. He was unhappy at the choice this little love-starved creature was causing him to make, but he had a few rules of conduct he had never allowed himself to break, and one of them was that he did *not* mess with virgins. Of course, once a loaf has been cut, he didn't see any harm in taking another slice; but this poor little girl snuggling eagerly closer to him was not only a virgin, but the daughter of a man he had come to like and respect.

"Patience!" he protested. "I don't think you ought to be doing this! And damn it, I don't want to!"

"Hush!" she cried anxiously, clamping her hand over his mouth. "Ma will hear you!"

He pulled her hand away and came up to a sitting position. "Patience," he whispered, his voice hoarse with urgency, "I do not seduce virgins."

"You ain't seducin' me, Marshal," she hissed furiously. "*I* am seducin' *you!* Now you just lie back and let me have my way with you!"

As she said this, she pulled back the entire covering blanket of his soogan, revealing him in the dim light in all his pale nakedness before her. She reached up and pulled him down so that her thick hair spilled over him as she nibbled on his collarbone. Longarm found his big arms folding about her lean, bony shoulders.

She *was* seducing him, the little devil! And who was he to shame her now by refusing her, by sending her from him? Did he have that right? He had a saying that fit a situation like this: Never take a woman against her will, but never scorn a woman when she was willing. No man had a right to be that cruel.

Still nibbling on his collarbone, she slid her hand down the front of his body, across his belly, all the way. Longarm lay there, aware that though she was a virgin, she was making all the right moves. She took his penis in her hand and began to play with it.

"It's growin' " she whispered happily. "Oh, it's gettin' so big!"

"Yes it is, ma'am," he told her, rolling onto her gently. "It sure is. Now this may hurt you. You sure you won't reconsider?"

She thrust herself eagerly in under him and hissed, "Don't you *dare* stop now!"

"Yes, ma'am," Longarm said, and with his big hands

under her tiny, firm buttocks, he positioned her just right, then let himself plunge into her. She was not as forbiddingly tight as he thought she would be, or as dry. She uttered a tiny, delighted squeal as he pushed still harder, then broke through and went in all the way. Her tightness almost made him lose his control, but he held himself back with grim resolve, and then slowly began to thrust. He was as gentle as he could be, and with each thrust, Patience uttered a smothered cry of delight. And then, inspired by her pleasure, she locked her legs around him and began moving and thrusting in perfect unison with Longarm.

He was proud of his control and they went at it for a long, long while, until gradually he felt her begin to build to a climax. She didn't know what was happening to her and she seemed a little frightened by it. Her breath came in short, excited pants, and he drew back and looked down into her eyes and thought he saw a trace of fear. He leaned forward and kissed her eyes shut and hugged her closer, never missing a stroke as he did so. She shuddered then, and began to hug him with a ferocity that amazed him. She started to open her mouth to cry out.

Swiftly he closed his mouth over hers. A long groan escaped from her lips and she flung her head to one side and arched under him, her legs tightening about his waist with such force that he had trouble catching his breath. Only then did he allow himself to climax . . .

"So that's it," she said softly, letting her finger explore his face in the darkness, slowly, caressingly.

"That's it, Patience."

"At first it hurt, so I thought that was what I was supposed to feel . . . and then it didn't hurt anymore." She snuggled close to him and hugged him, driving her narrow chin into his solar plexus. "Mmm! It was nice, so nice! Thank you, Mr. Long."

"Glad I could be of service."

She lifted her head off his chest. "So *that's* what they mean when they bring the bull into the pasture with the other cows!"

"Your education is proceeding at a right fine pace, ma'am," Longarm said, grinning at her in the darkness.

"Well, it sure is a mighty fine service, and that's a fact."

"Patience?"

"What?"

"You'll have to be less . . . bold in the future. More careful. Men get nervous when a woman gets too grabby, if you know what I mean."

"I know. I was just so anxious, that's all. And when I saw you, I just *knew* you'd be like this, that you'd understand." Then she punched him quickly on the chest. "That was *mean*, the way you wouldn't let me in that last time."

"It's like I said, Patience. Menfolks get a mite nervous when a woman grabs them down there. That's a sensitive spot, you know."

"Yes, I know," she said contritely. "I saw Josh get kicked there once. It was really something, the way he rolled around clutching at himself."

"Besides that, a man like to think *he's* the one doing the chasing, or he don't know how to play."

"Men!"

Longarm chuckled. "Now you're gettin' it, Patience. We are a caution, and that's a fact."

"You ain't."

He didn't respond. He just held her. After a while, he loosened his arms from around her. "Patience?"

"What?"

"I need to get some sleep. And you should be back in your bed by now."

"Can't . . . can't we do it again?"

"Ain't you a mite sore down there?"

"Just a little. But I tried to make myself ready for you, so I wouldn't . . . well, you know."

"I know. But I think that's been enough for now. And I do need to get some sleep. I got a lot of riding to do tomorrow."

"All right."

He got to his feet and pulled back the two barrels he had rolled over in front of the door. She stayed close beside him while he did this, a naked paleness that did not wish to leave him. He kissed her lightly on the lips, patted her bare backside, and sent her down the hallway to her room.

He closed the door and was about to start rolling the barrels back in place when he realized he didn't need to bother with that anymore.

Chapter 11

Longarm had decided to seek out Bide Hanson before he rode over to question Pablo. Waggoner had given Longarm directions, and it was late in the forenoon when he started angling down a slope and found himself within sight of Hanson's Bar H, just beyond the next ridge.

He saw a mule-eared rabbit shoot from cover and spring to the right and then to the left, its rear legs kicking high. He was still watching it when he heard from behind him the *chink* of steel on stone. Instinctively, Longarm's right hand reached across his belly; but by the time his hand had closed about the grips of his .44, a grinning puncher had ridden up beside him and Longarm found himself looking down the barrel of the cowhand's .45. Longarm slowly let go the grips of his Colt. The muzzle of the cowboy's blue sixgun looked like the entrance to hell, and all Longarm wanted was a peaceable chat with Bide.

A second rider pulled up on the other side of Longarm. This was Bide's foreman, to whom he had been introduced to in town on the day of Sir Henry's funeral.

"Howdy, Ben," Longarm said. "Thought I'd ride over and see how Bide was doing."

"Howdy, Long." The foreman smiled thinly. "I ain't sure Bide would be all that anxious for a visit from you, seein' as how you're such a big friend of them sheepherders."

"You got a point there," Longarm said agreeably.

He looked back at the cowhand with the .45 and saw that the fellow had holstered it. He felt a little better and looked again at Ben Collins, who had dark, stringy hair and a pocked face, and was somewhat round-shouldered. He wore black leather boots, leather chaps, a cowhide vest, cuffs on his wrists, and tan gloves. Inhabiting the darkness of his face were eyes that resembled those of the blind—a hazy, skimmed-milk blue that became even whiter when the man was under stress. At the moment they were the color of an overcast sky.

The foreman bestirred himself under Longarm's steady gaze. "Well, guess maybe it won't do no harm to let you talk to Bide. But I warn you, he ain't in a very gentle mood. I'd say he's about as sociable as an ulcerated tooth about now." Collins grinned then, like a possum eating yellow jackets.

"I'll just have to brave the man's fury then, won't I?" said Longarm, kneeing his buckskin on past the two men.

The foreman and his buddy kept a short distance behind Longarm all the way to the compound. When Longarm got close enough, he saw a fine-looking ranch. The main house was a long L-shaped building of shiny cottonwood logs, calked with clay and roofed over with soapmud. The barns—there were three of them, all good-sized—were constructed of rough, unpainted lumber hauled in from Ruby Wells. The numerous corrals were made of slim cottonwood saplings, and one corral—used to break the new strings—was almost circular, with a high pole fence. Here the timbers were huge and must have been hauled a good distance, from the Rubies more than likely.

Longarm saw Bide Hanson sitting on the veranda that stretched the full length of the main house. His wounded leg was propped up on a chair placed in front of him, a bright red pillow under his foot. Beside him stood a gaunt old man. As Longarm rode closer, he saw that the old man was totally bald. He wore a grease-spotted leather apron and a white collarless shirt. He was bent slightly at the waist, like an old twig.

Longarm pulled up within a few feet of the hitch rail and waited for Bide's salutation. The man let him sit his horse for a while without a word. Longarm heard his escort pull up behind him, their horses shaking their bits and stamping on the hard-packed ground. Longarm eased back in his saddle. The leather creaked under him.

"How's the leg, Bide?"

"How the hell do you think, lawman?" He pronounced *lawman* like an epithet.

"Well," responded Longarm, "from the color of your skin and the tone of your voice, I'd say the leg was in pretty bad shape. Might even have to amputate if all that poison bubbling up inside you ever gets into it."

"Damn you, Longarm. And damn your sheepherders. When I get back on a horse I'm going to kill that son of a bitch Erikson, and anyone else who gets in my way. Especially any federal *lawman* that tries to stop me."

"You didn't have to spell it out for me, Bide. I got your drift."

"You'd better."

"It's about Erikson that I've come. I'd like to ask you a few questions about him."

Hanson's eyes narrowed. "Go ahead," he said, "ask."

Longarm took a deep breath. "I'm tired of sitting this horse, Bide. I'd like to get down and stretch my legs, maybe get in out of this sun."

"Stay on the horse. It was your idea to come out here, not mine."

"Thanks, you son of a bitch."

Bide's face went blue with fury. He tried to move out

of his chair, then realized he couldn't. From behind him, Longarm heard the sound of steel scraping leather as both men drew. The anger in Bide's face faded. He looked past Longarm at the two men. "Put away them hoglegs," he told them. Then he looked wearily at Longarm. Sweat was standing out on his forehead from the pain that had erupted when he had tried to get up. "All right, Long," he said. "Light, if you've a mind, then give Cookie here a hand in getting me back inside."

The cook, despite his decrepit appearance, was surprisingly strong and helped Bide inside without Longarm's help. Once Bide was settled into a comfortable leather chair, the cook went out for Bide's chair and the red pillow. After Hanson was propped comfortably, Longarm sat down on a small divan facing the rancher, who made no offer of anything to drink, but just eyed Longarm coldly, waiting for the lawman to speak.

Longarm decided against taking out a cheroot. Hell, he was trying to quit anyway, wasn't he? "The thing is," began Longarm, "I'm not sure Erikson is what he pretends to be."

"You mean he ain't a goddamn sheepherder?" Bide exploded.

Longarm glanced around. The cook had vanished into what appeared to be the kitchen. He looked at Bide. "He's a sheepherder, all right. But where the hell's his sheep?"

"He's got 'em."

"So I'm told. But not enough to keep all those Basques he's employed. But let that ride for a moment. It's these attacks he's been complaining about. Waggoner says he's been coming into town for some time now, threatening to retaliate. That right?"

"That's what I hear."

"All right, Bide. And I want the truth now. How

many of those attacks on his sheep and his shepherds did you commit? You *or* your men."

Hanson held Longarm's gaze for a moment, then looked away and sighed, "One."

"On Erikson's camp last week."

"That's right. We killed some of his sheep. Shot some, clubbed others. And we shot out as many of his windows as we could. Wish to hell we'd of killed that son of a bitch himself."

"Why didn't you?"

The man moved uncomfortably in his chair and continued to avoid Longarm's eyes. "Oh, now, hell, Long. You know damn well why we didn't."

"Because you don't hold with killing someone just because he herds sheep."

"I didn't say that."

"No, but that's why, Bide. And if you'll think on it awhile and calm down some, you'll most likely see I'm right."

The man squirmed. Longarm took out two cheroots and handed one to Bide. He hesitated, then stretched his hand out, grunting, to take it. Longarm got up and lit the rancher's smoke, then lit his own and sat down again. The two men smoked awhile in silence while Longarm pondered his next question.

"Nice smoke, this," Bide said.

"I'm trying to cut them out," Longarm told the cattleman. "But I ain't doing too well lately."

"Might as well have *some* bad habits."

"Bide, some of Erikson's sheep were rimrocked not too long ago, and a young Basque, Manuel Alava, was killed. But the stampede wasn't what killed him."

"How's that?"

"I mean someone killed the Basque, threw him over the cliff, *then* stampeded Erikson's sheep off the bluff."

"How do you figure that?"

"A man caught up in a stampede doesn't try to stop

it with a copy of Webster's. He leaves it behind and starts running. The dictionary was found right beside Manuel. Someone threw it *and* young Manuel off that bluff."

Bide frowned. "And you think I did that."

"Did you?"

"Hell no! I didn't rimrock Erikson's sheep and I didn't kill that Basque."

"Then who did?"

"How the hell should I know?"

"Do you think Slade might have done it?"

"I told you, I don't know who rimrocked them sheep."

"I believe you, Bide. I don't think you did it, and I don't think you know who did."

"Even though I shot up Erikson's place last week?"

"Yes." Longarm looked carefully at Bide. "I think you did that because you'd been goaded into it."

"By whom?"

"By Erikson. He is a man who does not seem to want to let sleeping dogs lie. For a sheepherder, he makes an awful racket and stamps his foot a lot."

"He sure does, the son of a bitch." Bide looked at Longarm through suddenly narrowed eyes. "What are you driving at, Long? What's the bastard up to? Do you think he killed Sir Henry?"

"I don't know what Erikson is up to, and I don't know who killed Sir Henry. But I do know that Pablo Montalban did not kill him."

"He killed Slade's man."

"Yes. And saved my life and avenged his daughter's treatment by Cal Wyatt at one and the same time. But Sir Henry was another kettle of fish entirely. He had always been fair to Pablo, the way I hear it, even though he ranted and raved about the sheep along with the rest of you."

Bide looked shrewdly at Longarm. "Have you figured out why Slade brought Cal Wyatt along that night?"

"Of course."

Bide nodded. "Well, maybe Slade's your man. Maybe he's the one been ravaging Erikson's sheep and killing his Basques. You ought to ask him."

"Maybe I will," Longarm said, getting to his feet.

"I'd get up and see you to the door," Bide drawled, "but I ain't in no condition for the amenities. Thanks for the cigar, Longarm. Next time, maybe I'll have some coffee or something stronger when you stop by."

"I'll hold you to it," Longarm said, as he headed for the door.

As Longarm rode off—without the pale-eyed foreman and his silent companion with the big .45—he glanced back and saw Bide sitting again on his veranda, his injured leg up on that red pillow, Longarm's cheroot in his mouth.

Turning back around in his saddle, Longarm crested a low ridge and turned south for the Montalban sheep ranch, hoping to get there before dark.

He just made it.

The western sky was streaked with red, and Pedro was walking across the yard with his dog at his side, a staff resting on his shoulder. Longarm was able to glimpse, well beyond Pedro, on the meadowland across the stream, a large flock moving steadily closer, with a solitary herder walking behind them.

As Longarm dismounted, Carmen and Pablo stepped out of the ranch house onto the veranda. Pedro changed course as his father said something to the boy in their native *Euskera* tongue. The sounds resembled a kind of controlled coughing—or gargling. Pedro took Longarm's horse and led it toward one of the barns, while Longarm walked stiffly toward the veranda. Pablo allowed himself a slight smile and stuck out a tough, stubby hand. Longarm shook it and nodded to Carmen, who smiled brilliantly.

"Like to stay the night if I could," said Longarm.

"You are always welcome in my house, Longarm." Pablo glanced at Carmen. "Tell your mother we have a guest for the night." He glanced quickly back at Longarm. "We have good soup and coffee now. You eat supper yet?"

Longarm shook his head and placed a big hand over his stomach. "Matter of fact, I got a big hole right here." He grinned.

The Basque turned and led Longarm into the ranch house. Theresa smiled shyly at Longarm as he sat down with Pablo at the plank table in the kitchen. In a moment, a large bowl of lamb stew was placed in front of him. It was what Longarm had come to expect: a thick, delicious broth with chunks of lamb mixed with carrots and potatoes swimming in it. Theresa kept it simmering on the stove constantly, it seemed, so that it was always hot and ready to satisfy a man-sized hunger, while it sent a mouth-watering, stomach-rumbling aroma throughout the kitchen and the rest of the ranch house. Longarm knew that no cattleman would ever let himself be served—let alone eat—lamb, no matter how good it might taste or smell. At that moment, Longarm was grateful he was not a cattleman.

As he attacked the stew with a pleasingly large spoon, Carmen placed down beside it a heavy mug of thick, dark coffee, and alongside that a solid pitcher of yellow cream. Longarm thanked her and meant it.

Pablo, sitting across from him, sipped his own coffee, his dark eyes pondering Longarm's presence while his face showed the pleasure he felt at having the lawman as his guest once more. When Longarm had finished the stew and coffee, and resisted politely Theresa's attempt to place still more lamb stew before him, Pablo grunted, took out a long-stemmed pipe, and began to fill it.

"We smoke outside, Longarm?" he inquired.

Longarm nodded, took out a cheroot, and joined Pablo on the veranda. There were wooden chairs to one side of the door, and they sat down in the gathering dusk and smoked for a while in silence.

It was Longarm who broke it at last, when he saw two Basques carrying between them what appeared to be a sick lamb from one small shed to a larger one on the far end of the compound. The lamb was bleating pathetically.

"How many hands you got working for you now, Pablo?"

"Five."

That was two more than he had before, Longarm knew. He looked at Pablo questioningly. He shrugged slightly and took the long stem of his pipe out of his mouth. "Miguel and Felipe. They leave Erikson and come work with me. It is good. Carmen and Felipe . . . who know? Someday, maybe. . . ."

"What can you tell me about Erikson, Pablo?"

The man frowned. "He bring many Basque from California. That good. He know we make good shepherd. But he is not good sheepherder. This all the Basque tell me. I think soon they all want to work for Pablo."

"Why's that?"

He looked shrewdly at Longarm. "No sheep. Cattlemen kill all sheep, drive them off."

"Which cattlemen, Pablo?"

"I do not know this."

Longarm sat back and puffed awhile on his cheroot. It was dangerous to admit it to himself, but he found he could think a mite more clearly with the accursed leaf in his mouth, its tip glowing. He closed his eyes and puffed, twirling the cheroot slowly. He knew that Bide was not the guilty party. Longarm would bet his private store of cheroots on that. And certainly, Wally Waggoner was not the one. Nor did Stiff Mitchell or Pete Kitchen seem likely candidates. Even Dick Greer, despite his bloodthirsty talk, was an unlikely suspect. Longarm could not forget the horror on all their faces when he had patiently explained to them what they would have to do if they *really* wanted to get rid of the sheepherders. That left Sir Henry and Slade's Bar B.

Unless Kincaid had worked behind Sir Henry's back, the Lazy C was not guilty of rimrocking any sheep or driving them off. As Longarm recalled, Sir Henry had been upset at the rotting carcasses of those sheep at the foot of the bluff. He did not know who had done it, and there was no reason for the man to deny it if he had. His opposition to the sheepherders was up front and unashamed.

And that left Slade.

Longarm took the cheroot from his mouth and glanced at Pablo. "Carmen did not know about Slade's ranch when I asked her. How long has Slade operated the Bar B?"

"Only when he send his man Cal Wyatt to be foreman did we know that Bar B was his ranch. We think it belong to a man I never see. He call himself Winslow. But he is gone now."

Longarm nodded. Winslow would have been the front man. But Slade no longer felt it was necessary to hide his connections with that syndicate Rose had said was bleeding him white. No longer necessary or possible. The man was in a bind; he needed room to act. He could not afford to play it cozy any longer.

And what he needed was more room so that he could run more cattle.

Longarm puffed awhile on that, still not satisfied. It was Erikson who was the key to all this, but he was not sure just how.

"I'd like to talk to Miguel," he told Pablo.

Pablo stood up. "They are in the small bunkhouse. Come with me."

Longarm followed the sheep rancher across the yard. Pablo knocked twice on the door to a low, square, frame building. Someone called from inside and Pablo pushed opened the door. Felipe Alava was lying on a bunk in the corner, reading a book. Miguel was sitting up at a small table, carving with a very small-bladed knife what looked like a new *makhila*. For a fleeting moment, as Longarm saw Miguel put the staff to one side, he recalled Bide's fury at the death of Sir Henry and his suspicion that a Basque had knocked Sir Henry off his horse with just such a *makhila*.

It wasn't such a farfetched idea at all, Longarm realized, as he also recalled the way young Felipe had tumbled Kincaid off his horse with his well-aimed staff during that tense moment when Miguel had attacked Sir Henry.

Miguel was standing. Felipe had put down his book and was sitting up now on the side of his bunk, his eyes watching Longarm warily. The structure of their faces made it pretty obvious that they were father and son. Longarm wondered where the boy's mother was.

"The marshal wants to talk to you," Pablo explained to Miguel. "You know him."

A very slight whisper of a smile lit the dark face. "I know the marshal."

"Call me Longarm," Longarm said, taking a chair out from under the rough table and sitting down.

Pablo sat also as Miguel closed his knife and sat down across from Longarm. The boy remained sitting on the cot, his eyes still on Longarm.

"Miguel," Longarm said, "did you kill Sir Henry?"

The man's dark eyes grew wider. He glanced swiftly at Pablo, then back at Longarm. "No," he said. Again there was that faint ghost of a smile. "You would not let me, do you not remember?"

187

"Oh yes," Longarm replied, smiling. "I am glad you didn't, Miguel."

"And he had nothing to do with Sir Henry's death later, Marshal," said Felipe, his voice low, his dark eyes snapping angrily through the shadows of the small bunkhouse.

"Good," Longarm said, nodding pleasantly at Felipe, "I am glad."

"What you want with me?" Miguel asked.

"I'd like for you tell me what you can about Erikson—his ranch, the number of sheep he runs, things like that."

"Why you wish to know this?"

"Because I don't feel right about the man. He worries me. He bothers me. He ain't what he seems. And I don't like the company he keeps. I'm thinking of those two gunslicks he keeps by his side. They look like the type who might rob a train."

Miguel and his son exchanged a glance. The boy moistened his lips nervously. Miguel leaned back in his chair and looked for a long moment at Longarm. "You are right," Miguel said at last. "He is a strange one."

"How many sheep's he running on the range?"

"That is . . . not easy to say. He lose many sheep. The cattlemen take his sheep. They stampede them. He has many sheep one day, few sheep the next. I think he have to send back the men who bring him sheep."

"Basques like yourself?"

"Yes."

"Is that why you decided to work for Pablo?"

Miguel hesitated, then shook his head. "That is not the reason."

"What is the reason?"

The man started to speak, then looked at his son. "Felipe," he said, "come to the table."

The boy left the bunk and came over. Pablo pulled the table away from the wall while Longarm held the

188

lantern steady, and the boy sat across from Pablo, his back to the wall.

"Tell him, Felipe," said Miguel.

Felipe cleared his throat and told his story. He spoke softly at first, but at the end his voice was strong, and Longarm found himself wondering what this Basque had been reading, so fine was his vocabulary. It seemed that after Erikson reported the loss of one large flock that Miguel had tended the week before, Miguel, understandably upset at the loss, had gone to the benchland where the sheep had last been grazing.

He and his dog found the hoofprints of the riders who had driven off the flock, and followed them. And followed them. To Felipe's growing surprise, it soon became obvious that the sheep were being skillfully driven, not over bluffs or cliffs, but along another benchland that led at last into a winding ravine. Beyond the ravine was a swift stream, and across that stream stretched a rough but sturdy log bridge. To Felipe's further surprise, the sheep had been herded across that bridge.

It was dark by this time and Felipe was forced to spend the night under the stars. The next day he continued his trailing of the sheep, more and more certain that these sheep were not going to be killed, but were being stolen.

"Sheep rustlers," Longarm suggested, at that point in the story.

Felipe nodded, then went on.

Close to sundown of the second day, Felipe approached a long escarpment that stretched like a barrier across his trail—or rather, the sheep's trail. He followed the trail along the base of the escarpment and eventually came to a narrow canyon through which trickled a stream. He was about to follow the trail into the canyon when two rifle shots from somewhere above on the escarpment halted him. Both shots had been well placed, exploding the dirt at Felipe's feet. When Felipe hesitated, another rifle shot cracked and this time the bullet struck inches in front of Felipe's dog.

Felipe turned, calling his dog after him, and bolted back across the meadowland. He kept going until he judged he was out of range of the rifleman—or riflemen; he did not know how many there were up there. Then he stopped and turned about, his eyes searching the rocky battlements, looking for any sign of the man who had fired at him. A distant shot echoed, and Felipe knew it was a warning for him to keep moving away, to go back to where he had come from.

Felipe did just that and when he returned, he told his father what he had discovered. At the first opportunity, Miguel had contacted Pablo and asked him if he could work on his ranch. Pablo had been glad to hire them.

Felipe leaned back, his story finished.

"Felipe," Longarm asked. "What's that book you're reading over there?"

"Shakespeare."

"I thought so."

The boy smiled. "I also like to read your very funny Mark Twain. Soon he will be famous, I think."

Longarm nodded. Served him right for asking. "Felipe, why did you and your father decide to leave Erikson after this incident?"

"Because," Miguel said, speaking for his son, "this was not the first strange thing that happen with that man and his sheep. It is like you say—we do not feel right about him."

"And I don't like the way he rides that horse of his," said Felipe. "He tears up horses something awful, and they all have bloody bits. I don't trust a man like that."

Longarm nodded. He had what he wanted, he realized: something tangible he could follow up. He asked for and got a very good description of the trail Felipe had taken through the mountains to get to that escarpment. Longarm was pretty sure he could find it on his own.

And he would start for it first thing in the morning.

Carmen was shaking his shoulder. Cursing himself that it had taken that to waken him, he plunged his hand in under his pillow and sat up, holding his derringer out before him. In the darkened room, with only the moonlight filtering in through the single window, he saw Carmen's eyes as she jumped back.

"What is it, Carmen?" he asked.

"Riders!"

"Go get your mother and find a place to hide!"

She vanished out the open door. Longarm pulled on his boots and pants, grabbed his rifle from the pile of gear he had left in the corner, snatched up his gunbelt, and bolted down the short hallway to the kitchen.

Pablo and his son were kneeling by the window. Both had rifles in their hands. Longarm stood behind them, strapped his holster on, checked the Colt's load, then went for the door, rifle in hand. "Stay here!" Longarm told them.

He pulled open the door and stepped out into the cool night. It was, he judged, about three in the morning. The air was damp, clammy. The moon was low, hanging just above the roof behind him. The thunder of hoofs he had heard from the moment he entered the kitchen was getting louder with each passing second.

And then he saw the first rider, a dark smudge against the night sky, a torch held high in his hand, as he topped the rise coming from the meadow below. Another rider came hard after him, and this one also had a torch. The first one began to whirl the blazing brand over his head, preparing to send it onto the roof of a barn he was passing. Longarm sighted swiftly with his Winchester and squeezed off a shot. The rider lost his hat, and jerked back so suddenly the torch went zigzagging straight up into the sky. The second rider veered sharply and headed straight for Longarm, his torch also circling his head.

Longarm fired again and this time was not so lucky. The rider kept coming. A third, and then a fourth rider topped the rise and galloped into the yard. Longarm fired a second time at the oncoming rider. The man let his torch go, straight at Longarm. Longarm ducked. The torch struck the ground beside him, showering him with sparks. The rider was almost on him now. In the light from the burning brand, Longarm saw the rider's sixgun gleaming and fired almost straight up.

He heard the bullet strike solid muscle as the rider drove on past. Longarm rolled over onto one knee and squeezed off two more shots at the remaining riders, all of whom carried torches. The nearest one flung up his hands and lost the torch, then threw himself forward and grabbed his saddlehorn. The other spun swiftly, slumped a bit, and made a weak throw toward the house with the flaming brand.

It fell far short. Longarm got off his knee, levering rapidly, and sent another shot after this rider, who sped away back the way he had come, his dark form hanging forward over his horse's neck. The first one whom Longarm had shot was struggling to get back up into his saddle. His horse, with all the gunfire and rocketing torches filling the night sky, was not being very cooperative.

Longarm held back to let the fellow get back into the saddle. The other riders were also galloping from the yard, their attempt to fire the place having achieved nothing. The rider swung aboard then, hugging his horse about the neck, and urged it after his fellow night riders. That made three of them. There had been four.

Longarm turned. The rider he had shot from close range had pulled up in front of the ranch house. He was hanging onto his saddlehorn, his body sagging forward. Longarm covered him and walked slowly toward the rider, remembering the sound his bullet had made as it struck home. He was surprised the man had been able to stay aboard the horse. The rider was very still.

Longarm pulled up. "All right, mister, get down off that horse. Slow-like."

There was no response from the rider. The horse blew, then shook his head, his ears working. Out of the corner of his eye, Longarm saw Pablo and his boy emerge cautiously from the house. Both of them had their rifles trained on the slumped rider.

Longarm took a step toward the rider. The horse backed away nervously. As it did so, the rider tumbled slowly forward over the horse's neck. His hat went spinning off into the darkness, and when he came to rest he was lying faceup. Even in the darkness, Longarm could see the dark stain across his shirt front. He was a bearded man and didn't smell very good and was as dead as a losing poker hand.

Longarm relaxed and stepped closer to him. His eyes were closed. He might have been asleep. Longarm didn't recognize him. As Pablo and Pedro stopped beside the body, Longarm glanced at them. "Recognize him?"

As Pablo and his son shook their heads, the three became aware of distant shouts coming from well below the ranch. Longarm snatched his rifle and raced toward the outcry. Pedro and his father caught up to him by the time he was within sight of the stream below the ranch.

The night riders—no longer in sight—had stampeded the sheep into the stream. Barely visible, a gray smudge caught in the gleam of the moonlit water, they were being swiftly, helplessly borne downstream, some of them vanishing even as Longarm watched. The calls for assistance were coming from three of Pablo's men on the banks of the stream. They were wading into the stream, trying desperately to save what few sheep they could. At that distance, their calls for help came fitfully, plaintively. If the sheep were bleating in their distress, Longarm could not hear them.

It was a long run down the slope and across the flat to the stream. Halfway to it, Longarm became aware of Theresa and Carmen following after them, running almost as fast. Once he reached the stream's bank, Longarm dropped his rifle and waded in and began helping the Basques, who were struggling to haul ashore incredibly heavy, sopping wet animals that seemed unwilling or unable to help themselves.

They stood in water up to their necks and seemed frozen solid, their eyes starting out of their heads, paralyzed with fear. They did nothing to help themselves, and it took two men to carry some of them. There were a great many stranded in the shallows. Soon Longarm was soaked completely, his boots filled with water, his arms hanging out of their sockets as he lugged the waterlogged sheep from the water. Longarm and the others said little to each other, only enough to coordinate their actions, and they struggled this way, staggering with fatigue, until the sun was well above the horizon and every animal still within reach had been hauled ashore.

Then, wordlessly, bedraggled, stumbling with fatigue, they clambered up the long slope to the ranch. Longarm had decided earlier that he would leave first thing in the morning. Well, it was morning now, and he wasn't going to be leaving after all—not *this* morning, anyway.

Chapter 12

Longarm left Pablo's ranch later that same day, not long after two of Pablo's hands returned from burying the dead night rider.

They buried him somewhere in the foothills closer to the Rubies. It was an unmarked grave they had left him in, and no one would ever know exactly where his body lay. Like any ill-starred cowboy on a trail drive north who got struck by lightning or trampled in a stampede, this gunslick's flesh and sinew, his brains and marrow, the hard calcium of his skull and bones, would become finally a part of the living plains and thrusting mountains of this outsized land. It was not an unworthy tomb—and for that night rider, at least, it was a notch better than he deserved.

For whose brand those marauders rode, Longarm had no certain knowledge, and for now he was content to let the matter drop. He had another iron in the fire and he wanted to use it before it got cold.

It was after dark that same day when Longarm made camp well above Erikson's sheep ranch. He had cut around and approached from the west, coming out of the high country, hugging the canyon walls and cliffs and taking care not to expose himself by crossing long, open stretches. When he finally made his dry camp high above Erikson, he was satisfied that the sheep rancher had no inkling of his presence.

He was satisfied, but not certain.

For two days Longarm observed Erikson and his ranch. Each morning he would work his way down the rocks until he was close enough to the ranch to pick out individual fenceposts. Then he would lean back against a boulder, chew on some jerky he had brought with him, and watch. A little before dawn each day, the Basques would stir and, in the first, faint rays of the sun, move out to the small flocks Longarm saw bedded down surprisingly close to the ranch. Later, Erikson's two hired guns, Bigger and Pete, would emerge from their bunkhouse and straggle across the yard to the ranch house where they obviously joined the boss in a breakfast prepared by the Indian housekeeper. Then the daily business of the ranch would begin, which, for Erikson and his two ex-train robbers, did not seem to amount to much. Usually, by the end of the day, the three of them would be drunk, or close to it.

On the third day, the sheep were gone, as were the Basques. They had herded the flocks off the day before and had not returned by nightfall. At once, Longarm noticed a different tempo at the ranch. Shortly after sunrise, Erikson rode out with the two hired guns. Longarm scrambled back up the rocks, broke camp, and followed. A few miles from the ranch, Bigger and Paul turned off onto the wagon road leading to Ruby Wells, while Erikson continued north.

Longarm followed Erikson.

The setting sun was turning the rocks and hills to bright rust the following day when Longarm glimpsed the escarpment Pedro had described. It lay athwart Erikson's path on the far side of a long, sweeping flat. The flat was bisected by a swift, shallow stream that Erikson forded with little difficulty. Before the sheepherder could reach the first outcropping of the massive escarpment, he would have to travel another two miles at least across that open flat. It would be dark before the man reached the escarpment. Longarm reined in. If he followed Erikson across that open space, it was almost a certainty that Erikson would spot him. If Longarm did not follow him, the man would ride into one of the canyons that wrinkled the escarpment's ancient face, and Longarm might not know which one he had taken. The man would simply vanish.

Longarm sighed and dismounted, wishing he had binoculars. He would stay in the rocks until nightfall and hope he would be able to follow Erikson's trail by moonlight. He glanced skyward and saw a few pink puffballs floating by. It might stay clear through the night, he realized. It just might.

The moon was a bright silver dollar hanging before a velvet curtain. It was so bright it banished the stars. Too bright, Longarm thought, as he rode toward the stream that Erikson had forded so easily. If anyone was watching from the escarpment walls, it would be difficult not to spot him.

Longarm forded the stream and dismounted, comforting himself with the thought that Billy Vail had not given him a written guarantee that his assignments would be without risk. The comfort came from knowing he had not been misled. He found Erikson's tracks easily. The ground seemed somewhat softer on this side of the stream, and Longarm mounted up, experiencing little difficulty in tracking Erikson from the back of his horse. Not until the escarpment was shouldering ominously into the night sky and he found himself traveling over higher, rockier ground, did the tracks get difficult to follow. But by that time Longarm was in sight of a canyon looming straight ahead, a sharp cleft in the mighty wall of rock that looked as if it had been fashiond by a giant meat cleaver.

Once inside the canyon, Longarm found himself in a smothering cloak of darkness and decided it was time to camp. Dismounting, he led the buckskin around great hulking boulders until he came to an area of bald, worn rock. Here the canyon walls fell back and he could feel the open sky looming above him. Just beyond the caprock he found a thin stream coursing down the middle of the canyon, and from that he filled his canteen and let the buckskin drink. Afterward, he unsaddled the horse, hobbled him, and let him drift over to a patch of grass on the far side of the stream. Then he poked with his rifle barrel along the under edges of boulders, alert for snakes, until he found a clear spot for his camp. He unrolled his soogan and was soon asleep, his head resting on his saddle, his fist closed about the grips of his Colt.

He awoke quickly the next morning, aware at once of the gray light and disappointed he had not awakened earlier. Sitting up, he noted the wet tops of the rocks and felt the cold dampness in the air. He could see his breath in front of him. A bird, high up on the canyon wall, was trilling shrilly, evidently pleased with its echo. Longarm stood up and stretched, shivering.

He made a quick breakfast of sourdough biscuits fried in bacon fat, then saddled up and rode out, chewing on jerky as he went. It wasn't long before he sighted Erikson's tracks in the soft ground skirting the stream that wound through the canyon. He felt better after that, and hoped he would be able to get the man within sight before long.

The buckskin's shod hooves rang loudly on the rocky trail. Echoes snapped back from the walls. The stream ran along beside him swiftly, its cool sound a pleasure. Bluestem grew tall in its shallows. Glancing up at the canyon's rim, Longarm saw, on either side, huge slabs of red sandstone, hollowed out by wind and frost, hanging threateningly over him. Glancing ahead of him, he saw where older slabs of rock had already broken off and lay in shattered piles of rubble along the bases of each wall.

By midmorning the canyon widened and became a narrow plain. Along the shallows of the stream, the bark of willows gleamed red through silver leaves. Rabbit brush flared yellow over the low banks. Longarm kept going, following the stream now into the plain, and saw where beaver had cut more than a dozen small cottonwood saplings down. They were all lying aligned in one direction, ready to be dragged off. He came upon the beaver's dam further on. It had created a good-sized pond. Tiny cottonwood grew along the pond's margin.

Longarm was impressed. Beyond that forbidding wall of rock, Erikson had found himself a land lush and beautiful, a true "shining place." On the other side of the beaver pond stretched a parklike meadowland, through which the gradually broadening stream meandered lazily. As far as Longarm could see from atop his horse, the grasslands on both sides of the stream rolled away into gentle hills and a few cottonwood-topped ridges, with the purple slopes of the mountains lifting into the bright morning sky far in the distance, their snowclad peaks gleaming. It was a mite prettier than a picture, Longarm realized, and that was for damn sure. No single man with a brush and smelly oils could capture anything as grand and satisfying as this.

Longarm caught movement along the slope of a hill in the bright distance. Dismounting, he led his horse into a stand of cottonwood, then peered carefully through the trees. The distant slope appeared to be at least a mile away—and on it sheep were grazing. They streamed slowly across the bright morning freshness of the hill. Higher on the slope, Longarm could just barely make out the tiny figure of the sheepherder standing quietly, watching, his dog at his heels. Even at this distance though, Longarm could tell it was not a Basque. It was an Indian, more than likely.

For, by this time, Longarm was beginning to put it all together.

He mounted up and rode farther into the valley, keeping out of sight of the shepherd he had spotted, choosing to stay in the lower meadows between the hillsides. But toward noon, he was surprised as he came upon two enormous flocks that filled the valley ahead of him, including the sloping hills beside it.

There was nothing he could do but ride right on through the nervous, skittery sheep, going as slowly as possible so as not to panic them. When he reached the second flock, a ragged collie came pouring down at him from a crest to his right and began yapping at the buckskin's heels. Longarm soothed his buckskin and glanced up at the brow of the hill and saw an impassive Indian watching him, an ancient flintlock resting casually on his shoulder.

Longarm waved at him just as casually and kept going.

It was well past noon when Longarm, crouched behind a steep bank, sighted the cluster of low buildings and pens that had been built close by a grove of cottonwoods. They were set in under a sandy bluff, and the stream coiled placidly in front of them. A small but serviceable shack had been built under four tall cottonwoods to one side of the largest shed. It was a nice spot indeed for Erikson's other ranch, the one he used as headquarters for tending the sheep he was stealing from himself—or from the syndicate that hired him.

Longarm studied the layout carefully, waiting for some sign that Erikson was on the premises. At last he saw the man emerge from the small shack, empty a bucket of water on the ground, then go back inside. The man still wore his poncho and floppy hat. Longarm glanced back. He had tied up his horse well back out of sight beyond a bend in the stream. Looking at the shack again, he realized the best way for him to approach unobserved would be to follow the stream bank until he was behind the cottonwoods. He set out, keeping his head down.

There was no window in the rear of the shack. Longarm flattened himself against the wall, then moved around the side to the front, his Colt out by the time he reached the single front door and kicked it in. He strode into the dim place as the shack's door slammed against the wall, and leveled his revolver at Erikson. In the act of pouring himself a drink, Erikson held the whiskey bottle poised in his hand for a moment, then set it slowly, carefully down on the rough table.

"If you want a drink that bad, Longarm," Erikson drawled, smiling, "just ask. No need to kick the whole place down."

Longarm glanced around him. The single room was bare of everything but the necessities: a double tier of bunks on one wall, a single cot on the other. The cot was mussed, the mattress showing. A small potbellied stove sat close to the back wall.

"You can put that cannon away now," Erikson offered. "I ain't armed."

Longarm holstered his Colt, feeling just a mite foolish for the precipitous way in which he had entered this flimsy shack and threatened Erikson. It was a pure marvel the way this fellow kept him off-balance.

"Set a spell," Erikson said. "I'll get you a glass."

He found one on a shelf under the side window. It didn't look too clean. He blew into it. Dust flew out. He ran a finger around the inside, then slapped it down in front of Longarm and filled it halfway with whiskey. Then he finished pouring his own drink.

"Here's to bigger and better days, Longarm." He said, swallowing his drink.

Sitting down, Longarm sipped his drink and continued to look around. Erikson should have been more surprised to see him. Either that or he was the world's best actor. Longarm took another sip of the whiskey. He hated to admit it, but it was good stuff.

"Nice place you got here," Longarm said.

Erickson looked around the small interior. "Needs work, though."

Longarm nodded.

"But you didn't come all the way out here to compliment me on this ranch, did you, Longarm?"

Longarm shrugged. He decided he would let Erikson talk; the man seemed to need it. He was a little kid behind a barn who wanted to brag about his latest deviltry. His eyes were dancing as he looked at Longarm. He just couldn't wait to tell the lawman how clever he had been. Longarm leaned back in his chair and took another sip of the whiskey.

"I guess you know now what happened to all them sheep that's been stolen from me."

"Yep. I saw them. Looked pretty healthy to me."

Erickson smiled, delighted. "I'll be moving on soon, up north. Change my name and become a respectable sheepherder. No more being foreman to a bunch of black Spaniards who can't speak plain English."

"Your own spread, huh?"

"That's right. With sheep that the cattlemen around here destroyed, wiped out." He leaned forward, eyes gleaming. "The funny thing is, Longarm, they all think they did it, but they don't know which one of them it was. Bide suspicions it was Sir Henry's boys; Sir Henry must have thought for sure it was Bide."

"And all the while it was you."

"That's right."

"With a little help from Slade's riders."

"That's right. Of course, we always made it look a mite worse than it was, and then I drove such sheep as was left into this valley."

"You killed Manuel Alava."

"Had to, Longarm." He looked down at his whiskey, studied it for a moment, then tipped up the glass and emptied it. He rested the empty glass on the table and pondered some more. Then he looked at Longarm. "He followed me to this place. He was going to tell his father what was going on."

"You hit him over the head, threw him off that bluff, then stampeded a sizeable flock onto him."

"And I did it on Sir Henry's range," Erickson said, grinning. "Made Bide think for sure that old Sir Henry was in his corner. Made Bide all nervous to start the war right then."

"Did you kill Sir Henry?"

"No I didn't." The man appeared shocked that Longarm could consider him capable of such a deed. Curiously enough, Longarm believed him.

"Any notion who might've?"

Erickson grinned and refilled his glass. "You're the lawman. You tell me."

Longarm shrugged and took another drink of the whiskey. He was beginning to taste the dirt that had come loose from the inside of the glass. The whiskey was gritty.

"Mooreland had right fine stock," Erickson went on. "He wouldn't sell out to me. He didn't really have to kill himself. I never suspicioned he'd take it so hard, losing that dog of his."

"You stole what sheep were not killed when you dynamited his flock."

"Yes."

"Again, with Slade's help."

"You gotta understand, Longarm, no rider for the Bar B knows about this ranch. All they do is shoot up a flock, throw some dynamite, and club a few sheep, then scatter what's left. That's when I come along with my Indians and herd them to this place."

"Suppose they go too far and kill all the sheep?"

"They got their orders." He frowned suddenly. "You knew I was in this with Slade. How did you figure that?"

"I saw you and him exchange glances in the Palace after Sir Henry's funeral. It wasn't much, but it was enough."

"You got sharp eyes, Longarm, that's the pure truth. But you been givin' me some grief. I had the cattlemen pretty stirred up until you come along and settled things down." He smiled. "But I reckon I've taken care of that."

"Those were Slade's men who attacked Pancho's ranch?"

Erickson blinked, a bit startled. "How'd you know that?"

"I was there. We buried one of them the next day."

"Don't make no never-mind. Slade and Bide will ride together and wipe out the rest of Pablo's flocks and such sheep as I got left, as well. Just imagine how that's goin' to rile me. The law will be sent in to stop the range war, and I will limp off. My bosses in Kansas City will be wiped out. But I'll be in the clear. Neat, ain't it?"

"Very neat. How did you get Slade to throw in with you?"

"He needs the range that will be up for grabs when I'm gone, to handle the stock he's figurin' to run on this range—that he *better* run on this range if he figures to stay ahead of all the men he owes money to."

"And his backers."

"And his backers. They ain't fooled as easy as mine, I'm afraid. But that's Slade's problem."

"It'll be yours soon, as well. I'm sure your backers in Kansas City will be interested in learning how you've been feathering your nest at their expense. I'm taking you in, Erikson, for the murder of Manuel Alava." He smiled. "And for harboring two fugitives." Longarm reached across his stomach and took out his Colt. "We'd better get moving. We've got a long ride ahead of us."

Erickson leaned back in his chair, the smile still on his face, but a chill in his eyes that made Longarm uneasy. The man was going into one of his other personalities. Up until this moment, he had been like a pleased kid anxious to relate his criminal cleverness to Longarm. Now, at sight of Longarm's gun, he had turned into that other, less pleasant apparition—the one who mistreated horses and who had about him the aspect of an inspired and frightening madman. His eyes glinted malevolently at Longarm from out of his dark sockets. His long, filthy white hair seemed to frame his gaunt face in a kind of pale, unholy glow.

"Put that gun away, Longarm," he said softly. "You ain't gonna need it no more." He shook his head sadly. "You think I'd spill my guts to you if there was any chance—any chance in the world—that you'd be able to live long enough to use it against me?"

Too late, Longarm realized his danger. A shadow fell over Erikson as someone darkened the doorway behind Longarm. He turned swiftly. As he did so, a solid fist caught him on the side of the jaw. Lights exploded deep inside his head. He put his hands out to break his fall, but he kept falling—past the floor and past the rough laughter, into darkness. . . .

Chapter 13

The sun was slicing into Longarm's eyes. He turned his head and squinted up at the blazing sky. He moved his jaw slowly, carefully. A sucker punch, it was, and no doubt of that. His jaw must been hanging out there as big as life when that fist caught it on the tip. His jaw wasn't broken, but it sure as hell was sore.

He was lying on his back on the ground beside his buckskin. The horse's tail swept across his field of vision. Some of the tail's horsehair strands caught his nose and he almost sneezed. He turned his head. As he did so, he was kicked viciously in the shoulder. He tried to roll away from his attacker and found that his hands were tied behind him. Another sharp kick, this one bringing a grunt of anger from the lawman's clenched mouth, caused him to roll over onto his face. At once he was hauled roughly to his feet, then flung around to face his attackers.

Erikson was standing with Bigger and Pete. Erikson had a fixed, cold smile on his face. He stepped closer to Longarm and slapped him across the face, then backhanded him, putting all of his lean strength into it. Longarm's head snapped around. Again and again Erikson punished him in this fashion until Longarm was driven back against his horse's flank, his knees like water, his eyes stinging.

At last, exhausted, Erikson stopped and, panting like a madman, thrust his face inches from Longarm's and said, "You think I was going to let you get away with what you did to me in the Palace? I been plannin' this for a long time, you big son of a bitch. A long time. I let you push me around, I did. Oh yes! I let you think I was a nothing! I had to let you treat me that way! I couldn't let you know I was as smart as I am. You think I didn't know Bigger and Pete robbed that train when I hired them?"

He stood back, still panting. Then he took off his floppy hat and brushed off his forehead with the back of his forearm. Dirty streaks of sweat were running down his face. He looked completely mad.

"We let you kill Luke 'cause that left one less man we had to split that gold with. When we get rid of Trampas, that is." He smiled then, his yellow teeth gleaming in his dark face.

"You know Trampas?"

He laughed. His head tipping way back, he slapped his thigh and laughed. Bigger and Pete grinned too. "Sure I do! That son of a bitch!"

"Where is he?"

"You know what, Longarm? You are going to die without knowin' where that son of a bitch is. We know you been lookin' for him. Oh, we know that well enough, and it's goin' to pleasure us considerable to see you dead without you knowing where Trampas has been all this time!"

"He's hid the gold, you know."

"We know that! You ain't telling us nothing we don't know."

"Let me loose and I'll show you where he hid it." It was a barefaced lie, but Longarm did not let that bother him.

"You tell us where he hid it and I'll let you go. That's a promise."

"I'll have to show you the place."

Erikson laughed, then stepped forward and snapped

Longarm's head around with another vicious swipe. "You ain't a good liar, Marshal. But we don't need you to find that gold. We'll find it easy enough when we're ready to." He looked at Bigger and Pete. "Right, boys?"

They nodded. It was obvious they had all the confidence in the world in Erikson at this point. And from the look of things at that moment, their confidence was not misplaced.

"But we're wastin' time," said Erikson. "I shouldn't have let my damn fool anger put off what we've got in store for you, Marshal. Turn around."

Longarm turned. To his astonishment, he felt his hands being untied. As soon as he was able to, he flexed his hands. The blood rushing back into them made them tingle painfully. He kept flexing his hands until the tingling faded.

"Now mount up," Erikson told him.

Obediently, Longarm swung into his saddle. But when he looked down at the three men, he saw that Bigger and Pete were covering him with their sixguns. Erikson stepped close and, with a strip of rawhide, swiftly and securely bound Longarm's left boot to his stirrup.

"You're goin' to fall off your horse, Longarm," Erikson explained. "And your foot is goin' to get all caught up in that there stirrup, and you're goin' to be dragged to hell and back until they ain't nothin' left of your head but a bloody stump. Then we'll cut the rawhide. Someone will find you by your horse. A terrible accident. The kind of accident every horseman fears." He chuckled.

Longarm had to wait until the three of them had mounted up. When they did, he was told to ride ahead of them. The "accident" was not going to occur, obviously, until they were well out of this valley, much closer to Ruby Wells.

That was all right with Longarm.

They had taken his Colt, but they had left his holster on and had not taken anything else from his person, obviously so as not to arouse suspicion when his body was found. They undoubtedly planned to place his Colt back into his holster as well. In fact, they had not even taken his railroad watch or its gold-washed chain—and had overlooked one more seemingly minor item: his watch fob. Only in this case, of course, the fob happened to be a small, double-barreled .44 derringer.

As Longarm rode, he could feel the weapon's welcome heaviness against his belly.

Longarm seriously considered making his move while they were riding through the canyon that led from the valley. But the shadows were treacherous, he had only two rounds against their combined firepower, and the trail was littered dangerously with boulders and loose gravel. With his boot tied to the stirrup, it was a bad place to spook a horse with sudden firing. He decided he would wait for a better opportunity.

At noon they stopped by a stream to water their horses and rest up some. They left Longarm on his horse, his foot still securely tied to the stirrup. They were now in the foothills of the Rubies. The escarpment was well behind them, but they still had a long way to go before they reached Ruby Wells.

Nevertheless, Longarm's captors were getting eager for the treat. He could read the signs clearly. The three of them were beginning to whisper among themselves, dig each other with their elbows, and giggle furtively, like kids about to enter a whorehouse for the first time. The thought of how they were going to kill Longarm was getting their blood up.

They were in heat.

Longarm was still drinking from the canteen they had allowed him when he saw Bigger get up from the ground after a short exchange with Erikson and Pete, and start toward Longarm, a wide grin on his face that did not make Longarm want to smile back. As Bigger got closer, Erikson and Pete got to their feet to watch. The two were alive with anticipation. Longarm rested the canteen on the pommel and waited for Bigger to get closer, mentally calculating the odds of taking on three men with two bullets.

Bigger halted within a few feet, directly in front of the horse, and squinted up at Longarm. The sun was powerfully bright and perspiration was rolling down the man's heavy face. He placed both hands on his hips and leaned back happily.

"Why don't you shoot me, Longarm?" he asked loudly, his smile getting even broader. "Why don't you take out that little toy gun and shoot me dead!"

Longarm grabbed swiftly for the derringer, but even as he pulled it out, his heart sank. Its weight told him its two fangs had been removed. It was empty! They had known all along he had it!

"Gawdamn! Lookit his face!" cried Pete, pointing. The man was about to double up as he contemplated Longarm's shocked surprise. Erikson, too, was grinning hugely, while Bigger just tipped his head back and roared, his eyes squeezed shut with mirth.

Longarm unclipped the derringer with a single swift motion of his fingers and flung the weapon at Bigger's face. The pistol glanced off the outlaw's right eyebrow and sent him reeling back. Instantly, Longarm bent forward over the buckskin and clapped spurs to its flank. The horse, startled, lurched forward, its forelegs brushing Bigger, who went down on one knee before the charge, an arm held up to ward off the horse plunging over him.

Longarm heard and felt the sickening crunch as the horse's driving hooves came down on muscle and sinew, and kept spurring the horse, heading it now directly for Erikson and Pete. The two men broke in separate directions, Pete with his hogleg already out, Erikson still frantically clawing for his. Longarm veered after Pete. The man glanced over his shoulder, eyes wide, and threw a wild shot at Longarm an instant before the buckskin overtook him. A blast from behind Longarm caught the horse in the neck and it went down heavily on top of the sprawling Pete.

And Longarm went down with the horse, his left leg still tied securely to the stirrup. Fortunately, as the horse fell on Longarm, much of the weight of the animal was absorbed by Pete's body. The outlaw's entire torso was crushed under the horse. Longarm heard the man cry out once, then go silent. The horse quivered a couple of times, then lay still, his crushing weight sufficient to keep Longarm's left leg securely pinned.

Longarm looked around quickly, and raising himself as much as he could, he saw Erikson approaching cautiously from the other side of the fallen buckskin. He was bent well over, his hat off, his white, straggly hair wild.

"That's all right, Longarm!" he cried. "You ain't goin' nowhere with that dead horse on top of you!"

He stopped then, and aiming with both hands and holding the gun well out in front of him, he fired. Longarm had already ducked. The round thudded into the buckskin's side. Keeping down, Longarm reached in under the horse and tried to free his foot from the stirrup. But he could not get a firm grip on the rawhide.

He heard Erikson moving closer. The man was laughing softly. The excitement of the last few minutes appeared to have pushed him over the edge. Longarm started to pull his hand out from under the horse and felt it brush past something hard and metallic. At once he reached back and closed his hand about the barrel of Pete's revolver. He pulled it out from under the horse and looked up to see Erikson leaning over the horse, staring wild-eyed down at him.

"Can't get loose, can you!" Erikson cried.

"No, damn your hide," replied Longarm. "I can't. The rawhide is on too tight. I'm trapped under this dead horse. You got to help me get free, Erikson. I'll drop all charges."

Erikson shook his head quickly. "I don't believe you, Longarm. But I tell you what. I won't shoot you. I'll leave you here. It's perfect. You were chasing the two train robbers. They captured you and you tried to get away. Marshal Toady will be able to see what happened in a minute. If I shot you, there would be no way to explain the bullet." He straightened up. "So I'll just leave you like this."

As Longarm appeared to struggle to raise the dead weight off him, Erikson just smiled and holstered his gun. "The stench of death is on you, Longarm! Can't you smell it? Why struggle? It's all over."

"No it isn't, Erikson."

Longarm's struggle had been to slip Pete's sixgun around so his right hand could grab its butt. Now, as he spoke, he lifted the gun into view and leveled it at Erikson. The man was so startled he did not think clearly. Eyes wild, he went for his gun.

"Don't, Erikson!" cried Longarm, cocking Pete's Colt.

But Erikson was not listening. As his own gun cleared its holster, Longarm fired. The .45-caliber slug stamped a hole in Erikson's face just below his right cheekbone. Instantly the hole appeared to open and swallow the man's entire lower jaw. Erikson's head was snapped back and out of sight, his hands grabbing at his disintegrating face. He struck the ground behind him on his back and began rolling over and over until he was out of sight behind the buckskin's great bulk. For a while longer he flopped about on the grass, then grew quiet. A moment later Longarm heard his death rattle as he added his stench to that of Pete and the horse.

No longer working under the fierce urgency he had had to contend with before, Longarm was able at last to untie the knotted rawhide and free his left foot. Once that was accomplished, he slowly, gradually worked his way out from under the horse.

Erikson had not been entirely wrong in thinking Longarm would be unable to free himself alone. If it were not for the leverage Pete's body gave him, Longarm most likely *would* have been trapped. In any case, he was certain that Erikson would have hung around long enough to make sure he could not pull himself free.

Bigger died as Longarm examined him. The buckskin's hoof had sliced part of his neck away, and there were internal injuries as well. He died trying to form a curse to hurl at Longarm. Pete was also dead, his ribcage having been stove in by the tremendous weight of the falling horse. The buckskin, though unable to move, was still alive. He stared up at Longarm, his muzzle covered with a pink froth around which a horde of bluebottle flies were swarming. Longarm finished him with a shot just above and between the eyes, perfectly centered. The horse appeared to settle as Longarm looked away.

Longarm rode into Ruby Wells late the next day, aboard Erikson's mount. Bigger and Erikson, their bodies each wrapped in a slicker, were slung over Bigger's horse. Longarm drew up in front of Marshal Toady's office and went inside.

Craning his neck to see out the window past Longarm, Toady said, "What's that you got out there, Longarm?"

"Two dead bodies. I had to leave one more dead body and my horse back in the hills."

"My God, Longarm! Who are they?"

"Erikson and one of those hired guns he ran with. Bigger's his name, I think. Pete's the other one. He's the one I had to leave."

The man sat down heavily in his chair and chucked his hat well off his forehead. Then he grinned. "You killed that sheepherder! Son of a bitch!"

"Where's Slade?"

"In his saloon, I guess. What you got to see him for?"

"Thought he might know the name of that outfit in Kansas City that Erikson worked for. I figure I'll have to send them a wire to bring a new man out, now that Erikson won't be able to do the job anymore." He smiled thinly at Toady. "This is still good sheep country, Toady."

The man's pleasure faded. He shrugged. "Maybe it is, Longarm. But what makes you think Slade would know who Erikson worked for? Them two weren't thick that I know of."

"Not that you know of." Longarm turned and opened the door. "Take care of the bodies, Toady. Thanks."

A small knot of curious townspeople had already gathered on the boardwalk to look at the horse with its slickered burden. They were staying a good distance away. They knew what was under the slickers. Longarm pushed his way through the crowd and headed for the Drover's Palace.

It was before supper, and the Palace was not crowded. Judge Barclay, his skull-like head slumped forward over his forearms, was sleeping it off at a rear table. The girls were in a corner, giggling. Two serious drinkers were tossing down Scotch at the bar. They finished as Longarm entered, and strode out past him.

"Where's Slade?" Longarm asked the barkeep.

"In his office," the man said, indicating a door at the end of the bar.

"Thanks."

"Slade expecting you?"

Longarm glanced at the man. "Nope."

"Well, you can't just walk in there . . ."

"Yes I can," Longarm told him. "Watch."

Longarm reached the door, rapped once, then pushed it open and stepped inside. Slade was bent over his ledger, working diligently with pen and ink. He had just finished dipping the pen into the small bottle of ink when Longarm entered. He looked up in surprise and put the pen down as Longarm closed the door behind him.

He was not pleased to see Longarm, but he smothered his displeasure as well as he could and attempted a smile. "What can I do for you, Longarm? Nothing wrong with the whiskey, I trust."

Longarm smiled back at the man as he approached the desk. "Whiskey's fine, Slade. I just came in to get the address of that company Erikson works for in Kansas City. He said you would have the name around somewhere."

"Me?"

"He was probably asking for credit and gave you the name so you could check, something like that, I imagine."

Slade was disturbed, but he tried not to show it. "Well, yes, I do have their name, as a matter of fact." He opened a small drawer in his desk, took out a notebook, and flipped through it. "Yes, here it is. I'll write it down for you."

Longarm waited silently while Slade wrote it down, and thanked Slade as he handed it to him. Folding it carefully, he dropped it into the side pocket of his frock coat.

"What I can't understand, Longarm," said Slade,

getting to his feet, "is why Erikson couldn't have given you that address himself."

"Because he's dead."

Slade sat back down in a hurry, his face ashen.

"Now I'd like the address of that syndicate *you're* working for, the one that's backing the Bar B."

The man's face went from gray to red. He hauled himself angrily back up onto his feet. "Now what in hell do you need *that* for?"

"I'm going to have to wire this company in Kansas City about Erikson. Figure I might as well do the same thing for you."

Slade's eyes narrowed. "For *me?*"

"That's right, Slade. I'm taking you along with me for the murder of Rose O'Riley."

"The murder of Rose . . . !" He tried a smile and took a step back, away from the desk. "What in blazes has got into you, Longarm? Have you completely lost your senses? You know who killed Rose. Luke Twitchell. You went after him yourself!"

"And he resisted arrest and I shot him. Before he died, Slade, he told me who put him up to it. He said you wanted him to be sure and kill Rose before he got to me. That way it would look like an accident, like she just got in the way."

"He was lying! For what possible reason would I want Rose killed?"

"You needed full ownership of this place to keep yourself afloat. You were in hock to her already. When you saw a chance to get her share without buying it from her, you took it."

"Luke's dead! That means you can't prove a word of this!"

"A copy of that ownership agreement ought to tell me what I need to know. If it has a clause that says in the event of death, the surviving partner gets the other's shares, there won't be any doubt in my mind—or a jury's."

Slade was not wearing a holster, so his hand did not drop to his thigh. Instead, it flew to his belt. Longarm had expected the move and was already drawing his Colt as Slade brought up his belly gun. Longarm fired first. The .44 slug went into the heel of Slade's gunhand and ranged through his wrist and into his arm. The ugly little belly gun went off as Slade lost control of it, sending a small slug into a picture on the wall near the door.

Slade was clutching his shattered right hand in his left, and leaning sideways against the desk, uttering tiny little sobs of pain. Blood was streaming through the fingers of his left hand. Longarm heard the door behind him open. He turned. The barkeep was standing in the doorway, bringing up his sawed-off shotgun. Longarm flung himself to the floor just as the shotgun went off.

The detonation was deafening in the enclosed space, and caused Longarm to wince painfully as he fired up at the barkeep. His bullet caught the man in the shirt front, just under his string tie. The barkeep staggered back against the doorframe and seemed about to fire the other barrel at Longarm. Longarm fired a second time. The force of this round peeled the barkeep out through the open doorway. He dropped the shotgun, discharging the second barrel into the floor, then collapsed facedown on a table. One of the legs gave way under his weight and it crashed to the floor under him. A girl was in sight beyond the barkeep, her eyes wide, her mouth opening. As Longarm scrambled to his feet and kicked the door shut, she began to scream.

Longarm turned and looked back at Slade. The man was still on his feet, but only just barely. The shotgun's blast had sheared away much of his upper right torso.

His right arm and shoulder were mostly gone. He was gaping down at what was left of him. As Longarm hurried toward him, he collapsed to the floor, bouncing off the side of the desk as he did so. Thick, dark gouts of blood were pulsing weakly onto the carpet.

Slade was still conscious as Longarm bent over him. "You lied, you son of a bitch," the man gasped up at Longarm. "Luke never told you nothing. Erikson would've told me!"

"Guess that's right."

The man closed his eyes and groaned. Longarm was not sure it was because of the pain or because of what he had just learned.

"Slade! Where's the gold hid? Where can I find Trampas?"

Slade opened his eyes. "You tricked me, you bastard! I'm dead because of you!"

"You got no reason to hold back now, Slade. Tell me."

The man's eyes widened in fury. His head lifted an inch or two off the floor. "You're never going to find that gold, you son of a bitch!" He began to cough. "And you're never going to find Trampas, either! Damn you! I wish he'd done a better job . . . of killing you!"

His eyes closed then and his head dropped back to the floor, the fury slowly fading from his face, the lines growing less sharp, the face seeming to sink into the bone structure as the furious spirit that had animated his flesh fled the ruined body.

Chapter 14

Madeline seemed genuinely distressed that Longarm was not going to be able to stay longer. She had already wheedled Longarm into joining her and Frank Tully in a farewell drink before continuing on. But now Longarm was insisting once again that he had to get a move on if he hoped to reach the Montalban ranch before dark.

They moved out onto the veranda with him and watched while he mounted up. His mount had been waiting not too patiently in the sun, and was now anxious to get moving. The big bay crow-hopped a couple of times. Longarm held the reins lightly until the horse settled under him.

"Guess that animal's as anxious as you are to see all them sheep," Tully said, leaning back against a veranda post and folding his arms. He was no longer dressed to look like a riverboat gambler on horseback. His clothes had settled down some, and now he looked like what he was: the foreman of the Lazy C and, before too many more days, Madeline's husband and part-owner of one of the finest spreads in these parts. Madeline had been almost coy when she told Longarm of the engagement. His congratulations had been genuine; the impending marriage seemed to have done wonders for her outlook.

Longarm smiled at Tully. "Well, I don't know if

that's a fact. But this animal sure does want to get a move on."

"I meant to ask you," Tully said hesitantly, looking for a moment in Madeline's direction, "if you think Erikson might have had anything to do with the death of Sir Henry."

Madeline frowned, but spoke up firmly: "You can talk of it, Longarm. Don't mind me. It still hurts, but I guess I'd like to know myself if Erikson could have been responsible. Or even Slade. From what you tell us, they were both in this ugly business together."

"I guess the only way I can answer that truthfully, Madeline, is to say I just don't know. Both Erikson and Slade were trying to do everything in their power to stir things up, to get the sheepherders and cattlemen at each other's throats. And killing Sir Henry would sure be one way. You saw how Bide reacted. And that would have been just the beginning."

"Yes," said Tully, "if you hadn't happened along, Longarm."

"Then you think they might have killed Uncle Henry?" Madeline persisted.

Longarm shrugged. "All I'm saying is it fits the pattern. Beyond that, I don't know any more than you do."

"Good luck, Longarm," said Tully, unfolding his arms and straightening.

"Yes," said Madeline, smiling up at Longarm through the brightness of the afternoon sunlight. "Next time you're in these parts, you stop by."

"I'll sure do that," Longarm said, touching his hatbrim to her and pulling his horse around.

They were still on the veranda watching him as he rode through the gate. He waved to them once and they waved back, then turned and went inside. Longarm's horse got feisty a second time, so he let the animal have its run. A couple of Lazy C punchers got out of his way, waving their hats and grinning.

Longarm shifted his position slightly. The smooth face of the boulder, against which he had been resting his back for the better part of two hours, seemed to have developed a few bumps and other irregularities. His left leg was stiff, as well, and he was beginning to feel just a mite foolish. The Lazy C ranchyard below him was bathed in a bright blue glow from the brilliant silver-dollar moon, but the ranch house was quiet, the punchers were all in their bunks asleep if they weren't playing cards, and here he was, freezing to death on this chill bluff.

When Tully had asked him that afternoon why he was giving up his search for Trampas and the gold he had buried, Longarm had explained what he felt might have happened. Trampas could have been severely injured that night he killed Patty Wormser. He had galloped away over rough ground and it was a dark night. If he had been thrown and injured, it would have left him without a horse high in the Rubies; he could easily have died from his injuries and from exposure, allowing his knowledge of the gold's whereabouts to die with him.

It was a logical enough explanation, all right. The only trouble was that after what Slade had told him a few seconds before his death, Longarm could not possibly believe it.

He leaned forward and cocked his head slightly.

Yes, he was hearing right. Madeline and Tully. They were arguing, their voices drifting up to him on the night wind like faint, disembodied spirits. The door to the ranch house opened and a long finger of yellow light probed into the yard. Tully strode through the doorway with Madeline coming after him, a lantern in her hand. They continued to argue, but their words were hushed, urgent. Tully stepped off the veranda and headed for the horse barn, while Madeline, silent now, watched him go.

She stood in the doorway until he disappeared into the barn. Then she turned about and went back into the house. The door slammed and the yard was dim again in the moonlight. Presently Tully rode softly out of the barn and through the gate, the moonlight reflecting off his hat and shoulders.

Longarm got back to his own horse soon enough to pick up Tully's trail without much difficulty; but once they rode into higher country, the moonlight did not help as much. Twice he almost lost Tully. The first time it was the sound of a shod hoof striking stone that gave him the proper direction, and the second time it was a glimpse of Tully silhouetted against the night sky.

Now Longarm was afoot, approaching Tully from behind a thin screen of cottonwoods and willow alongside a narrow, swift-running mountain stream. Tully had left his horse to crop the grass along the bank while he proceeded to reach into the hollowed-out center of a dead cottonwood. When Longarm finally stepped into the clearing behind Tully, the man had already retrieved two bulging saddlebags and was perspiring freely from the exertion.

So intent was he on recovering the gold that he did not notice Longarm standing in the shadows.

"Trampas!" Longarm said.

Tully dropped the bags and whirled.

"You see? I found you after all." Longarm's Colt was out and leveled at Tully. When Tully saw its barrel gleaming in the moonlight, he slowly raised both hands over his head. "I'm glad you aren't rotting somewhere up there in the Rubies, Trampas, and that you didn't injure yourself riding off that night."

"May you fry in hell, Longarm. How did you know?"

"It had to be you—or Madeline—that shot me and killed Kincaid. It took me a while, but I finally remembered something I had forgotten about that. Kincaid recognized who shot me and seemed right pleased—a moment before you turned the gun on him. And just before he died, Slade said he wished that Trampas had done a better job of killing me. He wished that *you*, Trampas, had not bungled the job."

"You think the person Kincaid recognized was me, that it?"

"You deny it?"

"Hell, yes, I deny it! Wasn't *me* followed you and Kincaid from the ranch, it was—"

He never got to finish. A blast from the cottonwoods sent him reeling. He turned before he fell and sprawled facedown. He tried to push himself erect, then collapsed.

"Drop that gun, Longarm," Madeline said from the trees. "I can see you clearly, but I doubt you can see me. Drop it!"

Longarm tossed his Colt onto the grass and Madeline stepped into view, a .38 Smith & Wesson in her hand. "*You* killed Kincaid?" he asked.

"Yes. Frank heard he was planning something for you. I wanted to get rid of him, and this would be a fine excuse. I'd be saving your life."

"Woman, you nearly killed me."

"I was nervous and shot too soon. I hit you instead. When I stepped into the clear to get a better shot, Kincaid saw me. That was when he smiled. The fool! He thought I had shot you to save *him*."

"Why, Madeline? Why did you need to get rid of Kincaid?"

"He was such a damned pest! I wanted him out of my hair, so Frank and I could take the ranch from Uncle Henry. We'd planned it for a long time, Longarm. Back in San Francisco. All of it. The train robbery. Everything. Even to Frank's using that name, Trampas, with the other members of the gang."

"And now you've killed Frank."

"You heard him," she hissed. "He couldn't wait to spill his guts—to point the finger at me. I told him to wait until you were gone before coming here to count his precious gold. I told him that not until you were on that train to Denver would we be able to go near this gold. But he just couldn't wait. He had to make sure it was still here! He was a fool, like every other man I've known."

She stopped abruptly and took a step toward Longarm. Her red hair hung loose about her shoulders. She looked incredibly beautiful—and evil.

"Except you, Longarm," she said. "You're not a fool, not at all."

"Nice of you to say that, Madeline."

"We could share this gold, Longarm. The gold! The ranch! Can you imagine the life we'd have here in this country!"

"Sounds nice, real nice."

"You see! I knew, once you gave it a thought."

"Think maybe we could travel some?"

"Of course!"

"To England, maybe. To visit some of Sir Henry's relatives. His brothers and sisters. Sir Henry said he had a mother still alive back there. We could visit her too."

"Yes . . . I suppose so."

"How would that feel, Madeline? Having tea with the woman whose son you murdered. Would that bother you at all?"

"What . . . what do you mean?"

"You admitted all the rest of it. Couldn't wait to tell it all. Never heard a woman run on so. Why are you holding back now—about Sir Henry? Did it bother you that much?

"I don't know what you mean!"

"Did you ride the Appaloosa tonight, Madeline?"

"Yes."

"Your favorite mount, ain't it?"

She studied him bitterly before nodding.

"I saw you riding off on that Appaloosa the night we found Sir Henry. Wasn't sure what I'd seen at the time. But that's what it was, all right. You riding across that meadow on that horse of yours after you left Sir Henry in the shallows of the stream. Pablo or one of the other Basques—maybe Miguel—would get blamed, you figured."

She straightened, the small .38-caliber Smith & Wesson still leveled at him. She seemed to have come to a decision about him. "You do not want to share this gold with me, I take it," she said coldly.

"Why, sure I do, Madeline. You just put down that gun and we can start sharing that gold like crazy!"

"I was wrong about you," she snapped. "You're a fool too. Just like all the others. And maybe you're the biggest fool of all."

"Now that just may be, Madeline."

Longarm was doing a lot of talking, keeping her going, egging her on as well as he could—because behind her, that poor son of a bitch she had drilled earlier was getting slowly to his feet and coming at her. When Longarm saw Tully getting near, he took a single step closer to Madeline. She compressed her lips, took a small step backward, then held her ground.

"This isn't going to be pleasant, Longarm. But I don't really have any choice. I want you to be found here with Frank, the both of you dead. You were fighting over the money. I'll leave enough of the gold to establish that." She smiled thinly. "You see? It will work perf—"

With a sudden, desperate lunge, Tully had reached out and grabbed her from behind. As she rocked back, Longarm dove for her. While he wrapped his arms around her waist—or tried to—she slashed down at him

225

with the Smith & Wesson, stunning him. But Frank stayed with her and managed to grab the gun from her hand. Longarm pawed for her, trying to pull her down, but she spun free.

In a moment she was lost in the trees. Longarm rushed in after her, still groggy, but she had disappeared among the rocks. The moon was low now, playing tag with a cloud bank. While Longarm stumbled about trying to get some clue as to which direction she had taken, he heard her galloping off, the thunder of the Appaloosa's hooves filling the night.

Longarm went back to the clearing. Tully was down again, fumbling with the Smith & Wesson he'd knocked from Madeline's hands. He was probably attempting to shoot Longarm as he approached, but he was too far gone by then. His last spark had been expended in that futile attempt to bring Madeline down.

Longarm took the .38 from his hand and knelt beside him. The man looked up, closed his eyes, and died. Longarm stood up and looked down at Tully. If the man had kept away from the gold as Madeline had wanted, if he had waited until Longarm left for Denver, he would have made it. Longarm's suspicions alone would not have been enough to keep him in Ruby Wells indefinitely.

Tully *had* been a fool, all right. And it had cost him.

Madeline had not returned to the Lazy C by the time Longarm rode in the next morning with Frank Tully's body. The Lazy C hands were not very happy with what Longarm had to say concerning Madeline and Tully, since it meant they no longer had a Lazy C to ride for—and cowboys don't have pensions. A lot of them packed their gear and rode out that same morning, but a few older hands remained behind to help Longarm bury Tully and load the gold onto a couple of packhorses for the trip into Ruby Wells.

It was one of them, an old puncher called Stokey, who found Madeline.

He caught sight of something mottled, high in the rocks, on his trip back with the packhorses, and had left them with the hand helping him and ridden off to investigate.

"You better come with me, Marshal," the old cowpoke said. "It ain't pretty."

Longarm chose a few of the remaining hands to ride with him, and they followed Stokey high into the Rubies. They came across the Appaloosa first. It was in great pain, thrashing about on its side, its right front foreleg shattered. This was what Stokey had glimpsed from the trail below: the Appaloosa's pale, mottled hide lifting and thrashing among the rocks. Longarm had one of the punchers hang back and finish the suffering animal, and as the shot from the cowhand's revolver echoed among the rocks, Stokey pulled up on the crest of a rock shelf and pointed to a ledge far below.

Madeline was on her back, her arms flung wide, her thick plume of red hair a garish halo about her head. At this distance Longarm could not make out any of her features. From the way one leg was folded under her and from the crooked way she lay, he could tell that her back was broken. She was most assuredly dead.

Stokey was right. It wasn't pretty.

"How can you get down there?" Longarm asked the puncher.

"It'll be tricky," Stokey replied.

Longarm pulled his horse back off the rock shelf. "See to it," he said.

As Longarm rode back to the ranch, he found himself recalling Madeline during her kinder moments. There was no way he could tally that other woman with the one he had just glimpsed. But then, he knew enough about men *and* women by now to realize that there was no cruelty, no deceit, no abomination they would not willingly embrace in the pursuit of their various lusts.

"Marshal!"

Longarm pulled up until Stokey overtook him. For a while the two rode on down the rocky trail in silence as Stokey put together what he wanted to ask Longarm.

"Marshal," he said finally, "what I jest *can't* figure out is what that there woman was doin' way up there on that horse in the middle of the night. You told us she was fleeing, the last you saw of her. But you can't get to nowhere up there. And that there trail is as treacherous as a rattlesnake's kiss, even in broad daylight! Where in tarnation was she going?"

Longarm glanced at the old cowpoke. "Why, Stokey," he told him, "she knew where she was going. She knew perfectly well—and she got there, sure enough."

Stokey frowned for a moment as Longarm's words sank in. When it hit him, he glanced back at the rocks for a moment, then rode on beside Longarm, his old face somber, its expression matching perfectly what Longarm himself was feeling in his own heart.

Longarm was looking restlessly down at the narrow streets of Ruby Wells, debating whether or not he should leave his room and go down to the Drover's Palace for a nightcap. The new owner was stocking Maryland rye. Tomorrow Longarm would take the train out of this place and ride shotgun on the gold shipment he had recovered, to see that it reached, finally, its legal and proper destination. A telegram containing orders from Vail to that effect was in his pocket now. He had just returned from the telegraph office after wiring Vail to advise him he had received the orders and would soon be on his way.

Longarm's restlessness increased. As a rule, he never liked to hang around a place after finishing an assignment. There were always too many unpleasant reminders of the hellish gore he usually had to wade through—and for which effort no one usually stepped forward to thank him.

There was a soft rap on his door, a surprisingly soft rap. He had barely heard it. Frowning, he turned and walked across the room. "Yes?" he called through the door.

"Please, Longarm," he heard. "Let me in!"

He pulled open the door at once and drew Carmen into the room, closing the door swiftly behind her.

"Great balls of fire, Carmen!" he said. "What are you doing here?"

Her eyes were gleaming with excitement. "It is terribly wicked, is it not?"

"You must leave at once, Carmen!"

"Shh!" she said, removing the bandanna she had tied over her abundant hair, and then shaking her tresses out with a quick snap of her head. "Father is downstairs at the Palace with Pedro. They are talking to that one from Kansas City who wants him and Pedro to run all that sheep you find. It will be good! Soon Pedro will have his own ranch!"

"All right, Carmen, but do they know—"

She was stepping swiftly out of her long skirt. "It is all right, I say," she said. "I tell Pedro I go to say goodbye to the marshal. He understand and will drink to celebrate with father after the deal is made. But we must hurry!"

She had only a single waist-high petticoat under the skirt, and had soon kicked that off as well. Next came her blouse. She wore no chemise or corset under the blouse. He found himself looking at her smooth, dark nakedness as he backed slowly before her to the bed.

She held out her arms to him. "Do not worry," she said, smiling. "I am not a virgin." For just an instant, sorrow passed like a cloud across her face. "I visit Manuel many times while he tend the white-haired

229

one's flocks." Her arms were around him now, and she was pressing urgently against him. "You give me Manuel's dictionary. Now, like him, I study it. I will keep it forever and think of him. So now I thank you for that gift."

She pressed him back onto the bed and swiftly began to unbutton his shirt, her dark hair spilling over his face and shoulders, engulfing him in the sweet smell of her. He pushed his britches down across his hips and took her in his arms.

It was, Longarm had to admit, the nicest thank you he had received in a long, long time.

SPECIAL PREVIEW

Here are the opening scenes
from

LONGARM AND THE GHOST DANCERS

Twenty-second in the bold
LONGARM series from Jove

Chapter 1

It was a dull gray Sunday morning, and Denver looked dead as well as dry. A thirsty man whose health depended on it could always get a drink in Denver, city ordinance be damned. But that wasn't Longarm's reason for being up at such a ghastly hour on his day off. The tall deputy had a bottle of Maryland rye at his furnished room on the less fashionable side of Cherry Creek, so he wasn't searching for any side door to an officially closed saloon. He was on an unofficial mission for the Justice Department, or rather for his boss, Federal Marshal Billy Vail. The Justice Department might well have frowned on his spare-time activity, and Billy Vail said his wife would skin him too, if she found out about it.

Longarm sauntered up the steps of the city jail, took a deep breath, and went inside. It didn't work. Longarm had never been able to break himself of the habit of breathing, and the air inside reeked of stable tobacco smoke, disinfectant, and vomit. A desk sergeant eyed him curiously as Longarm strode to the desk, took out his wallet, and flashed his federal badge.

The Denver policeman frowned and said, "We don't have anyone in the tank that Uncle Sam could be interested in, Marshal."

Longarm wearily pushed his flat-crowned Stetson back from his forehead. "I'm only a deputy marshal

233

in the first place, but I understand you're holding a Miss Penelope Ascot on a charge of disturbing the peace."

The desk sergeant blinked in surprise and replied, "Oh, her? Yeah, we have her in the women's tank with some whores and another crazy lady. We were fixing to send her over to the county asylum for observation this afternoon. What in the hell does Uncle Sam want with a lunatic?"

"Material witness," Longarm said soberly. He didn't elaborate. Billy had said something dumb about bailing his old friend's kid out, but the local authorities had charged her with everything but typhoid, and what was the sense of packing a badge if you couldn't use it once in a while?

The desk sergeant looked at his charge sheets and muttered, "Federal witness, huh? According to the arresting officers, Penelope Ascot was engaged in the demolition of the Dew Drop Inn when they arrived on the scene. Prior to that, she'd also heaved a brick through a couple of plate-glass windows on Larimer Street, and the folks at the Silver Dollar want to know who's going to pay for a mirror and seventeen bottles that used to stand behind their bar."

"She's a caution," Longarm agreed amiably, "but what the hell, it's not like she killed anybody, and I have to report back with her." He saw the hesitation in the cop's eyes and added flatly, "I'm sort of in a hurry, friend."

The desk sergeant looked unhappy and said, "I don't know. You'll have to clear it with my captain. That crazy little gal owes a lot of money to the community for what she did."

"Where's your captain, then?"

"It's Sunday. He's off duty today. I think he said something about taking his kids to Cheeseman Park."

Longarm had known this before his arrival, but he looked surprised and sounded disgusted as he snapped, "Jesus H. Christ! You mean to hold a federal witness incommunicado while your captain takes his kids to the *zoo*? What's his name, Sergeant? If I don't show up with my witness, a federal grand jury figures to cloud all up and rain fire and salt on somebody. I sure don't mean to be the one standing underneath without a slicker, if you take my meaning."

The sergeant blanched visibly. "Hold your horses, damn it! I never said it was *impossible* for you to have her. I just said *some* damn body will have to pay for the damage she did last night!"

Longarm pasted a reasonable smile across his tanned face and said, "Hell, she's a member of the Women's Christian Temperance whatever, ain't she?"

"That's for damned sure! Those crazy ladies from the WCTU have been temperate as hell with their bricks and hatchets, lately."

"I know. But they're a nationally chartered organization, right?"

"I reckon so, but that still don't give them no call to go around busting up saloons, does it?"

"You're right as rain, Sergeant," Longarm agreed equably. "If I were you, I'd send a bill to the national headquarters of the WCTU for each and every bottle Miss Ascot busted last night!"

The sergeant brightened. "By jimmies, I never thought of that! Her outfit must have more in their safe than she had in her purse when we picked her up!"

"There you go, old son. Look how you'll be saving the county the expense of a sanity hearing and such, too."

The desk sergeant punched the call bell on his blotter as he said, "I'll mention that to the captain. Where's this here federal hearing being held, in case he asks?"

Longarm hesitated before he said, truthfully enough, "I can't say for certain. Like you said, it's Sunday. We'll get her statement from her this afternoon, of course, but it's hard to say when she'll be called before the jury."

A weary-looking turnkey limped into view and the desk sergeant said, "Gimpy, we're turning that WCTU gal over to this here federal man."

Gimpy breathed an audible sigh of relief. "Praise God from whom all blessings flow! Maybe we'll have some peace and quiet back there now."

As he turned away, Longarm followed. He knew the usual procedure was for them to bring a prisoner out to him, but the more he hung around the desk, the more lies he'd have to tell. The sergeant hadn't asked for his warrant, and with luck he might not even have to sign for her. He'd pointed this out to Billy Vail when the worried marshal had said the regular officers he knew might not be on duty over the weekend.

As he followed the limping turnkey back to the cell blocks, Longarm heard a young but strident voice, singing, "Lips That Touch Liquor Never Shall Touch Mine."

Off-key.

Gimpy stopped before the barred cell that the awful caterwauling was coming from and said, "Shove a sock in it and put your bonnet on, Miss Ascot. Uncle Sam has just taken you off our hands and tortured ears!"

As Gimpy unlocked the door, Longarm peered in at the five women in the gloomy cell. The one standing up was a surprisingly pretty little redhead in a severe black dress that almost completely concealed her figure. As she pinned her black sunbonnet on, covering her flaming mop of hair, she announced loudly, "I welcome my chance to stand trial, and I glory in my coming martyrdom!"

Gimpy told Longarm, "She's been talking like that ever since they brought her in last night. What charge are you boys holding her on?"

"Suspicion of bootlegging," said Longarm, soberly. He saw that Gimpy didn't have a sense of humor, so he quickly added, "You know that Lydia Whatsitsname that ladies take for female complaints? Well, we have evidence that it's eighty-proof alcohol and they've never paid a cent of the federal excise tax. Internal Revenue asked us to look into it."

Gimpy agreed, "Well, she's a female and she sure does complain a lot," as Penelope Ascot stepped grandly from the cell to face Longarm with a look of lofty superiority. Gimpy asked, "Do you aim to handcuff her, Deputy?"

Longarm smiled down at the tiny flame-haired terror and said, "I reckon she'll come quiet. How about it, Miss Ascot?"

She replied stiffly, "You have tobacco on your breath. Where are you taking me, sir?"

Longarm sighed and said, "I'll explain along the way. I can promise you it won't be a saloon. Let's go out front and get your belongings."

As Penelope Ascot walked between the two men, trying to look taller than either, a whore from the cell she'd just left yelled, "You're on the right track, sister! You just keep giving 'em hell, hear?"

"Convert of yours, ma'am?" asked Longarm.

Penelope sniffed and said, "Poor Flossy is another downtrodden victim of Demon Rum and men like yourself."

Longarm let it go. He could have said he didn't have to pay for it, and that if he did, he'd pick something better than Flossy, but he just wanted to get out of here with the crazy little gal.

Considering that he was getting her out of jail, she

sniped like hell all through the business of recovering her belongings and signing her out. The damned desk sergeant did insist on getting Longarm's John Hancock. How he and Billy were going to explain any of this to Washington was up for grabs. He knew he could get the owner of the Silver Dollar to drop the charges, but Billy was going to have to spring for some busted glass on the q.t.

They finally got outside and Longarm exhaled a long, relieved sigh as he took her elbow and said, "I hired a surrey for us. It's hitched just down the street."

"Where are you taking me, you brute?" asked Penelope.

He said, "I wish you'd stop mean-mouthing folks and *listen* to them once in a while, Penny!"

"Penny? How dare you call me by my childhood nickname, even as you drag me to durance vile! Have you been drinking? You look like a drinking man."

He gritted his teeth and hung onto her elbow as he half-led and half-shoved her toward the parked carriage. He said, "I called you Penny because that's who you were when Billy Vail was riding with your father for the Texas Rangers. I ain't taking you anywhere all that vile, and I sure aim to have a good stiff belt of Maryland rye when I get you there!"

Penelope Ascot gasped, "Oh, are you a friend of dear Uncle Billy's?"

He growled, "I *work* for Billy Vail, who, lucky for you, is the U.S. district marshal here in Denver. He had a fit when he heard about his little Penny going crazy last night on Larimer Street."

"Sir, I assure you I was perfectly rational when I attacked the forces of evil and corruption upon my arrival."

"Get in the surrey, ma'am. I'll unhitch the critter."

Penelope allowed him to boost her up behind the

dashboard, and sat primly as he untethered the bay gelding's reins and joined her. He backed away from the high sandstone curb and clucked the horse east toward Capitol Hill, up the street. He was dying for a smoke, but he'd been trying to cut down anyway, and this looked like as good a time as any to resist temptation. The little gal beside him seemed to be studying his profile as he drove. Finally she nodded as if satisfied, and said, "I didn't think Uncle Billy would hire a drinking man. You were just joshing me, weren't you?"

Longarm had lied enough that morning, so to change the subject, he asked, "How does Captain Buckeye Ascot of the Texas Rangers feel about his daughter running around scaring folks, ma'am?"

"My father, alas, died six years ago this fall. Surely Uncle Billy told you of his weakness, sir?"

Longarm shook his head and said, "No, ma'am. To hear Billy tell it, his old sidekick, Buckeye, didn't *have* any weaknesses. I'm sorry to hear he ain't with us anymore, but he must have been quite a man in his day. Billy never gets tired of jawing about the time the two of them stood off the whole Comanche Nation on the Staked Plains. I reckon that's why Billy wasn't happy about seeing you in jail."

"My father drank," said Penelope Ascot, flatly.

Longarm didn't answer. She'd already told him part of what was eating at her. He didn't remember hearing Billy say that Captain Buckeye Ascot was a drunk, but Penelope's father had been retired for some time since they'd ridden together, and it figured that a worn-out and cast-aside man might want to steady his nerves more than most folks might approve. Penelope was saying, "The doctor said it was cancer. They always cover up to spare the feelings of a drunkard's kin."

Longarm knew better. "Most of the death certificates like that read 'heart failure,' ma'am. Have you considered that your dad might really have had a cancer? A thing like that could account for any man drinking a mite, if folks took a charitable view."

Penelope wrinkled her pert little nose and insisted, "He drank when I was little. I used to smell the liquor on his breath when he came to tuck me in and kiss me goodnight."

Longarm shrugged and drove on. He'd already been told that she took her temperance work seriously. Penelope suddenly nudged him and said, "Stop! Did you see that saloon back there?"

Longarm reined in, puzzled, and asked, "Which one? We've passed a couple just now."

"*That* one, back there on the other side of the street, is *open*!"

Longarm said, "No it ain't, ma'am. The front door's locked with a grill and there's a 'closed' sign hanging in the window."

Penelope sprang down from the surrey with surprising grace and an ominous look in her eye as she insisted, "I saw men inside, through the plate glass! They were *drinking*!"

"Hey, come back here!" He called, as the little redhead strode grimly across the street with a ramrod up her spine, not looking back. He swore and ran the surrey to a curbside hitch rail before he jumped down and quickly hitched up. By the time he'd followed her halfway, Penelope had bent to one knee near the far curb and was gathering loose cobblestones from the poorly paved street. Longarm broke into a run and called, "No! Don't do it!" as Penelope straightened up, cocked her right arm, and pitched a rock right through the saloon's front window!"

There was an explosion of broken glass as two-thirds of the window shattered. Penelope wound up and fired an amazingly accurate pitch at the glass that was still

240

left, to leave the offending saloon's window gaping open in empty wonderment. As Longarm got to her side, he said, "I sure wish you'd stop that, ma'am."

The door was locked and grated, but men appeared in the new opening, and a man in a white apron shook his fist and yelled, "I'll kill you for this, you maniacs!"

Penelope threw again, and the bartender ducked as a paving block sizzled through the space his head had just occupied. His customers took cover too, as Penelope's barrage continued. From somewhere inside came the mournful sound of more glass smashing.

Longarm reached for her, but Penelope was advancing on the foe, singing. Off-key.

Longarm dove after her, missed, and groaned aloud as the little temperance fighter mounted the curb to stand in front of the busted-out window as she wound up again. It seemed impossible that she still had rocks left in that daintily hoisted skirt, but she'd armed herself with a mess of them, and seemed unaware that her striped stockings were showing above her high-button shoes. She threw the rock and spattered glass and liquor under the shattered mirror over the bar. But then Longarm grabbed her from behind and picked her up bodily to shake out the rocks she still had in her skirt.

She gasped, "Put me down! I've hardly started!"

Longarm lowered her to the ground, but hung on as he said, "Honey, you have just finished for sure, and it's time to vamoose!"

Then the bartender appeared at the window again with a double-barreled, sawed-off shotgun.

Longarm let go of the girl with one hand to draw his own double-action .44 as he said pleasantly, "I'd take it kindly if you'd point that scattergun somewhere more neighborly, friend."

The bartender roared, "You son of a bitch! First you bust my window, and now you're hiding behind a woman's skirts!"

Longarm said, "I never threw those rocks, old son. I've been trying to make this gal stop."

"Well, step away from her and let's have it out, anyway. I'm so riled I just have to kill somebody, and gals don't count!"

Longarm said, "I know just how you feel, neighbor. But we'll be backing off now."

"You yellow-bellied bastard! You know I can't shoot you with that gal in front of you!"

"It's unfair as hell," Longarm agreed amiably. Then he added, "*You* don't have any cover at all and, mad or not, this ain't a popgun I'm pointing your way. Don't you reckon we'd best quit while we're both ahead?"

"Who's ahead, God damn it? Look what you two lunatics just did to my saloon!"

"I'll chide her about it as soon as we're out of range," Longarm assured the infuriated barkeep. Then he let his voice drop a mite as he added, "It never would have happened if you hadn't busted the Sunday blue law, and I could see it as my duty to arrest you. But what the hell, I see you paid the fine already, so we'll just be on our way."

Considering that he'd just saved her life after getting her out of jail, Penelope Ascot sure sulked a lot. She hadn't said a word since he'd handcuffed her to the seat of the surrey so they could drive up Colfax Avenue in a more civilized manner.

He didn't drive her to Marshal Vail's home. Billy had some sort of arrangement with a widow woman who lived on Sherman Avenue, and he'd asked Longarm to meet him there.

Longarm drove into the backyard of the spacious brownstone, and was tethering the horse to a cast-iron post when Billy popped out of the back door to join them. The bald, pink-faced chief marshal grinned as he shouted, "I knew I could count on you, Longarm. How are you, Penny? My Lord, if you haven't grown up pretty as a—" He broke off, and his bushy black eyebrows met in a frown. "Longarm, what in thunder is Penny doing in those handcuffs?"

"She throws things," Longarm said. "I'll unlock her now, if you can swear you don't have a decanter of Madeira on the premises."

As Longarm freed her, Penelope nodded at Vail and said, "It's good to see you again after all these years, Uncle Billy, but I want you to fire this deputy. He actually laid hands on me and interfered with me as I was striving to uphold the law."

Billy looked dubiously at Longarm, who said, "I never laid hands anywhere important, and she was heaving paving blocks through windows at the time. You can fire me all you want. I'd rather herd *sheep* than escort her on my own time."

"Let's go inside," suggested Vail, taking Penelope by the arm to help her down as he added, "Lord have mercy, how you've grown, child. The last I heard of you, you'd married up and were living in St. Louis."

As the three of them walked to the back door, Penelope held her head defiantly and snapped, "If you must know, I'm divorced. They make beer in St. Louis, and the man I married seemed intent on drinking all of it!"

The two men shot appraising looks at one another over her sunbonnet. Penelope was starting to make more sense, if you wanted to call it sensible to wreck saloons.

Longarm had been inside the house before, but he hadn't asked, so he didn't know just what was going on between his boss and the attractive widow who met them at the door. He'd been told her name the first time they'd been introduced, but he'd forgotten it on purpose and had been sincerely glad that he had when, a month or so back, Billy Vail's wife had asked him in a desperately casual tone if he'd ever met Mrs. So-and-so. Longarm had looked sincerely blank. He'd been halfway home before he remembered that the name Vail's wife had asked about went with the somewhat younger and much prettier gal on Sherman Avenue.

So he studied the Boston ferns and maroon wallpaper, and tried not to listen as Billy introduced little Penelope to the graying but active-looking widow. He found the whole situation a mite distasteful, even though he knew human nature and himself too well to offer a moral judgement. He didn't care if other men fooled around on their wives, but he resented being drawn into a sticky bedroom farce in which he didn't get to sleep with any of the ladies involved.

As Longarm was trying not to hear their introductions, Penelope asked the widow, "Are you Uncle Billy's mistress, ma'am?"

The widow drew herself up like the Denver dowager she was and asked sweetly, "How would you like a punch in the nose, dear?"

Billy Vail said, "I told you Penny was sort of odd, honey."

But the widow said, "Impertinent would be a more accurate appraisal. Get her out of here, Bill."

Before Vail could answer, Penelope said, "Heavens, I wasn't trying to insult anyone. I just wanted to know. As a devoted follower of Miss Victoria Woodhull, I approve of free love."

"It's *drinking* she can't abide," Longarm offered laconically.

Vail said, "I'm sure you gals will hit it off, once you get to know each other. Why don't you sip some tea or something while me and Longarm have a private talk in the study?"

The widow looked grimly at the younger, smaller woman and said, "Come with me, dear. I'm sure there's some rat poison in the kitchen, if I really look for it."

Vail took Longarm's arm and steered him out of the room as the tall deputy murmured, "Billy, they're going to kill each other."

But Vail shook his head. "Naw. Jo's a sensible gal. You can see now why I didn't want you to bring Penny to my house, though. My old woman's sort of old-fashioned, and even as a child, little Penny was sort of outspoken."

As he followed Vail into the study, Longarm said, "Crazy would be more like it. What in hell do you aim to *do* with that little redhead, Billy?"

"Send her back to St. Louis, of course. Forget Penny. Me and Jo will see that she stays out of trouble, now that you've rescued her. I have a more important problem on my plate, and you're the one man I can think of who might be able to help me with it."

Longarm remained standing as Vail sat down in an overstuffed chair. He fished out a cheroot and a sulfur match and lit up before he said flatly, "It's my day off and I've had my fill of old friend's daughters, Billy. If you have anyone else you want me to get out of jail, forget it."

Vail said, "Sit down and shut up. I told you me and Jo had a handle on Buckeye Ascot's kid. This other problem is official."

Longarm sat gingerly on another chair and blew a thoughtful smoke ring before he muttered, "It's still my day off."

Vail nodded. "I know. You'll have time for that date you have with that Mexican gal tonight. I can't send you until we get the travel vouchers and such for you, tomorrow morning. I just figured as long as you were here . . ."

Longarm straightened abruptly, and his easygoing manner disappeared. "Just back up and let's talk some more about my love life," he said. "I've been polite as hell about the way other gents spend their time off duty, considering. Who in thunder gave you the right to spy on me?"

Vail shifted uncomfortably. "Damn it, Longarm, nobody's been spying on anybody, on duty or off. But a man hears gossip, and you have to admit that Mexican gal is sort of spectacular."

Longarm looked more annoyed than mollified by the compliment as he replied, "Well, in the first place, she's a single gal, and in the second place, she ain't Mexican. Tell your office gossips to take a better look before they carry tales to teacher. Everybody who has any call to mention the lady's name knows she's an Arapaho breed."

Vail brightened. "Do tell? That's even better. You going with an Indian gal, I mean. I told the War Department you got along with Indians better than any deputy I have on the payroll."

Longarm's eyes narrowed and Vail quickly added, "I didn't mention you going out with Indian gals, old son. I just said you spoke some of the lingos and had worked well with the Indian bureau in the past."

"Get to the point," said Longarm. "What sort of a mess have you gotten me into with the army, this time?"

Vail took out a smoke for himself and lit up with maddening deliberation before he said, "They're worried about that Paiute Messiah, Wovoka."

"The self-appointed leader of the Ghost Dance religion? Hell, I'm a lawman, not a missionary, Billy."

Vail shook his head and said, "Don't act so modest. You nipped some Ghost Dance trouble in the bud just a little while ago at the Blackfoot reservation, remember?"

Longarm looked pained and said, "*I* remember, but *you* sure don't! I only stumbled over one of Wovoka's Dream Singers while I was working on another case up there."

"Well, the point is, you put a sudden end to the son of a bitch."

Longarm protested, "I never did any such thing! One of the Indian police officers I had under me sort of got rid of the rascal on his own, and had I been able to prove it, I'd have had to arrest him."

Vail nodded and said, "I know your views on rough justice, old son. Officially, I'm only sending you up to Pine Ridge for a powwow with Sitting Bull." He flicked the ash from his cigar and added, "Of course, if the Sioux refuse to see reason . . ."

"Now hold on," Longarm cut in. "I'm not a missionary and I'm not the U.S. Army, either. If the War Department wants Wovoka or Tatanka Yatanka gunned, they have plenty of troopers drawing thirteen dollars a month and all the beans they can eat. Let them earn their keep for a change."

Marshal Vail looked confused and asked, "Who in hell are you talking about, old son? I wanted you to start by questioning Sitting Bull!"

"That's what I mean. Neither you nor the War Department knows the poor old geezer's name, and you're accusing him of all sorts of things."

Vail still looked puzzled, so Longarm said, "Tatanka Yatanka is what the Lakota call the gent you know as Sitting Bull."

Vail looked relieved and said, "Oh, right, the Heap Big Chief of the Sioux. We've heard the Ghost Dancers have been seen on the Pine Ridge Reservation, and Washington's worried as hell about it. I said I'd send you up there to straighten out Sitting Bull and his Sioux."

Longarm groaned aloud and muttered, "Jesus H. Christ. To start with, no Lakota's about to jaw with any white man dumb enough to call him a Sioux. Sioux means something between 'nigger' and 'enemy' in Chippewa, and the Lakota don't think much of the Chippewa, either."

Vail nodded sagely and said, "That's right. I forgot they call themselves Dakota."

"*La*kota, damn it. Dakota is another white man's word. If you'd let me finish, I'd get to the second point, which is that Tatanka Yatanka is not and never has been a chief."

"Hell, what is he if he's not the chief of the Dakota, Lakota, whatever?"

"He's what we call a medicine man. It doesn't translate too well. You might say the man we call Sitting Bull is somewhere between a judge and a priest."

"But he led his warriors against Custer at the Little Big Horn, didn't he?"

"No. I got it from some Lakota I know that he was nowhere near the battle. I got it from some Crow too, and since the Crow hate the Lakota, I'd say it was true."

Vail looked unhappy as he flicked away another ash and said, "Well, I know you're partial to Indians, but whatever the old bastard is, he's a troublemaker."

Longarm smiled thinly. "I'll pass on that remark about my being partial to Indians, since I've left a few squaws keening their dead in my time. But accusing Tatanka Yatanka of being a Ghost Dancer is dumb, even for the army. I just got through telling you he's a high priest of Wokan Tonka."

Vail said, "I know who the Great Spirit is. But Wovoka is an Indian religious leader too. So don't it figure they'd be in cahoots?"

Longarm shook his head and said, "I'll buy that when I hear that the Pope is plotting with the Grand Mufti of Islam. Wovoka's a *Paiute*, Billy. He talks a different lingo and prays to other spirits. None of the Lakota elders are likely to buy his fool notions about medicine shirts and such."

Vail got up with the expression of a cat that had the combination to the lock on the canary's cage, and stepped over to a sideboard to open a drawer.

"You're right at home here," Longarm observed.

Vail said, "Never mind about me and old Jo. I'd tell you it was platonic, if I wasn't so tired of you looking so damned know-it-all."

He took out a wadded-up leather bundle and spread it on a nearby table before he added mildly, "Tell me what this is and I'll tell you where they found it."

Longarm stared soberly at the painted buckskin garment, took a drag on his cheroot, and said, "That's a medicine shirt, or I've forgotten Wovoka's handwriting. Now you're fixing to tell me it comes from the Pine Ridge reservation, right?"

"It's tedious talking to a man who has all the answers. The Pine Ridge agency says there's more where this one came from, only the Indians get sort of truculent when a white man asks about them."

Longarm nodded and said, "All right. So some medicine-shirted Ghost Dancers have been to Pine Ridge. I still say none of the elders up there take Wovoka's nonsense seriously."

Vail asked, "What about the youngsters? The Sioux who claims he lifted Custer's hair was fourteen at the time. The Sioux haven't had a good licking for a while, and meanwhile, a lot of sullen kids have grown a few inches. I told the War Department I was sending you to investigate and report back to me, pronto."

Longarm protested, "Billy, I don't talk Lakota well enough to get laid. I got lucky up at the Blackfoot reservation that time because I do savvy a few words of

Algonquin, and because the men I was after turned out to be white. Sending me to jaw with Tatanka Yatanka is a pure waste of time."

Vail said, "Time may be just the ticket, old son. I may not know as much about Indians as you do, but I'm a fair-minded man, and we both know President Hayes keeps turning down the army's inflated budget."

"The President's a fair-minded man too, but get to the point, Billy."

Vail sat down again and said, "The point is that if somebody like you can't nip this Ghost Dance foolishness in the bud by making a few judicious arrests, the army will ride in whooping and hollering to do the job *their* way! There's more to this than the usual feud between Justice and the War Department, Longarm. We're both sworn peace officers, and there won't be a lick of peace this summer if we don't clean up this internal mess before somebody, on either side, gets hurt."

Longarm sighed and said, "You just touched a nerve. I scouted for the army one time, when I was young and foolish. I'll mosey up there and see if I can find anything out. But I sure hope you haven't any money riding on me doing any good."

Vail grinned and said, "There you go, old son. I knew I could depend on you."

Longarm loomed to his feet and answered, "You must know something I don't, then. I'm only willing to give it a try because I remember what the army did at Sand Creek and the Washita."

Vail walked with him to the door as he said, "I'm counting on you to keep innocent Indians from being massacred, Longarm."

Longarm shrugged and said, "Innocent Indians are only half of it, Billy. I remember what happened to a mess of white settlers at Spirit Lake, too."

• • •

Longarm boarded the northbound train late the next morning. He'd just had time to make it to the office and pick up his travel orders and warrants. He packed his Winchester and saddlebags aboard the coach with him for safekeeping, but his saddle and other heavy gear were riding up ahead in the baggage car. He found an empty plush seat and sat down to have a smoke and glance over the hastily typed arrest orders. Then, as the train chugged out of the yards, he muttered, "What the hell?"

Neither Wokova nor any other Indian he'd ever heard of was listed on the warrants, and Marshal Vail had tucked a coy note in among the papers before handing them to him on the fly. It read: "Indian religious matters are before the Supreme Court on constitutional grounds at the moment. So the judge refused us on Wovoka and other big medicine men. You'll have to get something more than praying and gourd-rattling on him if you mean to make a sensitive arrest."

Longarm swore and stared out the window at the passing prairie grass as he muttered, "Shit, the train's going too fast to jump, and my possibles are up forward, too."

What, he wondered, was he supposed to do when he arrived in Pine Ridge? The Indian police would have arrested the small potatoes on his federal wants by now, if they were anywhere near Pine Ridge and giving their right names.

He knew most Indians had more than one name. They gave one to the Indian agent when they came in for flour and beef; they used another name among their friends; they had a secret familiar name only close relatives knew; and, of course, they never told *anyone* the "real" name the spirits had revealed to them at puberty initiations.

How in hell was a strange white man to get a pissed-off Indian to admit that a name on a wanted notice was one he'd used, one time, to another white man?

He was on a fool's errand for sure, this time.

★★★★★★
JOHN JAKES'
KENT FAMILY CHRONICLES

Stirring tales of epic adventure and soaring romance which tell the story of the proud, passionate men and women who built our nation.

☐	05686-3	THE BASTARD (#1)	$2.75
☐	05238-8	THE REBELS (#2)	$2.50
☐	05371-6	THE SEEKERS (#3)	$2.50
☐	05684-7	THE FURIES (#4)	$2.75
☐	05685-5	THE TITANS (#5)	$2.75
☐	04047-9	THE WARRIORS (#6)	$2.25
☐	04125-4	THE LAWLESS (#7)	$2.25
☐	05432-1	THE AMERICANS (#8)	$2.95

Available at your local bookstore or return this form to:

JOVE BOOK MAILING SERVICE
1050 Wall Street West
Lyndhurst, N.J. 07071

Please send me the titles indicated above. I am enclosing $_____ (price indicated plus 50¢ for postage and handling for the first book and 25¢ for each additional book). Send check or money order—no cash or C.O.D.'s please.

NAME_____

ADDRESS_____

CITY_____STATE/ZIP_____

Allow three weeks for delivery. SK-17

REX STOUT

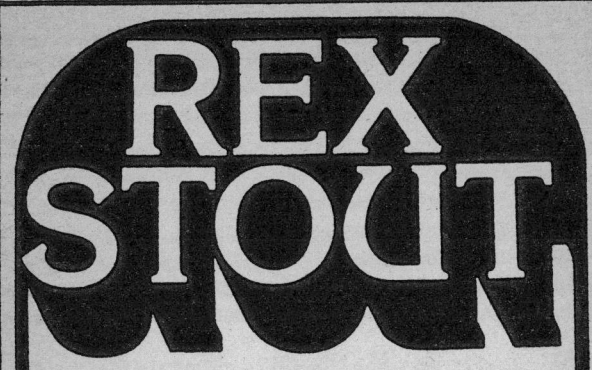

MORE BESTSELLING PAPERBACKS BY ONE OF YOUR FAVORITE AUTHORS...

Adventures of Nero Wolfe

☐	05085-7	BLACK ORCHIDS	$1.75
☐	05119-5	NOT QUITE DEAD ENOUGH	$1.75
☐	04865-8	OVER MY DEAD BODY	$1.75
☐	05117-9	THE RED BOX	$1.75
☐	05118-7	SOME BURIED CAESAR	$1.75
☐	04866-6	TOO MANY COOKS	$1.75

Other Mysteries

☐	05277-9	DOUBLE FOR DEATH	$1.75
☐	05280-9	RED THREADS	$1.75
☐	05281-7	THE SOUND OF MURDER	$1.75

Available at your local bookstore or return this form to:

JOVE BOOK MAILING SERVICE
1050 Wall Street West
Lyndhurst, N.J. 07071

Please send me the titles indicated above. I am enclosing $_____ (price indicated plus 50¢ for postage and handling for the first book and 25¢ for each additional book). Send check or money order—no cash or C.O.D.'s please.

NAME_____

ADDRESS_____

CITY_____STATE/ZIP_____

Allow three weeks for delivery.   SK-18